—

A Novel

Claudia Pemberton

iUniverse, Inc.
New York Lincoln Shanghai

Love Leaves No One Behind

iUniverse books may be ordered through booksellers or by contacting:

iUniverse
2021 Pine Lake Road, Suite 100
Lincoln, NE 68512
www.iuniverse.com
1-800-Authors (1-800-288-4677)

ISBN: 978-0-595-41402-4 (pbk)
ISBN: 978-0-595-67905-8 (cloth)
ISBN: 978-0-595-85753-1 (ebk)

Printed in the United States of America

To Rick

Thank you for being my best friend. And thank you for loving me enough to give me wings. You're always there to pick me up when I hit the ground hard, and hold on tightly to the rope when I soar too high. Without you in my life, I would be broken beyond repair.

To Perry
International Man of Mystery

Song Lyrics to:
"Love leaves no one behind"

Written by Julie Reeves/Danny Craig © BMI/ASCAP 2007
(Based on the novel by Claudia Pemberton)

Verse 1: Thirty eight years old, driving down a desert road
Thinking about the last twenty years
So many soldiers lost their lives, and he still wonders why
Must be a reason he's still here
He never left one behind, the faces never leave his mind
No regrets, he'd do it all again

Chorus: Cause a friend is forever, when push comes to shove
Everything we are inside, is nothing short of love
You'll stand up and fight, when others run away
You're a hero to a heart, when a heart begins to break
It's just his state of mind, love leaves no one behind

Verse 2: She was twenty nine years old, stranded on that desert road
Prayin for a miracle to appear
He came along just in time, and she looked into his eyes
And she knew, her miracle was here
He couldn't leave her behind, and now she never leaves his mind
No regrets, he'd fall in love again

Chorus: Cause love is forever, when push comes to shove
Everything we learn from life, is what we're made of
You'll stand up and fight, when others run away
You're a hero to a heart, when a heart begins to break
It's just his state of mind, love leaves no one behind

Bridge: Love will take you places, you never thought you'd go
It'll give you strength you never knew you had
It will help a friend in trouble, No matter what the cost
It'll help you find your way back home again

Chorus: Cause love is forever, when push comes to shove
Everything we learn in life, is what we're made of
You'll stand up and fight, when others run away
You're a hero to a heart, when a heart begins to break
It's just his state of mind, love leaves no one behind

Tag: It's just his state of mind, love leaves no one behind

ACKNOWLEDGMENT AND GRATITUDE

As far as I'm concerned, one of the greatest rewards in getting my book published is that it affords me the opportunity to publicly express my sincerest appreciation to my very own personal heroes: U.S. Army Rangers First Sergeant John P. Tompkins (ret.), Ranger Perry (ret.), Staff Sergeant Justin Gingrich (ret.), and Sergeant Major Brendan Durkan.

I would like to thank each of you for your invaluable contributions to the fulfillment of my dream and for your kind encouragement and inspiration. But most of all, thank you for breathing life into the character of Jesse, endowing him with the heart of a soldier and the soul of a gentleman. For that gift, I will be eternally grateful. Thank you so much for sharing your insight and expertise.

I feel the need to say a special thanks to you, John and Perry, for answering my initial call for help and for faithfully sticking with me from the very beginning. Thank you both for tirelessly and patiently answering all of the incessant technical questions that I fired at you for months and months on end. But most of all, thank you for never once entertaining the notion of leaving me behind.

The story I set out to tell in my first novel was a simple love story, although it ultimately refused to be written as one. For the leading man in my story, I wanted to create a larger-than-life character, a man of honor and integrity, one who would be trustworthy and true. Ultimately, I came to the obvious conclusion, for me anyway, that he should be a soldier. For several reasons, I decided that my character would be a

U.S. Army Ranger. The single most deciding factor in my decision came when, while researching my character, I happened across a copy of the Army Ranger Creed. One of the belief statements in that creed declares that a Ranger will never leave behind a fallen comrade. That one supremely selfless ideal personified the type of character I was trying to create.

When it comes to writing, I've always heard that one should write about what you know. But since I've always done things the hard way, I thought to myself, why change now? Although the story I was telling was a work of fiction, it was my fervent desire to make the history of the events and the main character's training and career as true to life as possible. Since I knew very little about the military or the lifestyle of a soldier, specifically an Army Ranger, I set about doing some extensive research on my leading character. This personal search for information ultimately led me to John, Perry, Justin, and Brendan. I soon discovered that these men epitomized all of the characteristics that I expected a Ranger to have. Under their expert tutelage, I quickly learned one thing: I had certainly chosen the correct career for my larger-than-life character. The real versions—the real U.S. Army Rangers and all other soldiers in all other branches of the U.S. military—are already larger than life. There was no need to embellish my character's personal attributes or tendency for heroics in the least.

I have come away from this endeavor with a greater understanding of the fortitude and dedication that an American soldier exemplifies. I cannot pretend to comprehend the bravery and honor that they carry in their hearts every day. I do know, however, that I do not have it—but I couldn't be prouder of those that do. To me, soldiers are a breed above and apart from the rest of us. It is my belief that God has truly blessed this nation of ours. And I believe that He has entrusted its guardianship and protection to a special group of brave souls who will always be standing firm—ready, willing, and able to unselfishly defend her to the death. I can't imagine a more noble calling.

To that end, I would like to extend to each and every soldier who has ever served this great nation of ours—past, present, and future—my personal and deeply sincerest "Thank You." I am profoundly appreciative and humbled by your courage, dedication, and most importantly the personal sacrifices you make in service to our country. I thank you from the bottom of my proud and grateful American heart!

And guys—John, Perry, Justin, and Brendan—just in case I haven't told you before … thank you for being my buddies; I couldn't ask for better.

PROLOGUE
A GLIMPSE OF EVIL

"We each get to choose our own path in life.
We can choose to be good, or we can choose to be evil."

—Granny Mae

Hidden amidst the desolate woods, void of any signs of life or humanity, the rustic log cabin stood nestled deep within the forest. It was as much a part of the trees as they were of it. Through the eye of any photographer it would be a rare and intriguing subject, lending itself to an image of serene beauty from the outside, with absolutely no indication of the unspeakable horror to be found on the inside. The events unfolding within this dwelling were anything but picturesque, giving credence to the age-old saying that looks can be deceiving.

What remained of the sane and vibrant young woman who had been abducted and forcibly brought here three weeks earlier, appeared emotionless and defeated, tightly bound to a rigid wooden chair. The unthinkable physical and emotional torment she had been subjected to during her captivity was more than enough to strip away any and all desire to continue living. She closed her eyes as if relinquishing all hope of ever being rescued. Her will to live seemed to be ebbing away with each reluctant breath she took.

The captor observed his prisoner from across the room. Once captivated by her resiliency, he found her belated, but peaceful surrender equally as mesmerizing. Although her physical body was obviously fighting the prospect of dying, her spiritual body seemed to be welcoming it. He wondered … *could she possibly see death as a blessing?*

Her despondency caused a foreign, albeit fleeting, pang of remorse to course speedily through his demented mind, an almost inconceivable amount of regret for what he was about to do to her. He had grown quite fond of her, more so than with any of her six predecessors. He indulged himself in his deranged fantasy of their love affair, even permitting himself to call her by name, something he had never done with any of the others. But Sallie was different. She was quiet and submissive, cooperative and more than willing to satisfy his every desire. But she wasn't fooling him, nor was he fooling himself. Though she was flatteringly convincing at times, he knew full well that her efforts were not born of pleasure or affection, but merely to prolong her own life. Still, he had become emotionally attached to her, going so far as to allow this misguided fondness to precipitate his decision to end her suffering now, well ahead of the appointed time of death in his otherwise inflexible transformation ritual.

As he walked toward her, she remained still and resigned, as if waiting patiently for the inevitable, but praying that it would come soon. Standing directly behind her chair, the sound of his deep, menacing voice disrupted the silence. Although spoken at a startling volume, his words failed to induce so much as a flinch from his captive. She no longer feared him—that was obvious. Although he had complete control of her fleshly body, mentally she was far and forever removed from his grasp. The winsome smile on her face bared evidence to her blissful absence from reality.

"Sallie, I'm going to put the gag back on now," he told her solemnly, knowing as the words exited his mouth that they were a lie. He had no intentions of replacing the thinly folded fabric between her dutifully parted lips. The fact that he lied to her about his intentions puzzled him. He had never before lied to protect a person—only to lure or hurt her in some fashion.

With the gag pulled taut between his hands, he looped his arms over her head and lowered them slowly past her face, lingering just inches below her chin. Holding the cloth weapon poised and ready just millimeters from her fragile and fatally exposed neck, he paused. The image of her body's violent reaction to this form of strangulation once again caused him a momentary measure of grief. Although the desired outcome would be death, it wouldn't come quickly enough and the pressure and subsequent crushing of her larynx would cause her excruciating pain. Selfishly, he thought about the resulting damage and discolorations that the ligature would produce, leaving her attractive face and neck swollen and bruised.

Having made his decision, he raised the piece of cloth back up to her mouth and gently placed it between her lips. He then proceeded to tie it loosely behind her head.

Filled with a semblance of compassion, he began stroking her hair. Starting above her temples, he allowed his fingertips to slowly follow the length of her voluminous blonde tresses, pulling the hair away from her face and shoulders, and draping it gently down her back. With each stroke, his hands moved closer and closer to her throat, until finally his fingers were touching nothing but the soft and supple skin of her neck. He continued moving lightly up and down either side of the front of her delicate throat. Once his fingers located the area of the carotid arteries, he could feel the strong, steady throbbing of oxygenated blood being pumped to her head and brain. Following the course of the life-sustaining vessels, he aligned his fingers along the pathway of the flow.

As his fingers pressed in firmly on the carotids, he leaned over and kissed the top of her head. Her body remained still and calm as if she felt no pain at all. She made no attempt whatsoever to free herself from his grip. Within ten short seconds, and without so much as a whimper, she drifted away into unconsciousness.

After only two more minutes of sustained pressure to the arteries, her life was over. The empty shell of who she once was belonged to him, now and forever, just as he had planned from the very first day he saw her.

He cradled her limp and lifeless body in his arms and carried it into a small, but separate room inside the cabin—his makeshift workshop and sanctuary. He laid her down on the plastic-lined, wooden surface and promptly started removing her clothing. Working with practiced precision, he went about the task of preparing the body, speed being of utmost importance in order to circumvent the onset of rigor mortis and the resulting damage it would inflict upon her perfect face.

Making the deep incision into her femoral artery, he used the razor-sharp scalpel to lacerate the alabaster skin of her groin. The honed instrument penetrated her body as though passing through warm butter. He then inserted the canula into the gaping blood vessel and secured the plastic tubing in place.

With the quick flip of a switch, a small, motorized pump began to siphon the still-warm blood from her body. The natural pink hue of her skin began to gradually fade as the machine hummed steadily in the background. Leaning against the side of the table, he gazed at her perfectly shaped physique. Compelled to touch her, he began moving his hands lightly and slowly over her cooling naked body, delighting in the way his fingers rose and fell amidst the curves of her voluptuous shape. Leisurely, he trailed down the entire length of her form and back up again. Pausing momentarily, he cupped her firm, adequate breasts in his insatiable hands, his fingers tugging playfully at her soft, pink nipples, attempting to coax them to erection. Teasing them to react to his touch as they had several times before, he was dismayed at their lifeless response. Closing his eyes, he allowed his hands to continue their blind exploration of every inch of her perfect anatomy. The sensual sensation of his fingers entering her soft femininity filled him with animalistic desire. The act aroused him into such a frenzied state of excitement that rubbing his lower body against the table was the only physical stimulation necessary to bring him to climax. He moaned loudly as the pleasurable pulsation coursed through his body.

Waiting for the last faint throb of ecstasy to pass, he opened his eyes and stared at her pale and unresponsive body on the table before him. Although sexually satisfied for the moment, he immediately regretted that he hadn't gratified himself inside of her just once more before ending her ability to respond.

With pity only for himself, he sighed heavily as he picked up her small, cold hand and laid it across his palm. It was delicate and flawless, having taken on a porcelainlike appearance. He marveled at the perfection of her skin and fingers, especially her fingernails. They were her natural nails and showed evidence of the painstaking care that she had taken to keep them meticulously manicured and polished. Reaching for his smallest scalpel, he decided that it would be a shame to discard them along with the remaining parts of her body that he no longer needed.

By the time he finished the repetitious ten-finger task, the humming of the pump motor had ceased, indicating the completion of its intended purpose. He slowly straightened his torso and stretched his aching back. Painstakingly, he removed the canula and plastic tubing from her body.

For the final step in this part of her transformation process, he would need his largest #22 surgical scalpel. The brand-new, stainless steel instrument was razor sharp and ready for use as he removed it from its designated slot in the red, velvet-lined storage case.

Returning to the table, he stood alongside her, just above the area of her waist. He paused momentarily to appreciate her beauty in its entirety for the final time. It saddened him that this part of their experience together was over.

Placing the thin surgical knife next to her ghostly pale skin, he began the penetrating incision in the area below the delicate hollow of her throat, just above her clavicle. With the expertise of a veteran surgeon, he continued the cut that would eventually sever the only part of her anatomy that he would preserve and keep with him forever.

Try as he might to maintain his concentration, he could not keep his mind from wandering. He found himself envisioning his next female conquest. What would she be like? Would she be as sweet and fulfilling as the one lying on the table in front of him? The mounting anticipation of the hunt ignited a burning desire inside of him that consumed any false remnants of regret still smoldering in his dysfunctional heart for Sallie.

I'll know her when I see her, he surmised. *But, the question is … where will I find her?*

Chapter 1

SAYING GOOD-BYE

"God will never place a mountain in our path
and leave us there to climb it alone."

—*Granny Mae*

Surrounded by the familiar scent of spring lilacs, Mikayla drove slowly down the tree-lined, gravel driveway that led to the only home she had ever known. Their home had been filled with so much love and happiness over the years that she wondered how such a small structure could have contained it all.

She had been certain when she awoke this morning that she had finally gathered enough strength to come here. Now that she was here, that certainty was fading fast. As she turned off the ignition key, the monotonous hum of the engine was replaced with utter silence. Mikayla closed her eyes. Someone dear to her once told her that if you closed your eyes and opened your heart, your mind would replay years of stored memories in your head, just like a movie projector. Finding this to be true, she indulged herself for a few moments in the comfort of her treasured memories.

Opening her eyes, she was greeted with a reality that quickly brought her attention back to the task at hand. As she surveyed the scene around her, she tried desperately to memorize every single nuance of the home she loved so much.

The spring perennials in full bloom around the porch were held in check by large, whitewashed stones bordering them all around and down along the walkway. Along the base of the porch were huge clumps of pink and white peonies, their beautiful blossoms drooping slightly, the stems straining to support the enormous masses of color. The stately iris blooms, clothed in deep purple and lavender velvet, served as nature's delicate announcements that spring had come again. Meticulously arranged between the taller flowers was a colorful array of bright yellow and crimson tulips, surrounded by clusters of fragrant and dainty lilies of the valley. The garden could not have been more perfect if it were painted by a master.

The two-story, white frame house hadn't been structurally altered since Mikayla's great-grandparents first built it in 1925, save an occasional rotten board or leaky roof. She smiled at the sight of the old place. It was more a living entity to her than just a place to live. It always had been, even from her earliest childhood memory. Now, as a grown woman of twenty-nine, she still could hear its resounding heartbeat.

The faded wicker swing hanging on the front porch swayed in the breeze as if beckoning for someone to sit and talk awhile. How many hours of laughter and conversation had they shared together sitting on that comfortable swing, listening to the crickets and watching millions of flickering fireflies on a warm and starry southern summer evening? As the precious memories came flooding back, Mikayla's mind and heart raced, trying desperately to comprehend the reality that this would be the last time she would return to her beloved home. Fighting back the pending flood of tears, she stepped out of the car and onto the crunch of gravel.

As she made her way down the shady and damp redbrick pathway that led to the front porch, she paused to steady her trembling legs and gather her composure.

In the three months since her loss, she had merely been going through the motions. But she didn't want to do that today. She was here to say good-bye—good-bye to her home, to the only way of life she had ever known, and to the beloved grandmother who was everything to her. Granny Mae was not only her grandmother; she was also her mother, her best friend and confidante, her spiritual guide, and anything else Mikayla had ever needed her to be. Granny Mae loved her "all the way up to God's house and back down again," as she used to say. Granny meant it, and Mikayla believed it.

The weathered screen door creaked on its hinges as Mikayla stepped inside. It was as if she was just coming home from school or work or an evening out. Everything still looked the way it always did—clean and tidy, warm and inviting. Even though the furniture and fixtures ran the gamut of style from 1925 to 2005, they seemed to meld together perfectly. In fact, that was exactly the way that the new owners wanted it. They insisted on it. They had purchased everything—the house, the furniture, and the kitchen fixtures. They wanted it all. That was part of its charm, they said. Mikayla was here for one reason, and that was to gather her personal effects and nothing more.

With that in mind, she retrieved an elastic band from her purse, gathered her long, auburn curls into a thick ponytail, and got to work. She decided to start in the kitchen, "the heart of the home," as Granny Mae called it. The buyers understood that Granny Mae's china was not part of the contract. It was, no doubt, a valuable antique, as was almost everything else in the house, but it was priceless to Mikayla, and she had no intention of losing it, too. She had lost enough already.

Opening the door to the cabinet, she started removing the heirloom tableware that had once belonged to her great-grandmother. Carefully, she wrapped each piece in sheets of protective plastic. Running her fingers over the raised blue pattern of the Victorian country scene, she recalled some of the delicious meals Granny Mae had served on these lovely dishes. She was truly an amazing cook, one of the many gifts she had passed down to Mikayla. Granny had spent countless hours patiently teaching her precious granddaughter how to cook by touch rather than by measurements. She would add a pinch of this and a handful of that. "Eye-ball it" was one of Granny's most frequently used cooking terms.

Granny could make anything taste good, which was lucky for them because they didn't have much money. She had been widowed at a young age, only two years before Mikayla was born, left to support herself and a rebellious sixteen-year-old daughter. Work was hard to find. She had a small income from her husband's retirement and social security, and an even smaller education. After a few odd jobs, Granny was blessed to get a housekeeping and meal preparation position at the home of Edward Carmichael and his family. The Carmichaels were one of the wealthiest families around town and also one of the kindest. Over the twenty-three years that she worked for them, they treated her with respect and paid her a fair wage for her hard work. After Mikayla came along, they afforded the devoted grandmother flexible work hours, so that she could be waiting when her baby girl arrived home from school every day. It was important to Granny Mae that Mikayla have a safe and stable childhood—to know that she was loved and protected.

Since there were just the two of them, two peas in a pod, as Granny always said, they learned to make the most of what they had. A small garden in the backyard provided most of their meals in the summer, and Granny would "can up" extra fruits and vegetables for the winter months. Every Sunday morning before church, she always made Mikayla's favorite blueberry drop biscuits with blueberry cream spread. That was one of the first recipes to be placed in Mikayla's recipe box. (It was really just an old shoebox, but Granny said it served the purpose just fine.) Granny had started the collection for her when she was just a little girl. Each time Mikayla would master a new recipe, Granny Mae would add it to the box. Now yellowed and soiled from years of handling by sticky little fingers, that box was the last thing Mikayla removed from the china cabinet.

The remainder of her morning was spent boxing up items of sentimental value and trashing those with none—her wedding album being one of the latter.

That was a waste of four years of my life that I would just as soon forget, Mikayla thought.

After years of struggling to make her marriage work, Travis simply decided one day that he didn't want to be married anymore. But, that turned out to be just another lie. Only three months after the divorce, he was remarried, this time to Mindy Greenly, eight years his junior. It seemed that he had not only graduated from pharmacy college, but to a better life as well. Lucky for Travis, his new wife's father just happened to own Greenly's Drug Store, a successful business in town.

"May they live happily ever after," Mikayla said out loud as the photo album hit the bottom of the trash can with a resounding thud. It had grown easier now that five years had passed, but she still recalled how devastated she was the day the divorce became final. Of course, as she had been so many times before, Granny Mae was there for her that day. She was always there, whether Mikayla needed advice, someone to listen to her problems, or just a soft shoulder to cry on; Granny always knew what to say or when to say nothing at all. On this day, however, she offered some of her sage advice. Granny Mae had a wonderful way of conveying her opinion by way of insightful and clever sayings. "Baby Girl," she said—that's what she called Mikayla when she really wanted her attention—"You're gonna have many devastating things happen in your life. You'll have many glorious things happen in your life as well. The secret is how you perceive the bad ones. You can see these devastating things as the end, or you can see them as the beginning. Is this spoiled marriage of yours going to be the end of your life or the beginning of a whole new exciting life for you? It's entirely up to you and how you perceive it. It doesn't change the past one bit, but it can certainly change your future." Mikayla was having a hard time picturing her future right now without Granny Mae there to love and guide her.

She found some comfort in the fact that she still had Granny's letters. In the nightstand beside her bed, the bottom drawer was full of letters Granny had written to Mikayla over the years. There was a letter for every important event in Mikayla's life and even some not-so-important events. Mikayla once asked Granny why she wrote letters instead of just putting her thoughts down in a diary.

"The way I see it … a diary is for someone's own remembrance," Granny Mae explained. "My writing is for your remembrance. I don't think I'm likely to forget how much I love you, and I don't want you to forget it either. Did you know, baby girl, that I love you all the way up to God's house and back down again?" At the end of every one of her letters, Granny always affirmed that infinite and unconditional love with those very same words.

Mikayla placed the letters in one of the empty moving boxes. As she made her way toward the bookshelf, her eyes searched out her photo albums and scrapbooks—"memory books," as Granny called them—stacked neatly together on the first shelf. Granny had been adamant about preserving Mikayla's childhood memories, beginning the day she was left with her at the tender age of two months. That evening, Granny placed the very first picture on the very first page of Mikayla's very first memory book. Holding the book close to her heart, Mikayla walked over and sat down on the edge of the bed and opened the cover. On the first page was a picture of a tiny baby girl wrapped in a powder-pink blanket in the arms of a young and beautiful Granny Mae. The woman's shoulder-length chestnut brown hair fell in natural curls. Her vivid green eyes seemed to dance with happiness. She looked delightfully content cradling the little infant in her arms. The handwritten description beneath the photograph brought the sting of tears to Mikayla's own green eyes: "An unexpected gift from Heaven, Mikayla Mae (age: two months), May 9, 1976."

"Oh, Granny … how lucky I was to have you in my life," she whispered. *What would I have done without you? My mother simply dropped me in your lap one day and left in search of her own life—a life that didn't include me. But instead of viewing me as an inconvenience and disruption to your life, you opened your arms and your heart and welcomed me inside. You considered me a gift and a blessing and loved me unconditionally. There is no greater gift you could have given me. You encouraged me to dream big and search for my place in a world full of limitless possibilities.*

There are no adequate words to express my love and thankfulness to you, Granny Mae. I know that I was loved by you every single moment since the day I came into your life, and I know that I'll miss you every day for the rest of mine.

Sighing deeply with bitter sadness and loneliness, Mikayla reluctantly closed the book and tucked it lovingly away in the moving box.

Glancing one more time around the room that she had grown up in, she tried desperately to absorb all of the priceless memories lingering in the hallowed space. The room had been her sanctuary from everything bad or hurtful. She had not one unhappy memory of this room—only wonderful, magical ones. The sounds of Granny's nightly lullabies still lingered in the air, mingled with an abundance of melodious giggles and laughter. The enticing aroma of freshly baked chocolate chip cookies still hung heavy in the room. The sweet treats had served as special rewards when Mikayla had been a good little girl, and sometimes even when she hadn't. She recalled the time that she had done something bad, and although she dreaded the thought of being punished, she was devastated that she had disappointed Granny Mae.

She had unknowingly used a curse word during Sunday School and Granny had overheard her. Mikayla couldn't figure out why everybody was so upset. She had heard Mr. Gregory use the word *bitch* many times talking about his hunting beagles. Why was she in so much trouble for saying it?

After all these years, that memory was as vivid in Mikayla's mind as if it had happened only yesterday. She kept this one in the forefront, as it was the first time she could remember actually *feeling* the depth of her grandmother's love.

Granny had a special way of dispensing discipline. First, she reached out and scooped her teary-eyed, heartbroken little girl up onto her lap. Hugging her tightly, she comforted her and explained about the evils of using curse words. When she was certain that Mikayla understood, she told her, "Baby Girl, even though you did a bad thing and Granny is a little upset with you, I want you to know that you could never ever do anything bad enough that would make me not love you anymore. Granny will always love you. Do you understand?"

Recollecting the precious moment, Mikayla could almost feel her grandmother's tender touch upon her face, wiping away the tears as she pulled her close and kissed the top of her curly little head.

"And just so you know, Baby Girl," Granny had told her as she lovingly patted Mikayla's chubby bare legs, "Even when you're as good as you can be, you could never ever do anything good enough that could make me love you any more than I do at this very moment."

Comforted by the priceless memory, Mikayla smiled through the tears as she recalled the next words out of her loving grandmother's mouth. "Now that we've got that all settled, how's about we have ourselves some cookies and milk?"

Mikayla walked resignedly out of the room. Looking back for one last glance, she gently closed the door to her happy childhood. With a heavy heart, she proceeded to the final room to be packed—the one right next to hers—Granny Mae's room.

Upon entering the comforting space, she closed her eyes against the brightness of the radiant afternoon sun beaming through the cascading, white lace curtains. As if in a trance, she just stood there, momentarily unable to will herself to move. There were so many different emotions battling for her immediate attention that she had no other choice but to simply stand still and wait patiently for the dominant feeling to take over. When it finally did, she smiled softly, feeling wrapped in the love that emanated from this sacred room.

As a child, when she became frightened by a strange sound or the sharp crack of a spring thunderstorm, she would creep silently into the big poster bed next to her grandmother where she would instantly feel safe and secure. As a teenager struggling to grow up, Mikayla and Granny had many late evening conversations sitting on the edge of that bed. Most of those conversations began with tears and ultimately ended with laughter. The two of them shared everything and had no secrets.

Granny Mae was her staunchest supporter, especially when it came to getting a quality education. Mikayla had been attending the University of Alabama for almost a year when she met and fell in love with Travis. Six months later they were married, at which time she dropped out of school to support Travis' education and career. Her turn would come later—at least that was the plan. After the divorce, Granny had persuaded her to go back to college to complete her degree in advertising and marketing. But, even with grants, student loans, and a part-time waitressing job, there just wasn't enough money. To make matters worse, her unreliable old car was no longer safe for the two-hour trips back and forth to school. Even though Mikayla stayed in a small apartment near campus Monday through Thursday, she always came home on Friday to spend the weekend with Granny Mae. She wouldn't have it any other way. So, with tuition, rent on the apartment, and the need for a new car, it just didn't seem to be in the cards for her to get her degree. But then Granny decided to get a small mortgage loan on the house—enough to fund Mikayla's education and even put a down payment on a slightly used car. Although Granny didn't believe in borrowing money or charging things she couldn't afford to pay for outright, she still insisted on acquiring the mortgage loan. Mikayla reluctantly agreed. The bank set up the loan over a ten-year period, so the payments were relatively small. Everything was going according to plan, until nine months ago when their world came crashing down.

Shaking her head gently from side to side as if she could toss out those painful memories, Mikayla fought to get her mind back on task. Methodically, she removed the delicate handmade quilt from the bed and began to fold it. Made in the traditional Dutch Girl pattern, the quilt was Granny Mae's most prized possession. She affectionately referred to it as her "recollection quilt," because she had fashioned it from scraps of Mikayla's favorite dresses from when she was just a little girl. Pausing a moment, Mikayla examined the painstaking precision of every hand-sewn stitch and each colorful Dutch girl dressed up in remnants of her own happy childhood.

On the dresser next to the bed sat Granny's old jewelry box. Mikayla smiled as she picked it up, recalling the many times she and her best friend, Diana, had "plundered" (as Granny called it) through the box, putting on necklaces, earrings, and bracelets as they played dress-up. She removed her favorite piece from the box and clutched it in her hand. It was the only piece that had been strictly off limits to the two girls: a beautiful cameo pendant hanging from a short string of delicate ecru pearls. The pendant was a petite and elegant oval silhouette of a graceful Victorian lady's profile set against a mauve-colored background. It had been a wedding gift to Mikayla's great-grandmother from her groom on their wedding day. It was truly stunning, and it still beguiled Mikayla as much as it had when she was a little girl. She had been born with a romantic's heart, Granny used to say.

Carefully, she placed the cameo necklace back into the box.

The mental exhaustion of the day was beginning to take its toll as Mikayla sat down on the edge of the bed. Her eyes were drawn to Granny Mae's family Bible on the nightstand. Lying within arm's length of the bed, the book was creased and discolored with signs of its years. As she reached over to pick it up, she noticed how worn and fragile the pages had become from frequent use by someone who had patterned her life by its teachings. Sorrow gripped Mikayla's heart as she ran her hand over the cover and held it close to her heart. Slowly and with overwhelming sadness, she turned to the family record section at the beginning of the Bible. Pausing to steady her trembling hands, she let a tear fall onto the thin, delicate paper—joining those long left by Granny Mae. On the page designated for the recording of family deaths, Mikayla wrote the name of her cherished grandmother: Tinessa Mae Mitchell—February 1, 2005. Tearfully, Mikayla whispered, "I miss you so much Granny." *I'm so alone,* she continued silently. *I'm trying to be strong, but I'm so afraid to go on by myself. You were supposed to be here with me. I wanted to take care of you the way you always took care of me. You knew how much I loved you, but I wish I could have told you just one more time … just one more 'I love you' … most of all, Granny, I wish I could have thanked you again for loving me. All of my life you told me what a precious gift I was. Although I never really believed it myself, it meant everything in the world to me that you believed it.*

It took all the strength Mikayla had to raise herself from the bed. Looking around to make sure she had packed everything, her eyes fell to one last item: a brightly colored cross-stitch piece on the wall next to the door. The panel of beige cloth, perfectly stitched with painstaking detail, was displayed in a wooden frame. Granny's own hands had formed this masterpiece. She had stitched a little brown frame house in the background, with a bright red heart in the center. The embroidered caption beneath it read: "Home is Where the Heart is." Mikayla removed the frame from the hook and held it close to her hollow chest, trying desperately to understand how to let go and move on.

Reading the words once more, the reality of their meaning sank in. If home truly is "where the heart is," Mikayla knew she would be leaving hers here.

No longer able to contain the tears that welled from the depths of her broken spirit, she allowed the bitter release to flow freely down her cheeks.

Chapter 2

THE LAST PRINCE

"There's no greater treasure on earth
than the love of a treasured friend."

—*Granny Mae*

Weary and emotionally drained from packing Granny Mae's things and battling the grief the task had caused, Mikayla's mind and body had no recourse or desire to fight the blissful escape of sleep. She knew she would need a good night's rest to face the events of the following day. Since the new owners had refused her request for one last night at home, crashing at a small motel in town, just thirty minutes away, seemed the perfect solution.

Mikayla inserted the keycard into the door and entered the sterile-smelling room. She had picked up a sandwich at a drive-through restaurant on the way to the hotel and ate it in the car. She hadn't realized it had been so long since she'd eaten anything, so she had been famished. With the hunger problem solved, the only thing left on her mind was a hot, relaxing bath, which she hoped would ease her stiff and aching muscles.

With her long, thick hair still damp from an hour-long soak, Mikayla lay down across the blue floral covering on the king-size bed. It was still daylight outside, only 6:00 in the evening. The vibrant orange sun was beaming through the partial openings in the vertical window blinds. The cozy, gentle sunlight blanketed her face and body, offering streaks of welcome warmth in the chilly, air-conditioned room. The pain and emptiness in her heart had subsided somewhat back to the level that she had become accustomed to since Granny had passed away three months ago. She wondered whether the pain from her loss would ever lessen past that point. She never expected it to go away completely. Her only hope was that the intensity of it would diminish enough to allow her to enjoy life again. While drifting off to oblivious sleep, that hope was her only comfort.

When she opened her eyes, night had turned to morning, and she had awakened in the same position in which she had fallen asleep. Her physical and emotional burden seemed considerably lighter, the obvious result of fourteen hours of unconsciousness. She arose rested and eager to have breakfast with her best friend, Diana. Critiquing her own reflection in the bathroom mirror, Mikayla ran her fingers through the alluring mass of dark curls that fell gracefully onto her shoulders. For the first time in a long time, the vibrant green eyes that stared back at her didn't appear quite as gaunt or empty. Blessed with a flawless, ivory complexion, she used very little makeup. A little blush and mascara did the trick.

After slipping into a favorite, green cotton dress, Mikayla gathered the remainder of her things and was ready to face the day. Actually, this day would mark the beginning of the rest of her life, as Granny Mae would say. After breakfast, she would embark on a 2,400-mile excursion across six states to the promise of a lucrative career that would provide her with the expertise and finances for fulfilling her plan—a plan that would require her to temporarily leave her hometown of Guntersville, Alabama.

Standing at the hotel checkout desk, Mikayla heard a familiar male voice behind her.

"You do realize, don't you, that Diana will spend every penny we have on phone calls during the first month alone?" It was the voice of her best friend's husband, Rick Owens. He was Mikayla's best friend as well, by default, she always said in jest.

"Don't you know by now that we're much smarter than you are?" She laughed as she turned around and held a prepaid phone card exaggeratedly close to his handsome, smiling face.

"What! That thing's only good for a thousand minutes. That won't last you gabby girls more than three days," he rebutted jokingly.

Rick and Mikayla had teased and picked on one another since the first day they met. They just seemed to bring that playfulness out in each another. It had been their ongoing game for the past fourteen years.

"Yes … but we each have our own calling card, at a bargain price of only three cents a minute," she mocked. "That means we're good for at least six days for only thirty dollars, if we pace ourselves. After that, we can use up our cell phone minutes, and then there's always e-mail." She returned his genuine, glowing smile—a smile that up until that moment she had so often taken for granted. She knew that she was going to miss it terribly. Granny was right. We seem to have no idea what we have—smack dab under our noses—until it's gone.

"Did you sleep okay here?" Rick asked with noticeable sadness in his voice. "We wished you'd stayed with us, especially since it was your last night in town."

"Oh yeah," she replied, shaking her head sarcastically. "And crash the intimate celebration of your tenth wedding anniversary? I don't think so," she said with a grin. "I was fine right here. Besides, I wouldn't have been very good company anyway."

"Well, that's never stopped you before," he joked, his smile returning with a vengeance. "Since when have you ever been good company?"

"Well, thank you very much," she retorted, pretending to be insulted as she playfully poked him in the chest. "That was a good one, by the way."

They laughed together as they had done so many times before—almost always at each another's expense.

Not quite ready to say good-bye to him just yet, Mikayla continued. "Hey, since you're the boss around here, can you sneak away for a while and have breakfast with me and Diana?" she asked enticingly.

"I wish I could, Mikayla, but I think you two girls need this time alone. Besides, we're going to be swamped around here. There's a group of a hundred or so party animals checking in this morning. They're coming here to celebrate their twenty-fifth high school class reunion. We're gonna be having some disco-dancin' fun around here tonight." He laughed as he broke into his personal rendition of the infamous disco pose. "You sure you don't want to stay and join us?"

"As tempting as that sounds," she said, giggling at his antics, "I have to hit the road if I'm gonna get to California in time for my interview next week. I'm already traveling with a handicap since I'll be following those maps you drew up for me."

He grinned affectionately at her good-natured insult. "Just trust me, smarty pants. I'm good with maps. All you have to do is follow the yellow brick road. Do you think you can manage that?" he asked, laughing instantly at her usual nonverbal response of sticking her tongue out at him.

Mikayla knew that Rick had labored for days mapping out the whole trip for her, highlighting the entire route with a fluorescent yellow marker. By his best calculations, it would take her about five days to get to Monterey. Rick said that he wanted her to drive during the daylight hours only, for a maximum of eight or nine hours a day, with sufficient caffeine and food breaks in between. She promised she would stop when she got tired or sleepy. As he was reiterating his concerns, he reminded her of an old red hen mothering a baby chick—one of the many reasons why she loved him so much. Rick was the kind of friend who always put her needs before his own.

His family had moved to Guntersville from Athens, Georgia, at the beginning of Mikayla's freshman year. On his first day at the new school, in third-period math class, he nervously took a vacant seat next to Mikayla. Sensing his apprehension and shyness, Mikayla offered him a reassuring smile—and then asked him to go and sit somewhere else. The moment he returned her mischievous grin, they became instant friends. During lunch, she introduced him to Diana, and the two were immediately smitten with each other. From that day on, the three best friends were inseparable.

Although graced with a relatively quiet personality, Rick was kind and good-natured, not to mention drop-dead gorgeous. Mikayla used to tease him about his good looks, calling him Prince Charming because he was so handsome and virtuous. Even with the blessing of a beautiful face and a smile that lit up a room, Rick was never the least bit struck by his own attractiveness.

Standing before her today, Rick looked the same as the day they had met—tall and lean, with a gorgeous head of shiny, midnight black hair that had just a hint of natural curl. His telling facial expressions matched his personality exactly. He had amazing, bluish-green eyes that squinted slightly closed when he laughed, exposing a kidlike sweetness. Even Granny Mae couldn't help but comment about how perfect he was, inside and out. She often told him that he reminded her of an angel that had just dropped out of heaven.

Not only good-looking, he was highly intelligent, too. Majoring in business and management, Rick had become the southeast district manager for a successful national hotel chain in just a few short years.

Mikayla knew that she would never find more loyal friends than Rick and Diana, not that she ever planned to look. For now, however, fate had dealt her a new hand, one that was taking her away from her home and friends. She vowed that their estrangement would only be temporary. She had no reason to believe that fate would be so cruel as to separate her permanently from the only real family she had ever known.

She and Rick had already said their farewells over the two weeks following her decision to go, but today would be their final good-bye. Preparing to leave her dear friend, Mikayla turned to lay her handbag down on the counter. She knew she would need both arms free to hug this man whom she loved like a brother. Turning to face him, she wrapped both arms tightly around his neck. She spoke quietly into his ear through the already flowing tears.

"I love you, Rick ... I hope you know how much. You are, and will always be, a special part of my life." Barely able to force the heartfelt words past the painful lump forming in her throat, she whispered, "I'll miss you most of all, scarecrow."

Smiling, but swallowing hard, he returned her hug with as much affection as it was given. Lovingly, he kissed her damp cheek. "I'll miss you too, Dorothy," he told her.

They stood there quietly, holding on to each other for a few moments longer, unable to speak through the sorrow and the tears, but drawing comfort and strength from the awesome power of unspoken friendship.

Chapter 3

THE PINKY PROMISE

*"A promise between friends
is a pledge between hearts."*

—Granny Mae

Pulling into an open parking space at the Country Cookin' Restaurant, Mikayla spotted her best childhood friend, Diana, sitting in one of the rocking chairs in the outdoor waiting area. Her pretty blonde head was buried in the morning edition of the *Alabama Daily Herald*, which was obviously making for some interesting reading. Mikayla couldn't help but smile when she saw her. They had been best friends since either of them could remember; and they had declared that nothing would ever change that, not even 2,400 miles. Actually, Mikayla and Diana were much more than best friends—blood sisters, in fact. When they were eight years old, they had a secret ceremony to officially seal their pledge of sisterhood. One warm summer evening they had an all-night back-yard campout in Diana's father's hunting tent. It had taken several hours of relentless pleading on their part, but finally Mr. Gregory succumbed and heroically assembled the hunting tent for the giggling girls.

Armed with flashlights under the cover of darkness, each of them bravely stuck her pinky finger with the end of a safety pin. Squeezing the spot, Mikayla and Diana waited until a small drop of blood oozed to the surface. While touching their pinky fingers together, they vowed to be blood sisters for life. They believed in their friendship then and to this day had no reason to doubt that it would last for the rest of their lives.

Diana and her parents, Will and Bessie Gregory, moved in next door to Granny Mae and Mikayla shortly after the girls were born. Their homes were on adjacent lots divided by a majestic row of towering, blue spruce pine trees. The massive branches of the soft blue pines flowed all the way to the base of the trunks and then spilled out gracefully onto the ground. Each tree's branches interlocked with the branches of the trees on either side, as if creating an impenetrable line of defense. In a child's imagination, the trees were easily transformed into a massive row of tall Confederate soldiers standing at attention. Undaunted by the thickness of the pine barricade, the determined friends burrowed a tunnel through the dense limbs that was large enough to allow them to crawl through without receiving a single scratch. This hidden, damp passageway allowed for quick and easy access to each other's homes—which in the whimsical world of little girls, is of vital importance at times.

One of Mikayla's first memories of her dear friend was from first grade, when they had gotten their fannies paddled by "mean ol'" Mrs. Healy because they were giggling in class. What Mrs. Healy failed to realize was that laughing was completely beyond their control, especially in school and, God forbid, sometimes even in church. In the very places that they knew they shouldn't, something would invariably trigger an episode of "the giggles." Like when old Mr. Bennet would start snoring in church or when Mrs. Healy didn't realize that she had a long strip of toilet paper streaming from the heel of her shoe. Then there were those times when they giggled for absolutely no reason at all, laughing so hard at absolutely nothing that they almost wet themselves.

After many futile attempts to stifle them, it seemed Granny Mae simply conceded defeat, glad that the two girls had such a special relationship and that they were blessed with such carefree and happy little hearts. Her standard explanation in their defense was "something has switched on those girls' giggle boxes again."

At the age of twenty-nine, both women were continually amazed at how often that phenomenon still occurred after all these years.

"Hey, you big goof. Are you ready to eat breakfast, or are you gonna sit there in that chair all day, pretending you know how to read?" Mikayla kidded as she approached the rocking chair.

Startled by her friend's stealthy approach, Diana looked up and smiled broadly. "Hey, curly top. You shouldn't sneak up on someone like that. And to answer your question, I'd rather feed my face than read any day of the week."

After sitting and ordering pecan pancakes with extra whipped topping, crisp bacon, a single order of hash browns to share, and two coffees, Diana handed her friend a small, wrapped package. "I know we said no more gifts, but this one's from Rick. He got me one, too. Actually, they're not for us at all; they're for his own peace of mind."

Giving a nod of understanding, Mikayla accepted the gift and quickly tore off the paper. Reaching inside, she removed the contents and read the label aloud.

"Body Guard: Self-Protection Pepper Spray. Hmm … and just who am I protecting myself from, exactly?" she inquired with a half-hearted grin.

In a silent answer to her befuddled friend's question, Diana unfolded the front page of the morning paper and held it up in Mikayla's direction. The bold and eerie headline read:

"NIGHT CRAWLER CLAIMS SIXTH! DECAPITATED CORPSE FOUND IN SHALLOW GRAVE"

"This is the sixth young woman they've found dead in the past eighteen months," Diana reported sadly. "Each one of them was abducted from somewhere in Alabama, Mississippi, or Tennessee. There was another girl kidnapped a few weeks ago, Sallie … something. The police think she may be his seventh victim, but they haven't found her body yet."

"Why did someone dub him the 'night crawler,' anyway?" Mikayla asked, shaking her head in obvious disapproval.

"Apparently, it was some police officer's idea of a joke, and then the media somehow got a hold of it. It has something to do with the method he uses to abduct his victims. The police aren't saying," Diana answered, wide-eyed with fear and fascination.

"Maybe they should put forth a little more effort in trying to catch this nut rather than thinking up clever little names for him," Mikayla added.

"I agree," Diana said. "The authorities don't seem to have a clue to his identity. They have no idea if he is a transient or an upstanding citizen with a job that requires him to travel. Who knows? The killer's M.O. is always the same though, and there hasn't been one single witness, even though the women were abducted in open public areas." Gesturing with her fingers, Diana counted the victims in an effort to emphasize the point she was about to make. "Two of them were taken from a mall parking lot, one from a grocery store lot, one from a self-serve gas station, and two were driving to or from somewhere alone at the time of their abduction—which brings us to you. Rick and I just want you to be safe out there on the road all alone for such a long trip. Except for when our senior class went to Myrtle Beach after high school graduation, you've never been out of the state of Alabama."

"Well, thank you very much for pointing out that riveting facet of my exciting life." Mikayla responded with humorous sarcasm.

"I didn't mean it that way, and you know it," Diana replied in a shaming tone. "Rick and I just want you to be watchful and prepared. Sometimes living in a safe little town like we do can cause us to get complacent about what's going on out there in the real world. The thing that scares me most about this whole thing is the fact that this guy isn't an endangered species. There are plenty more human predators out there just like him. So, I need you to promise me you'll be careful."

Diana's worried countenance was something Mikayla had seldom seen, and it hurt her to know that she was the one responsible for her friend's uneasiness. Hoping to relieve her anxiety, Mikayla met her serious gaze. She reached across the small table, took her by the hand, and promised that she would be extra careful. She even pinky promised, but only after they had both vowed to be more cautious.

Diana's mother approached the table with their breakfast orders in hand.

"I knew when I saw this familiar order come through that my girls were out here," Mrs. Gregory said with a smile. "How you two can eat like this and still stay so thin is beyond me."

Momma Gregory, as Mikayla called her, had been the kitchen manager at the restaurant for many years. She was a slightly round and petite woman of fifty, with blonde hair and deep brown eyes, just like her daughter. Both women had the same delicate facial features, with soft peaches-and-cream complexions. She had a sensitive, caring spirit and was a perfect mother to her only child, Diana. But Mikayla knew that in Momma Gregory's heart, she had two daughters. She loved Mikayla dearly and had always treated her as one of her own. As she sat the plates of food down in front of them, Mikayla rose from her seat to stand next to her. Adequate words to express her feelings had been escaping her increasingly these last few months. Simply saying "thank you" or even "I love you" didn't come nearly close enough to describing the intensity of what she was feeling inside. Losing her cherished grandmother had given her a deeper and stronger appreciation for the loved ones that she had left.

"I don't know how to thank you, Momma Gregory, for everything you've done for Granny Mae and me. I just ..." she stopped midsentence, her words trapped in her throat.

"Sweetheart, whatever are you thanking me for?" the older woman asked. "You and Tinessa Mae are my family and always will be. You've been nothing but a blessing in my life, and I'll love you for as long as I live. You'll always have a home and family here with us, baby, and we'll be right here waitin' for you when you come back." Mrs. Gregory hugged and kissed her, all the while insisting that there be no more tears and that Mikayla sit down to eat before her food got cold.

With a concerted effort to remain positive, the two friends began eating their breakfast. Soon, they were chatting like schoolgirls, doing surprisingly well at pretending that this was just another day like the countless other days they had spent together.

Diana's unwavering support of her friend's decision had been instrumental in giving Mikayla the courage she needed to take this first step toward fulfilling her ultimate goal.

"So, if you land this one-year internship, can you realistically make enough money to come back here and open up your own advertising agency?" Diana questioned.

"To tell you the truth, I really don't know," Mikayla confessed. "I can maybe save up enough for a down payment on a business loan, but money isn't the main issue with this internship." Mikayla explained that the company's founder and sole owner, Alesander Dantoni, was only thirty-three years old, his company was only nine years old, and he only had fourteen employees, yet Dantoni Advertising had risen to the top of the field in a relatively short time. "The knowledge and perspective I can get from this guy is much more beneficial in starting my own agency than any amount of money," Mikayla said.

"Yeah, but it takes money to start your own business," Diana pointed out.

"I know—I know," Mikayla laughed. "Luckily, the salary is phenomenal, especially for an internship position, and there are hefty bonuses if I'm lucky enough to help land any big accounts. You can believe this, I'm going to work harder than any employee this guy's ever had. Let's just hope I can nail the interview. He pretty much told me I had the position—pending a favorable face-to-face meeting."

Diana glanced at their almost-empty cups and waved to the waitress carrying a full pot of coffee. "Why would someone of this guy's stature want to offer an internship?"

"Well, according to a magazine article I read last month, this is Mr. Dantoni's way of screening candidates for a new position in his company. Apparently, if the new intern performs well during the year, he or she may be hired on permanently as one of his top executives. Of course, this poses a dilemma." Mikayla paused for a sip of coffee and looked questioningly at Diana. "Do I tell him that I only plan to stay for one year to learn all I can, and possibly risk losing the internship, or do I keep that tidbit of information to myself?" She shrugged her shoulders in indecision. "I guess I have plenty of time to think about that on the way. Speaking of which, it's 11:00, so I guess I'd better get started."

Even though they had spent more than two hours talking over breakfast, it seemed like only two minutes.

They walked out of the restaurant arm in arm and stopped in an open area out of the flow of traffic. Appropriately, the weather had turned gloomy. Ominous dark clouds were releasing sprinkles of rain, with the imminent threat of more to come.

Tears were already pooling in Mikayla's eyes, threatening to spill over at any moment. She turned around only to find them already streaming down Diana's cheeks. "Hey, I thought we said no more tears," she said as she reached out to hug her dear friend.

"We did, but we didn't pinky it." Diana tried to laugh through the tears, but the attempt was futile. Her sorrow was much too powerful to subdue. "I have no idea how to say good-bye to you after all these years," she managed to whisper while the friends held on tightly to one another.

"This is not good-bye," Mikayla declared adamantly. "I'll be back in one year. I promise. Actually, I'll be back for Christmas in only six months. The time will pass so quickly, we won't even miss each other." She was trying to convince her friend, as well as herself, that being separated by so many miles wasn't going to be like losing a part of herself, but deep down she knew better.

Diana stepped back and seemed to be searching Mikayla's eyes for an honest answer. "I just want you to be sure that you're doing the right thing. Are you sure?"

"As sure as I can be," Mikayla answered honestly. She could see by Diana's expression that she needed to elaborate, so she paused to find the words to convey what was in her heart. "I guess for the first time in our entire friendship, I haven't been totally straight with you these past few months," she said, unable to look her friend in the eye, knowing that if she did, she would not be able to continue. "I just didn't want you and Rick to worry about me any more than you already were. Even though there was nothing you could do to help me, I knew that you'd try." Glancing up, she could read Diana's anticipation, so she continued. "After Granny got sick, it was like I lost my balance—my stability—you know what I mean? I lost my grounding, because I was losing her. She was my anchor. Then when I really lost her, I lost my heart, too. It's broken so badly, Diana, that I don't know if it'll ever fully mend." She paused and reached out for Diana's hand. "To lose a parent who loves you so unconditionally, to lose that foundation of support, is so completely devastating. Then, just a few months later, I lost our home, too." Fighting back the flood of tears, she paused and took a deep breath.

"I'm so sorry, honey," Diana whispered comfortingly.

"It's just that I felt like such a complete and utter failure, you know?" Mikayla questioned, as her sadness gave way to anger. "I can't tell you how mad I've been at myself. The loan balance wasn't even that much money, but with the doctor and hospital bills to pay, I just couldn't pay that, too." Mikayla explained how the guilt had been weighing heavy the past few months because she had blamed herself entirely—mostly because at twenty-nine years of age, she should have been farther along in her career. She should already have a good-paying job. If she had, the money wouldn't have been a problem. She shouldn't have married Travis and wasted over four years of her life. If only she had gone back to college sooner. "I've made so many mistakes—mistakes so big that they cost me our home. Granny was right, you know. We do have to pay for the bad choices we make in life."

Pausing again, she stared into the face of her best friend. Diana's sympathetic eyes gave Mikayla the strength to continue.

"But do you know what else Granny Mae said? She said that we shouldn't allow ourselves to stay bitter and angry at the consequences of those choices. We should just try to make better ones in the future. So, somehow, I have to come to terms with everything I've lost, the sadness in my heart, and the anger at myself. I just don't know how I can do that if I stay here. I think I need a little distance for a while, to gain a little perspective," she said with a timid nod, hoping for much-needed assurance from her friend. "I'm so sorry to lay all of this on you just as I'm ready to leave. This is so unfair to you, but I just couldn't let my feelings out until this very moment. I'm so sorry. I hope you understand …?" Her eyes pleaded for support and forgiveness.

"Of course I understand." Diana answered, as she gripped her friend's trembling hands. "I know you, Mikayla. I knew you were suffering more than you were letting on, but I also knew that I had to give you space to grieve. I knew you'd open up to me when you were ready. I'm sorry too, honey. It hurts me to know that you've been bearing all of this sorrow alone. For your sake, I wish you could've shared it with me sooner, but I'm glad you finally did."

"I am too," Mikayla whispered. After a deep sigh of relief, she continued, "I know this sounds cliché, Diana, but thank you for being such a wonderful friend. I don't know what I'd do without you and Rick, but I do know that I want my life back and I think I know what I have to do to get it," she declared, her voice growing stronger with conviction. "I have to find my own happiness, and I have to find it in myself, first and foremost."

Mikayla had come to the conclusion that the best way to begin her journey was with her career. She knew that her chances were slim that she could come back to Guntersville in a year and be able to start her own business right away, but she saw no harm in working toward that end. "I have to set a goal for myself, a goal that will give me a purpose to strive toward. It's definitely not about the money. It's not that I want to be rich. I just want to live a fulfilling life, with a little bit of security, working at something that I enjoy doing. It could never be about the money for me," she said with a faint smile.

"What's that reflective look all about?" Diana asked.

Still smiling, Mikayla explained. "Even though Granny isn't with me anymore, she has become this still voice in my head, kind of like my own personal compass for life." Mikayla explained that at certain times, she could hear the words of wisdom that Granny shared throughout her life. She smiled reminiscently. "About money, or the lack of it, she used to tell me, 'Baby Girl, we never want to have so much money that we don't need God no more.' So, thanks to Granny, I know better than to let money become a driving force in my life."

The friends shared a moment of common grief at the loss of the woman who had meant so much to both of them.

Mikayla felt better sharing her feelings with Diana. It helped sort out some of the confusion in her mind, making her decision to go seem a little more certain and her ultimate goal a little more attainable. In the smile of her precious friend, she saw the level of compassion that only comes from unconditional love. In an attempt to fend off pending tears, Mikayla tried to lighten the mood. "Besides, what else do I have to focus on but my career? Let's face it; I'm batting a big fat zero in the game of love. As you know, my personal search for Mr. Right has been far less than successful," she said with a fleeting grin. "Even if I found a man, I don't think I could find a large enough piece of my heart to give to him right now; not to mention, you apparently snatched up the very last of the princes out there anyway. All I'm doing is wasting my time kissing a bunch of big ol' frogs."

With that, Mikayla and Diana began to laugh. After all, how could they part any other way?

"Walk me to my car, you big goof," she teased, looping her hand through Diana's arm.

Standing by the open car door, the friends hugged each other one last time. Mikayla wondered how many times one poor heart could break. With a trembling voice, she somehow managed to coax the words past the painfully familiar lump in her throat. "I love you, Diana ... I'm so blessed to have your friendship. It means the world to me. Please don't think it will end here and now. I'll be back ... I promise."

Diana pulled back to look into the face of her beloved friend. "I won't believe it unless you pinky it."

Smiling through the tears, the friends joined their pinky fingers. "I pinky promise you that I'll be back," Mikayla pledged.

"I love you, curly top." Diana made a fruitless attempt to laugh.

The lump in her throat was so agonizing that Mikayla could only manage to mouth the words, "I love you, too," as she closed the car door.

Placing her pinky finger against the window, Mikayla smiled faintly. Diana returned her smile as she touched her own finger to the glass. Mikayla was nostalgic for the days of childhood when a pinky promise was an absolute guarantee and all the assurance she needed to be completely satisfied and secure in the outcome of that promise. Mikayla sadly thought how that was one of the most amazing attributes of youth forever lost in the process of growing up—the ability to have unwavering faith and utmost trust in a promise that one is powerless to keep.

As Mikayla turned to drive away, the two best friends smiled bravely and waved good-bye. But try as she might, Mikayla could not dismiss the sudden, unnerving feeling that she might never see Diana again.

Chapter 4

A RIDE OF DESPERATION

"Sometimes God uses detours
to get us where we need to be."

—Granny Mae

It had been less than one hour since Mikayla had bid a fond farewell to her old life, and a somewhat timid hello to the new. As if mimicking the swift pace of her life lately, the interstate traffic flowed quickly as she merged assertively into the I-20 lane bound for all points west.

Her five-day journey toward the promise of a bright new future had begun. By the close of this day, she would have crossed the border of her home state of Alabama for the first time in twelve years. Not only that, she would have traveled across Mississippi, Louisiana, and into Texas as well. If someone had told her nine months ago that this would be her reality today, she would have thought the person totally insane. Yet, here she was on a cross-country trip, and for the first time in her life, she was completely on her own. Granny was right; lives can change with every beat of the heart.

Determined to be positive and upbeat on the first day of her trip, she switched on the radio and popped in one of the CDs that Rick had made especially for her. "Only happy and fun songs for the road," he promised. She giggled happily as the first song began to vibrate from the surrounding speakers: arguably the most recognizable tune of the past twenty years and easily identified after only the first few notes, "Achy Breaky Heart" by Billy Ray Cyrus was the first track. She turned up the volume and began to sing along, welcoming the levity that the catchy tune inspired. She, Diana, and Rick had line-danced the night away to "Achy Breaky Heart" at their high school prom. She marveled at the power that this simple song wielded, flaunting its ability to conjure up fun, heartwarming memories at will.

As Mikayla continued to sing along to the blaring music, the miles on the odometer seemed to quickly roll by.

By the end of day one, she was 468 miles closer to her destination, and by 7:30 in the evening, she was checking into a roadside motel in Monroe, Texas. She was a little tired and hungry but proud of the fact that she was right on schedule and hadn't gotten lost all day. Rick would be very proud of her. She was right on track with the trip itinerary he had configured for her.

Subsequently, days two and three of the cross-country trek came and went as planned, yet they were vastly freeing. Forsaking the music during those two days of the trip, the seemingly endless miles of serene solitude had a hypnotically quieting and thought-provoking effect. This peacefulness of spirit, although comforting, felt foreign to Mikayla, as it was in such sharp contrast to her tumultuous feelings and emotions of late. During these quiet hours of reflection and reasoning, she found herself reiterating her thoughts verbally. She talked aloud to Granny, to God, and to herself. Putting voice to her thoughts seemed to help solidify, in her own mind anyway, the conclusions, resolutions, and plans she had made. But most importantly, she finally made peace with her own heart, discovering that although the mind is designed to navigate and dominate our thinking, the heart has a mind of its own—and sometimes it knows best. The heart is much more powerful and persuasive than any amount of intellectual reasoning.

In the end, Mikayla allowed Granny's words to lead her to the closure she so desperately needed. She could hear the voice in her head as plainly as if her grandmother were in the seat next to her. "Just because something unthinkably painful happens to you one day, Baby Girl, doesn't mean it has to happen to you every day. The key to having joy in your heart is to learn to accept the past and leave it where it belongs—in the past. How can you find happiness in the present and excitement for the future if you keep living in the past?"

Granny's unending love and foresight gave Mikayla the courage she needed to finally leave the anger, pain, and the guilt of the past few months behind her. But just because she was putting the past behind her didn't mean that she wasn't bringing her inspiring and loving memories of Granny Mae along to keep her company for the rest of her life.

❀   ❀   ❀

Beginning her fourth day of travel bright and early on Tuesday morning, Mikayla realized that during the past three days of travel, she had been all but oblivious to the magnificent country she had been traveling through. She spent the night in a reclusive, family-owned motel in Santa Fe, New Mexico, adhering precisely to Rick's planned itinerary.

It was decorated in historic Spanish fashion and had peaceful gardens with winding brick walkways in which one could get lost. Early in the evening, after a delicious dinner in the café on the outdoor terrace, she took a leisurely walk through the lush green gardens filled with wisteria and fruit trees. The blossom-laden lilac bushes in their beauty and fragrance reminded her of home.

Mikayla was pleasantly surprised by the rustic and colorful Santa Fe décor in her room, and she sat in the corner of the spacious area that was perfect for reading or corresponding. At an old roll-top desk, she addressed a picture postcard to Diana and Rick.

After a long and restful night's sleep, she went down for breakfast in the café. At 7:00 in the morning, the air was crisp and clean. The grounds were even more breathtaking in the morning light than they had been last night. Breakfast was delicious. She had tart cranberry-walnut muffins slathered in cream cheese and served with scrambled eggs and freshly squeezed orange juice. She indulged and allowed herself extra time spent sitting in the garden with her favorite morning drink, a frothy mocha latte with a shot of raspberry syrup. Mikayla felt like she was on vacation, so she decided to act the part. Since checkout time was not until 11:00 and she was traveling on schedule with time to spare, she decided to take in a little sightseeing before commencing her trip. The Santa Fe landscape was truly majestic and awe-inspiring, the beauty of which was indescribable. She took lots of pictures to share with Diana and Rick and picked up a pretty handmade necklace for her best friend in one of the local shops.

All too soon, it was time to hit the road. Grabbing a few snacks at the convenience store where she stopped to fill up the tank, Mikayla was off in pursuit of her day's destination: Topock, Arizona. Merging onto I-40 West a few moments later, she settled back in the seat for the next 517-mile leg of her journey.

Several hours later, near the small town of Seligman, Arizona, she spotted in the distance the one thing that strikes sheer terror in the heart of any interstate highway traveler: seemingly endless miles of glowing red brake lights—as far as the eye could see. "Oh, great," she muttered under her breath, as the flow of traffic all but stopped. Although she was only moving at a snail's pace, Mikayla didn't take her eyes away from the car in front of her as she reached over to feel for the map on the passenger seat. Surely there was an alternate route or bypass she could take. She was less than two hours away from Topock, and thanks to the most annoying trait of her fierce type A personality, she wanted to stay on schedule as much as possible. Mikayla vowed that someday she would work on this particular personality flaw, which insisted on perfection in every facet of her life, but not today. There had been enough changes in her life lately. One more change just might push her completely over the edge of sanity.

Shifting her gaze for only seconds at a time from the taillights of the creeping car in front of her, she quickly scanned the open map. *Aha! The Historic Route 66 turnoff is just a few miles up ahead. The detour will add a few extra miles in a roundabout way, but the scenery will be well worth it.* Pleased with her newfound navigational abilities, she refolded the map and returned her attention to the brake lights only inches in front of her.

Unfortunately, those few miles to the turnoff ended up taking about ninety minutes. When Mikayla finally merged onto the exit for the two-lane stretch of blacktop known as old Route 66, she could feel the anxiousness begin to slowly drain from her body. By then it was about 7:30 in the evening, and the sun was just moments away from reaching the straight, thin line where land meets the heavens. Mikayla decided she needed a break and a chance to stretch her legs, so she pulled over at one of the tourist shops conveniently located along the side of the road. As she was getting out of the car, she found it impossible to shift her eyes away from the horizon and the vibrantly illuminated sunset. It was absolutely breathtaking. Even the imaginative names of the most exotic colors in the fattest box of crayons couldn't describe this amazing Arizona sunset. Mikayla quickly retrieved her digital camera from her handbag to capture a few snapshots of Mother Nature's awesome display. Watching in wonderment, she continued to click the shutter as the distinctive, bold colors intensified and then ever so slowly began to diffuse, until finally, but far too quickly, they faded away, leaving only a soft glow of golden illumination in their wake.

Mikayla smiled as she recalled Granny's unique explanation for sunsets. The memory was tenderly ingrained in her mind. She could see herself as a happy little barefoot girl, sitting on the porch swing, snuggled up in the lap of her doting grandmother, watching the sun go down on a clear, warm Alabama evening. Granny would take Mikayla's tiny hand and point to the brightly colored sky, explaining that it was time for God to go to bed and that He was turning out all the lights in Heaven. Then, the two of them would sit quietly and watch as God slowly turned out the big light to the world. As the blazing glow of the huge, orange sun faded away, they would both wave good night to God.

Laying her hand to her chest, Mikayla was thankful for the understanding that it's not the passing of time, as the old saying goes, that mends the broken heart. Instead, it's the healing embracement of one's own cherished memories that bonds the broken pieces of the heart back together, tightly mending all of the painful cracks so that only the love is sealed inside.

❦   ❦   ❦

By 8:30 that night, Mikayla was back on the road. By her calculations, she was less than two hours from her destination. At any moment she expected to see the I-40 West highway signs guiding her back on course. She was looking forward to a relaxing hot bath or maybe even a luxurious soak in the hotel Jacuzzi. As miles of desert sand flashed by in the beams of her bright headlights, Mikayla's thoughts turned to her immediate future. As the end of her long journey grew near, she was at the same time optimistic and yet a little apprehensive. After just one more day of driving, she would reach her destination. She should arrive in California on Wednesday. That would give her plenty of time to find a suitable hotel, decompress, and prepare herself for the interview with Mr. Dantoni on Monday morning. Mulling over whether she should wear her moss green dress or her royal blue suit to the interview, she felt an unpleasant foreboding creep into her consciousness. As Mikayla looked around, the highway seemed dreadfully deserted. Even though there were many areas in Arizona where development was sparse, this area seemed unusually desolate. Just as she decided to pull off the road to check her map, she felt the car engine suddenly begin to hesitate. After only a split second of sputtering, the engine completely stopped. Immediately upon losing power, but still rolling from momentum, she tightened her grip on the steering wheel and strong-armed the now heavy and powerless vehicle to the side of the road and out of the way of approaching cars—not that there were any other cars in sight. She was relieved when she felt the tires fall off the low berm of the blacktop and onto the dirt, verifying that she had indeed gotten completely off of the road. Although rightfully rattled, she systematically turned on the emergency flashers, turned off the ignition, unbuckled her seatbelt, and took in a deep, calming breath. She was thankful that the headlights were still beaming and that the interior lights came on when she reached up and flipped the switch. Putting her hand on the ignition key, she uttered a quick prayer and turned the key forward in hopes of restarting the engine. Instead of the prayed-for sound of the restarting motor, there was no sound at all—not a click, a moan, or any other sign that there was life under the hood of her car.

"Okay, Mikayla, don't panic," she said firmly, as if talking to someone other than her own frightened self. Digging her cell phone out of her handbag, she dialed 911. Instead of the reassuring tones of the three numbers being dialed and the anticipated ring on the other end of the line, she heard the dreadful beep-beep signal and saw the flashing black words on the bright green screen announcing "searching for signal."

"Oh no! Not now. Please don't do this to me." she pleaded as she frantically rolled down the driver's-side window. Holding her phone outside of the car, she tried once again to call for help, only to receive the same disheartening response.

Despondent, but trying not to panic, Mikayla opened the door and stepped out onto the eerily deserted, two-lane highway. Hindered by the consuming darkness, she peered down the straight, flat highway in both directions. There was no evidence of a home or business in sight in either direction. Her car headlights and the glowing full moon were the only sources of illumination for as far as she could see.

Standing in the road, she weighed her options. Thinking she might get a signal a little farther down the road, she slowly began walking in the direction lighted by her headlights. After a distance of a few hundred feet or so, she tried the cell phone and again received the disappointing "searching for signal" response.

"What good are these things if they never work when you need them?" she mumbled to herself. Turning to walk back toward the car, the ghostly silence was interrupted by a sudden rustling in the bushes beside the road. Startled, she paused momentarily, thinking about what she should do. Not willing to wait for the thought process, her feet decided to break into a flat-out mad dash toward the car. If she was going to be eaten by some kind of wild animal, it was going to have to catch her first. Only a fool would just stand there, waiting to be devoured. Running as fast as she could, she didn't once look behind her—or even to the sides, for that matter. She kept her eyes trained on the open car door and the safety it represented. Breathlessly, she made it to the vehicle and threw herself inside, slamming and locking the door behind her.

Although she had run only a short distance, her heart was pounding as if she had sprinted a mile. And what a quick sprint it was, too. Feeling safe for the moment in her locked, animal-proof sanctuary, all at once the thought of her little "running fit" struck her funny bone. *Boy, I bet even Superman couldn't beat that time.* she thought, laughing out loud at herself, having been scared silly by what was probably just the wind rustling the bushes. *Just wait until Rick and Diana hear this story.*

As she was trying to catch her breath and calm her racing heart, Mikayla caught a glimpse of something on the road ahead, about fifty feet away. It stood frozen in time, caught in the high beams of the headlights. A creepy realization of the danger that lurked in the darkness washed over her, leaving her skin cool and clammy. The menacing animal resembled a large gray dog. She assumed it was a coyote. The animal stood perfectly still, staring straight ahead in the direction of her car, its demonic eyes glowing bright green in the reflection of the light. After a few more moments of intimidation, the animal turned and crept silently back into the bushes.

Well, so much for walking in the desert at night, she concluded to herself. *I guess the only thing to do is sit tight until dawn or until someone comes by. At least when it's daylight, all of the nocturnal, people-eating creatures will be asleep, and then I can walk a little farther down the road in both directions and maybe get a call out on my cell.*

Thinking it wise to save what battery power she had left, Mikayla turned off the high-beam headlights in exchange for the small parking lights. Anxiously, she clicked off the annoying emergency flashers.

It was about 11:30, and she was beginning to feel the chill of the desert night air, so she leaned over the back seat and dug some socks and a lightweight jacket out of her suitcase. There was a blue crocheted afghan in the backseat as well, one that Granny had made for her to keep in her car in case of an emergency. She felt sure that tonight qualified.

A few minutes later Mikayla was snuggled under the afghan, trying not to freak out. She closed her eyes and took some deep breaths in an attempt to extinguish the overwhelming fear slowly welling inside of her. Her mind was spinning with scenarios. *What if no one comes by, or worse—what if someone does come by and he happens to be a murdering maniac? What if Cujo comes back and attacks the car—what if* ... She fell asleep with these frightening thoughts running through her head, which would explain why she awakened a few hours later with a blood-curdling scream loud enough to wake the dead from their eternal slumber.

After a moment of haziness, reality returned to remind her of her precarious predicament. Glancing at the clock, she saw that it was 1:30 in the morning. She flipped on the headlights and once again saw nothing but deserted highway ahead. Reaching for her bottle of water, Mikayla took a tiny sip. She was trying to limit her intake of liquids for the obvious reason that what goes in, must come out, and she had no desire to step one foot outside of her car again tonight.

Clicking the headlights off, something in the dense darkness ahead immediately caught her eye. Straight ahead, but far off in the distance, she saw a single, tiny white dot of light. Her body stiffened to attention in the seat. She watched as the glow slowly increased in diameter. Breaking into the deadly silence of the night, with the exception of an occasional serenade of insects and animals, emerged a faint, soft, humming sound. The sound grew louder as the glowing dot grew larger.

It didn't take but a few more minutes for her to realize it was either a car with only one burning headlight or a motorcycle coming toward her on the opposite side of the two-lane road. She didn't know whether to be relieved or terrified. Forgoing her fear, she decided it best to boldly announce her presence, so she flipped on the high-beam switch of her headlights.

As the seconds passed and the sound grew louder and closer, her anxiety level grew in tandem. Her heart was pounding so hard and fast that she could see it thumping through her jacket. *Just keep a clear head, Mikayla, and don't do anything stupid,* she instructed herself.

Within a few hundred feet of reaching the illumination of her headlights, Mikayla recognized the sound as a motorcycle engine, and she could tell by the sound of the decelerating motor that the rider was preparing to stop.

Just a few feet inside of her headlight beams, and off to the left side of the road, she saw the ominous, dark motorcycle slowly emerge from the night. After rolling a few feet closer, the rider placed his feet down on the pavement as the bike finally came to a complete stop. The figure straddling the bike was dressed in black from the top of his helmet to the tip of his boots. At least she assumed it was a "he". For a moment, she felt a fleeting glimmer of hope as she thought it might be a woman on the bike.

As the rider dismounted his ride, positioned the kickstand, and removed the revealing helmet, Mikayla's momentary lapse of relief quickly disappeared. A tall and foreboding, dark-haired man with a short, scruffy beard began walking slowly toward the car, stopping just a few feet short of the driver-side window.

Since the interior lights were still on, the man could clearly see her through the window. She knew that it must be immediately apparent to him that she was alone and frightened. Since he had to communicate through the window that was still tightly closed, he had to speak rather loudly.

"Howdy, ma'am. Are you okay?"

She gave no response, and after a moment, he continued, "It looks like you might be havin' some car trouble. Can I do anything to help?"

In sharp contrast to what she had expected, he had a smooth, mellow voice with a bit of a slow country drawl. He certainly didn't sound like a lunatic, but neither did Ted Bundy (not that she had ever spoken with Ted personally she reminded herself); but as Granny always said, first impressions can be deceiving. Keeping the lunatic possibility in the forefront of her mind, Mikayla slowly lowered the window about an inch for communication purposes. Peering through the glass she saw the man leaning down to the level of the window. He had almost shoulder-length, chestnut-colored hair, a mustache, and several weeks' overgrowth of facial hair. Looking into the stranger's unwavering eyes, a chilling shudder traveled down her spine, causing her whole body to shiver. Even though she had Rick's pepper spray clutched in her right hand, her index finger poised and ready on the nozzle, it did nothing to relieve the sheer terror of the moment.

Mikayla tried to disguise her trembling as shivers from the cold night air, rubbing her arm with her free hand as though trying to warm herself.

The stranger didn't seem convinced, but courteously replied, "It's cool out tonight. Most people have no idea of how chilly it can get out here in the desert when the sun goes down."

"I'm okay," she muttered, managing somehow to coerce the words through her tightened larynx, "But my car isn't so lucky. I was driving down the road, and it just stopped. Would you make a call for me on your cell phone, please?"

"I'd be glad to—if I had one," he answered. He seemed to have noticed her obvious disappointment as he quickly added, "But since I can't do that … if you pull the release latch, I'll take a look under the hood and see if I can tell what the problem might be." He was already walking toward the front of the car before she could voice any protestations. Seeing no harm in his looking under the hood, she felt under the dash and pulled the lever.

As he raised the hood, the tiny light bulb came on inside the motor compartment. The small space between the dashboard and hood provided her with a thin peephole through which she could see his hands probing around the engine. She saw him check the battery cables and remove the cover over the air filter. He then proceeded to check the spark plug wires, requesting from time to time that she try to start the engine. Each attempt to revive the lifeless motor failed. After only a few minutes, he straightened up and closed the hood.

Standing next to the car once again and speaking to her through the small crack in the window, the stranger explained, "Ma'am, I believe the trouble is with your distributor. The battery's holdin' the charge and the engine's getting fuel, but there's no spark to the plugs. I think your distributor module is bad."

Mikayla held her breath. Somehow she knew what was coming next, and began shaking her head before he had even completed the sentence, "I'd be glad to give you a ride to the next town where you can get some help."

"No, thank you," she replied, still shaking her head.

"Ma'am, I can't just leave you out here on this deserted road all alone. I'm sorry; I just can't do that," he said politely but sternly.

"If you think I'm getting on the back of that motorcycle with a total stranger in the middle of the desert, in the dead of night, you've got another think coming, mister!" Mikayla stated firmly, summoning every ounce of conviction she could muster.

"Well then, we've got ourselves a little problem, 'cause I'm not leavin' you out here all alone," he stated, sounding just as determined as she had. "So, if you're not comin' with me, and I'm not goin' without you, then I guess we're both just staying put," he said dogmatically, emphasizing his decision with an obstinate stare.

"Why can't you just go on alone to the next town and send a tow truck back for me and my car?" As far as she was concerned, this was the perfect solution.

"Ma'am," he began with a sarcastic chuckle, "I don't know if you realize it or not, but you're in a very dangerous situation here. If I leave you here alone, any number of unspeakable things could happen to you. Number one—you could sit here for days before another living soul comes down this road. Number two—worse than seeing no one at all, a couple of 'good ol' boys' could come down through here and see you as nothing more than a few hours of fun. Number three—what are you going to do when you have to go to the bathroom?" He smiled smugly. "Have you given any of that a minute's thought?"

"Well, if I have to go to the bathroom, I guess finding a private spot won't be a problem." she responded, returning his irritating sarcasm—although the thought of peeing outdoors had been causing her serious concern ever since her earlier encounter with Cujo.

She could almost see his patience thinning. "Ma'am, do you have any idea what kinds of animals are in this particular desert?" Not giving her time to respond, he continued. "Well, I do. When I was a kid, I spent every summer of my life in this desert, so I believe I know a thing or two about the wildlife who call this place home. Trust me when I say they're not 'girl-friendly' creatures." He raised his hand and gestured toward a small clump of weeds on the side of the road. "Sooner or later you're gonna have to go to the bathroom. Suppose you squat down out there next to a sidewinder rattler, a scorpion, or a big ol' Gila monster—all of which are poisonous, by the way. How would that be for ya?" he questioned cynically. "If it were me, I'd take a nice motorcycle ride any day of the week."

Crossing her arms as she spoke, Mikayla hoped he couldn't sense her wavering conviction in her decision to stay put. "How do I know you're not just trying to scare me? Besides I have never heard of a Gila monster. It sounds like something you just made up to me."

"Well, when you get back home you can look it up for yourself on the Internet." His eyes widened as if to emphasize the danger. "But for your information, it's a big ol' venomous lizard that can grow to more than two feet in length. They have big, razor-sharp teeth and, more to the point, these little beauties feed only at night."

"Are you telling me the truth?" she asked, slowly realizing that she had no other choice but to accept his offer for a ride.

"Yes, I'm tellin' you the truth. I never lie," he affirmed with a stern and convincing expression. "I can tell you this as pure fact, too—I, myself, once saw a Gila monster devour a whole stubborn woman in less than five minutes, and she was a lot bigger than you, too." He ended his little tale with a wide, disarming grin. He seemed to be trying his hardest to put her mind at ease.

Making an attempt to return his smile, Mikayla thought to herself, *How do I know you're not a bigger monster than all the animals in this desert put together?*

The decision to go with this stranger was one of the most frightening and difficult decisions she had ever made. But, for the life of her, she saw no other alternative. As she pulled the handle and slowly opened the door, the stranger took a few steps back.

"Do you happen to have an extra set of car keys?" he inquired.

Thinking this a somewhat unusual question, she unzipped her purse and pulled out a single key. "I have a valet key. Will that do?"

"That'll do perfectly." He took it from her hand, walked around to the back of the car, and placed the key inside the tail pipe. In response to her questioning expression, he said, "For the tow truck driver," as he walked past her toward the motorcycle.

Looking doubtfully at the way she was dressed, the man said, "The jeans will be warm enough, but your jacket's awfully thin. Do you have a heavier one in your car?"

Shaking her head no, Mikayla reluctantly closed the car door. Her heart sank as the clicking noise made by the locking mechanism sounded the "Amen" to her separation from safety inside the vehicle. Trying not to appear as terrified as she felt, she kept her right hand jammed into her jacket pocket, tightly clutching the bottle of pepper spray.

"Well, I'll see what I can do about keeping you warm," he told her, as he walked over to his motorcycle and opened the flap on the left saddlebag. "You can bring a small overnight bag with you as long as it will fit into this compartment—if you want to," he offered politely.

Deciding it best not to turn her back on this stranger to pilfer through her car looking for toiletries, Mikayla declined his offer with a simple "No, thank you."

Pulling a lightweight jacket out of the saddlebag, the man removed the heavy leather coat he was wearing. Putting his arms through the sleeves of the lighter garment, he pulled it on and zipped it up. Walking toward her, he handed her his heavy leather coat and instructed her to put it on.

As she raised her hand to decline his gentlemanly gesture, he stopped and slowly ran his fingers through his thick, wavy hair. As if summoning patience to deal with this difficult female, he took a deep breath and released a long sigh. "Lady, have you ever let anyone be nice to you? Would you please put this coat on so you won't turn into a human icicle on the back of my bike?" he pleaded with what Mikayla imagined was all the tolerance he could muster.

"Thank you," she said quietly, as she reluctantly surrendered and took the coat from his hand. Quickly, she slid into the bulky garment that still radiated with the comforting warmth of the stranger's body heat. She discreetly, transferred her right hand from one pocket to the other, all the while maintaining a death grip on the life-protecting pepper spray.

The man straddled the seat of the motorcycle and started the engine. Mikayla winced as the loud rumble shattered the deadly silence of the night. She turned back toward her disabled vehicle and beeped the security button on the keyless remote. The lights flashed with the assurance that all was locked up safe and sound. She just hoped it stayed that way until a tow truck could get there and retrieve her car, along with everything else she held near and dear locked away in the trunk. Obligingly, Mikayla put on the helmet that the man placed into her trembling hands.

"Sorry it's not a cool one like mine," he teased, "but it came free with the purchase of the bike, and I wasn't expectin' company."

"It will do fine, I'm sure." Momentarily releasing her grip on the pepper spray, she buckled the helmet strap beneath her chin. She tried to offer a faint smile in appreciation of his humor, but her heart just wasn't in it. It seemed that fearing for her life had taken precedence over humor at the moment.

Mikayla took hold of his outstretched arm as he effortlessly, with one quick motion, hoisted her up into the seat behind him. For the next few seconds, she just sat there stiffly, both hands buried in her pockets.

It was the stranger who finally broke the awkward silence. "If you don't put your arms around my waist and hold on, what's gonna keep you from flying off the back of the bike when I take off?" he asked with a chuckle.

"Sorry," was Mikayla's one-word response as she wrapped only her left arm around his body. "I haven't been on a bike in a long time." Then, deciding to be painfully honest, she further confessed, "Actually, I've never been on a bike in my entire life."

"Oh, man. That's a real shame," the stranger announced loudly, releasing the clutch and feeding gas to the powerful machine. "A gal's first ride on a motorcycle really should be with someone who actually knows how to ride one."

Even though her heart was still racing from the terror of having her life depend on the kindness of a stranger, she couldn't suppress an inward chuckle at his quirky sense of humor.

Mister, she thought, *I don't even know your name, but I hope that you truly are what you seem to be—a kind gentleman with honorable intentions of helping someone in distress—and not the stark-raving lunatic that I know you could be.*

Speeding down the road on the back of his bike, Mikayla prayed that she had made the right decision.

It didn't take but a few minutes for the vibration of the bike against the pavement to alert her attention to a whole new problem. Try as she might in this vulnerable seating position, her attempts to keep her body pinned against the backrest of her portion of the seat were in vain. Preventing her body from scooting forward and touching and bouncing up against him was a constant battle—one that she was clearly losing. And even though the last thing in the world she wanted to do was inadvertently arouse him, Mikayla eventually realized the fruitlessness of her efforts and abandoned the attempt at keeping distance between their jostling bodies.

Once she had admitted defeat in the battle against gravity, her attention quickly returned to her fervent prayer that this was not the worst decision she had ever made in her life. Even if she did happen to live to tell the story, she knew that Rick was going to be furious when he heard about this. Not to mention, poor Granny must be rolling over in her grave. "Sorry Granny," she whispered, as she clung to the stranger, not knowing if he was a saint or a demon.

Chapter 5

JESSE DAULTON

"Risking momentary embarrassment from confessing the heart
is far less painful than saying nothing
and forever wondering, 'What if?'"

—*Granny Mae*

Mikayla knew it was well after 2:00 in the morning when she sped off on the back of a total stranger's motorcycle, but keeping track of time since then had become impossible. In ways it felt as though it had been hours, but she was sure it hadn't been. For one thing, it was still dark. Regardless of the duration, the trip had been defined by one persisting constant: darkness. There had not been one single sign of civilization, nothing but miles and miles of desert, brush, and rocks, highlighted with an occasional glimpse of a moon-cast shadow during an infrequent break in the clouds. Other than that, there was only the seemingly endless strip of blacktop on which the two had been traveling. The chilly dryness of the desert night air was stinging Mikayla's face. Her eyes were burning and weary. Her mind and body were fatigued from hours of harboring a generous amount of nervous tension, anxiety, and fear.

Once again, she leaned her head slightly to the left of the stranger's body in front of her, searching for anything but the dismal blackness of night. Finally, signs of human existence began to peek through the obscurity of the dark desert veil. At first, there was only the haloed glimmer of highway lights far off in the distance, but as the bike rumbled closer, Mikayla could see towering billboard signs advertising fast-food restaurants, lodging, and fuel. In the forefront was a massive, neon yellow sign announcing the entrance to a brightly lit gas station. Mikayla vowed to herself that she would never again take the existence of electricity for granted. As if slowly releasing a tightly wound rubber band, she felt the anxiety-induced tension in her muscles begin to gradually loosen.

As Mikayla's salvation grew closer, she felt the motorcycle begin to gear down in preparation for pulling into the gas station. The bike finally rolled to a complete stop at the self-serve island. Barely able to contain her relief and thankfulness for safe harbor, Mikayla wasted no time in jumping off the bike and removing the helmet from her head. The stranger did the same and then busied himself with filling the tank.

This time, it was Mikayla who broke the silence. "I'd like to thank you, sir," she said, taking a timid step toward him. "I really appreciate your help, but … do you have any idea where we are?" she asked hesitantly, scanning the area for a road sign or landmark that would identify their location.

His expression softened into a sentimental smile. "Yes, ma'am, as a matter of fact I do. We're in Santa Claus, Arizona." His grin grew larger, as he continued. "When I was a little fella, my Uncle Clinton used to bring me here for the horse and pony auction. He had me convinced that this was where Santa Claus really lived … that the North Pole was just where the toys were made."

Although appreciative of his laid-back attitude and sharing mood, Mikayla was still more than a little anxious about her own situation.

As the stranger placed the nozzle back into the pump receptacle, he seemed to sense her increasing apprehension. He wiped his right hand on his pant leg and then extended it to Mikayla. "Jesse Daulton, ma'am, nice to meet ya."

For the first time in hours, Mikayla released the pepper spray from her intensive grip and extended her curled, stiff fingers to shake his hand. "Mikayla Mitchell. Thank you for the ride … although I don't think I was very gracious about accepting it." Letting go of his firm, warm grip, she felt the need to apologize for her rudeness. "I'm sorry about that. I think I let fear overshadow my good manners."

He accepted her apology with a nod but said nothing as he turned and opened the left saddlebag to retrieve her purse. As soon as he placed it in her hands, she immediately opened one of the zippered compartments.

"Please allow me to give you something for your trouble," she said as she held out a fifty-dollar bill.

Backing up as if she were contagious, he replied, "No thanks, ma'am; I was comin' this way anyway." After pausing for a second, he quickly added, "But thank you just the same; I appreciate the gesture."

As Mikayla reluctantly put the cash back in her purse, he took a step toward her. "Would you mind if I offered you some advice?"

"Well, Mr. Daulton," she said as she glanced around the deserted lot, "I could actually use some advice about now, especially from someone who seems to have knowledge of the area."

"First of all … it's Jesse," he said with a pleasant smile. "And, if you don't mind me asking, since you're obviously not from around here, where're ya headed?"

"Well, my goal last night was Topock, Arizona, and from there on to Monterey, California. I have a job interview there on Monday."

"Well … unless you have a specific reason for going to Topock, I have a suggestion for you to consider," he said diplomatically. "A few miles south of here is a road, Route 68 West, which will take you straight to the little town of Bullhead City, about an hour's ride from here. There's a reputable dealership there, and Bullhead City is only thirty minutes from I-40 West, which will put you right back on course to Monterey." Surprisingly, she was listening to him without fear or prejudice, and apparently he must have sensed it, because he continued. "I think it'd be in your best interest to get your car repaired at a dealership. I have an old friend out in the boonies of Ray Place, which is about sixty miles from where you broke down. I can give him a call and see if he can get your car towed to the dealership—if you want." Looking at his watch, he saw that it was 3:45 AM. "Although I'd better give him a couple more hours of shut-eye before I ask him for a favor." Jesse pointed to the right of the gas station in the direction of a small motel. "You could get a room there for a few hours sleep and catch the bus to Bullhead City in the morning to meet up with your car."

Truly astonished at his generosity and willingness to help, Mikayla voiced her acceptance to his suggestions. She took off his coat and handed it back to him, immediately missing the warmth it had provided.

"Thank you again, Jesse, for all your help." This time it was she who extended her hand to offer a sincere handshake of gratitude. He reached out and accepted her hand, his grip as gentle and reassuring as the smile on his handsome face.

As she turned to walk toward the motel, Jesse spoke up again. "Um … Miss Mitchell … this is just a thought … I don't know if you'd want to, but I'm actually headed toward Bullhead City right now. If you want to hitch a ride, I have no objections. That way you can be there when your car arrives in the morning. Maybe that would make it easier to make arrangements to get it repaired."

Mikayla stopped momentarily to consider his suggestion. She had never felt more alone and vulnerable than she did at this moment. She hated that feeling. It was never easy for her to need people, and since Granny's passing, it had become even more difficult for her to rely on anyone. It was important to her, especially at this point in her life, to be self-sufficient and independent. But putting those feelings aside, the important thing right now was getting back on the road to California.

As Jesse patiently waited for her decision, she reviewed her options. If she stayed at the motel for the next few hours, she had no idea when, or even if, a bus would run to Bullhead City in the morning. Jesse was right; making repair arrangements would be easier if she was there. Basically, the decision came down to a matter of trust. She could spend the night in this sleepy town of strangers or trust the one standing in front of her. She in no way relished the idea of once again putting her life into the hands of a man she barely knew, but deep down, something in her heart told her that she could trust him, even though the only thing she knew about him was his name. Although she knew it was completely irrational, still for some reason, she felt perfectly safe with him.

Making her decision, Mikayla looked into his eyes. Jesse stared back at her with what seemed to be unblinking sincerity.

"Well, first of all … it's Mikayla," she said with a hint of a smile. "And yes, Jesse, I'd appreciate a ride … if I can have that jacket back."

❦   ❦   ❦

Just before 5:00 in the morning, Mikayla and Jesse arrived in the charming town of Bullhead City, Arizona. The welcome sign proudly boasted a population of 38,960 residents.

A few blocks down the street, Jesse wheeled the motorcycle into the parking lot of a brightly lit restaurant, where the large overhead sign flashed "Open 24 hours." Looking around, Mikayla spotted a small motel directly across the street. The thought of a long, steaming hot shower and a nice, comfy bed seemed almost too good to be true. She heaved an audible sigh of relief.

Jesse chuckled. Waiting for her to jump off the bike first, he asked, "I take it you're glad we finally made it?"

Mikayla leaned backward to stretch her aching back. "You have no idea how glad I am." Straightening up, she paused and caught his eye. "Yes, I'm glad we made it … I'm glad to be near food and a motel … and I'm definitely glad that you really do know how to ride a bike." Grinning at him, her levity quickly switched to earnestness. "But most of all, Jesse Daulton, I'm glad *you* were the one who found me on that deserted road. Would you like to have breakfast with me, as my way of properly thanking you?"

Nodding his head yes, they had already started toward the door when he added charmingly, "But only if you let me buy."

Immediately after being seated and ordering breakfast, they both headed to the restroom to wash up. Mikayla returned to an empty booth. After sliding into her seat, she glanced around the restaurant and spotted Jesse standing by the exit doors talking on a pay phone. He was close enough that she could hear his voice but far enough away that she couldn't make out the words.

Watching him as he talked on the phone, she took notice of the man who had just come to her rescue. He was quite tall, probably six foot two or so, and very well built. She could see the definition of his biceps beneath the sleeves of his dark green shirt, which was unbuttoned and hanging open like a jacket. Underneath he wore a white V-necked shirt tucked neatly into the waist of his form-fitting black jeans. He had combed his wavy, chestnut hair, which was a little longer than she usually liked on a man, but it seemed to suit him perfectly. After observing him for a few minutes, she found herself smiling at the thought of how he would measure up against the "Rickter Scale." Thinking about the Rickter Scale sent a sharp pang of homesickness through her heart. She missed her best friends.

Together, she and Diana had devised a measuring device—a scale of sorts—which they fondly referred to as the Rickter Scale, appropriately named in honor of the man on which it was based. As they both saw it, Rick was clearly a perfect ten, acing all three of the standards necessary to qualify him, or any other man, as the ideal soul mate: number one—strength of character, number two—personality, and number three—appearance. After the establishment of this useful scale, every new man in Mikayla's life was subject to measurement and scrutiny against this nearly impossible standard. The highest scorer she had ever dated rated only a low six. But, even though she had just met Jesse a few short hours ago, something told her that he could measure at least an eight.

She was startled out of her train of thought when both her rescuer and the waitress returned to the table at the same time.

Jesse stepped aside and waited patiently for the waitress to deliver their breakfast orders.

Making eye contact with the smiling server, he issued a polite and sincere, "Thank you, ma'am." As he sat down, he immediately transferred his attention to Mikayla. She felt self-conscious under his appreciative stare. She glanced up to find that his facial expression openly revealed that he was not the least bit disappointed in what he saw.

He seemed slightly embarrassed that she had caught him staring. Looking down into his cup, he took a sip of hot coffee, and then raised his eyes once again. "Well, we're in luck," he told her cheerfully. "I called my friend in Ray Place, and he's gonna bring your car down to the dealership in a few hours. He says he should be here around 10:00 or so. He's gonna call you over at the motel across the street when he gets here."

"What do you mean bring it? Does he own a wrecker himself?" she asked, spreading grape jelly on her biscuit.

"No, but he has his own car hauler," Jesse explained. "He restores old muscle cars in his spare time, so he's always travelin' around haulin' cars and parts. He's glad to help you out, and he'll be a lot cheaper than calling a towing service. His name is Logan Brice, by the way." Mikayla looked up and caught Jesse watching her. He smiled slightly. "Logan's a pretty good guy," he added quickly.

"You must be tired of hearing this by now … but thank you, Jesse, for all your help." She continued the sentiment, hoping he could sense her sincerity. "I wish you would let me pay you something or pay for a room for you at the motel. You must be exhausted! If you don't mind me asking, where were you headed on that desolate desert road in the middle of the night anyway?"

Although he didn't raise his eyes from his plate, she could see him smiling as he slightly shook his head from side to side. "I don't mind tellin' you where I've been, but I'm not sure about tellin' you where I'm headed." Looking up, he answered her perplexed expression. "I don't want you to think I'm following you or anything but, like you, believe it or not, my ultimate destination is California," he confessed, still wearing an alluring smile. "My younger brother, Joe, opened up his own restaurant in Napa a few years ago. Things are going so well that he's thinking about expanding or even moving to a larger location, so I am goin' out there to visit him and help out for a while … or longer if I … well, if I decide to make my home there." There was a hint of sadness on his face as he continued. "I haven't seen him for a long time. Last night, when I happened across you, I was on my way to spend a few days with my sister, Annie. She lives in Walapai. I'm sort of on a cross-country mission just to visit and catch up with family members and friends that I haven't gotten to spend much time with lately." After a second's pause he continued, the tone of his voice clearly conveying his remorse. "I've been pretty much out of touch for the past twenty years."

Out of touch? Mikayla wondered, as she quickly shifted her gaze from his eyes down to her half-eaten breakfast. *Where could he have been for the past twenty years that would have secluded him from his family?*

The answer hit her as sure as if someone had spoken it into her ear. *Oh my God!* she surmised silently. *I bet he's been in prison. I knew he was too good to be true. Where else could he have been for the past twenty years? Oh my Lord, I just hitched a ride with a convict!*

She nervously tucked her hair behind her left ear. Deep in thought, she chewed on her bottom lip as she played with the leftover food on her plate. When she looked up and caught Jesse's eye, he started laughing—out-loud laughing—a manly, sexy laugh.

"Mikayla … shouldn't you ask me where I've been for the past twenty years before you start jumping to conclusions?" With a charming but ornery chuckle, he leaned across the table and whispered, "Where do you think I've been—*in prison*?"

Finding his humor contagious, Mikayla began to laugh along. "Well, the thought did cross my mind," she admitted. "You weren't—were you?"

"No," he said emphatically, his laughter trailing away to just a disarming grin. "I haven't been in prison. I can't believe you thought that," he said, acting as though he were insulted.

"Well, then … where have you been for the last two decades, Mr. Daulton?" she inquired humorously.

"Actually, I just recently retired from the military after twenty years of active service in the army, Miss Mikayla." He raised his right hand and gave her a jestful salute and a good-natured wink.

Obligingly, she returned his smile. "Way to make me feel like a jerk for thinking you were a convict. Thank you very much." Her face felt warm, so she knew her cheeks had to be sporting a fairly noticeable pink glow. Much to her surprise, she wasn't sure whether the heat in her face had originated from her embarrassing assumption of Jesse's recent whereabouts or from a response to the intensity of his gaze from across the table. Whatever the reason, he seemed to be enjoying himself immensely at her expense. "Seriously, though," she continued, hoping to divert his attention to anything but her, "now I'm really intrigued. Would you mind elaborating a little on that career bombshell you just dropped, pardon the pun?"

"Sure, I don't mind at all," he said as he took another sip of coffee. "Just before I turned eighteen years old, I realized that maybe becoming a cowboy, like my Uncle Clinton, wasn't the best career choice for me anymore, and since … well, let's just say I seemed to be lacking a little discipline in my life," he added mischievously, "I decided to join the army and volunteered for the Airborne Ranger Regiment upon enlistment."

Now Mikayla's curiosity was really aroused. "I've heard of it, of course, but what exactly is the Ranger Regiment?"

Jesse explained that the Rangers are the army's premier rapid-deployment special forces unit used for conventional infantry tactics and special ops missions. Rangers are 'wheels up' and ready within eighteen hours of being called and are most often the first forces deployed, usually with a direct action mission to raid, seize, and secure a specified target area. Attempting to simplify his rather technical explanation, he added, "We make it safe for the insertion of other forces—so they can come in and do their jobs."

Mikayla nodded in understanding as he continued. "After four years in the service, I felt like it was the profession for me, so I decided to make it my career—that is, until I turned thirty-eight a few months ago and started thinking that maybe there was a little more to life than being the ultimate soldier. So I passed the baton and came home." Turning his intense hazel eyes to meet her gaze, he finished his story. "I have to stop there. If I tell you any more than that, I'll have to kill ya." He broke into another gorgeous grin. "Now, it's your turn, Miss Mitchell. It is Miss, isn't it?"

"Yes, it's Miss." She answered his contagious smile with one of her own. "How about you? Are you married?"

"No, ma'am, not married, except to the army. Now quit stalling and spill it," he joked, pushing his empty plate to the side and resting his elbows on the table.

"Let's see," she paused, as if deciding where to begin. "Last Saturday, I left my hometown of Guntersville, Alabama, on my way to California for a job interview. My car broke down and you rescued me." She stopped and took a drink of lukewarm decaf.

Acting somewhat offended by her coyness, Jesse replied, "If that's not just like a woman. I spill my guts, and then you tell me nothin'. I think I've earned more of a history than that, don't you?"

Raising her eyes, she looked into his incredibly handsome, smiling face. He seemed to be looking at her with all of his attention, as if she were the only other person in the world. She found herself staring into the most mesmerizing hazel eyes she had ever seen. They were a captivating light shade of brown, highlighted with dark green flecks and outlined with thick, dark lashes. Lost in his gaze for a moment, Mikayla tried to decide what part of her history, as he put it, she wanted to share with a total stranger. She would probably never see him again after today, so she figured a little divulgence wouldn't hurt.

"Well, in May I graduated from the University of Alabama with a degree in advertising and marketing. I'm on my way to California in hopes of landing a one-year internship with a company called Dantoni Advertising. I plan to learn all I can from the very best in the business, and then after the year is up, I'm going back home with a head full of knowledge. And as soon as possible—that is to say, after I've saved enough money," she said with a smile, "I'm going to start my own agency. I hope to help some of the local merchants market their home-made products and services. Plus, I want to buy a home."

Jesse seemed to take in what she had said. "It sounds as though you have your life all planned out. What makes you so sure you won't like California and want to stay on there?"

Drawing her eyes down as if that was the most ridiculous thing she had ever heard, Mikayla expounded on her thoughts about home. "Home and friends are the most important things in my life. I plan to live out my life within spitting distance of the place where I grew up."

Smiling, he said, "Well, that's a rather graphic description, but I think I get what you mean. So you must have had a pretty happy home life, huh? Do your parents and family still live there?"

Unwilling to share any more of herself at present, she was grateful when the waitress chose that moment to refill their coffee cups. Since they had finished their food almost an hour earlier, the server's patience for her lingering customers was obviously wearing thin. Making eye contact, Jesse flashed the girl one of his disarming grins and apologized for their extended stay. After Mikayla agreed to one more cup of coffee, he promised the waitress that they would soon be on their way. Returning his engaging smile, the server's mood changed abruptly as she poured the hot, black beverage into their cups.

"Is there anything else I should know about you?" Jesse asked as he raised the steaming cup to his lips. "You were about to tell me about your family, I think."

"Well, I guess there is one thing I should tell you," she said seriously. "I'm a really great cook."

"Oh, I doubt that," he said, shaking his head and laughing as if that was a preposterous notion. "You don't look like any great cook I've ever seen."

"Is that so? Well, tell me Mr. Daulton, what does a great cook look like? I can hardly wait to hear your expert critique," she said as she crossed her arms, trying her best to look insulted.

"You're much too thin, for one thing. Great cooks love to cook, and they love to eat. You don't look like you eat much to me. Besides that, a person can't just declare herself a great cook. That fact must be proven—not by the cook, but by the eater."

"Well, I'll just have to cook dinner for you sometime, then." she proclaimed in answer to his good-natured challenge. "Not just to prove my cooking abilities, but to thank you for being such a considerate stranger."

"Hey now woman, don't tease me about somethin' as serious as a home-cooked supper unless you're serious about deliverin'," he said, just as the waitress passed by their table again with a large tray of food. After she was out of earshot, Jesse leaned toward Mikayla and asked quietly, "Before she throws us out of here, I wonder if I could ask you for a favor."

Intrigued as to what kind of favor she could do for him, Mikayla nodded her go-ahead.

"While I was on the phone up front, I noticed some maps of Arizona up by the register. I don't mean to imply that you are incapable of reading a map by yourself. You've already proven your prowess at map-reading," he said teasingly, inducing a chuckle from Mikayla. "But I would appreciate it if you'd indulge my need for chivalry and allow me to point out where we are on the map and how to get back on your route. I'd feel a lot better about leaving you here all alone."

Mikayla appreciated his kindness and concern for her well-being, and since her own maps were locked in her car somewhere in no-man's land, she saw no harm in accepting his offer.

"Actually, I'd appreciate that very much."

After paying the cashier, Jesse returned with the map and stopped at Mikayla's side of the booth. "Would you mind if I sit down beside you? It'd be kinda hard to do this upside down from the other side."

In response, Mikayla scooted over to the far edge of the rather small booth. Sliding in beside her, Jesse began unfolding the map as she cleared the cups and water glasses out of the way.

Placing the partially unfolded map on the table, he pointed out their specific location. Running his finger along the thin lines, he told her with precise detail how to get back to I-40 West and back on track to California. Once he seemed confident that she understood how to proceed on her way, he refolded the map.

Mikayla reached out and touched his hand. "Wait a second. If you don't mind, would you show me where I was when you found me? I'd love to know exactly where I was and how in the heck I ended up there."

Wishing he hadn't moved his hand from hers so quickly, Mikayla watched as he unfolded the map once again. Using his index finger, he traced backward—to the north of their present position—to a tiny road just south of Dolan Springs. "You were right about here," he said, pointing to the tiny spot on the map.

"How in heaven's name did I end up there?" she asked, feeling somewhat inept and embarrassed for being so far off course.

"Well," he hesitated. "I assume you were comin' west on I-40, correct?"

"Yes, until I hit a humongous traffic jam and decided to take a detour around it, by way of Historic Route 66. I assure you that from this day forward, it'll always remain 'historic' to me," she said with a cynical giggle.

He laughed pleasantly. "Well, I would guess that when you exited Route 66, amid the twists and turns to get back on I-40 ... well ... right about here," he said, pointing to a tiny spot on the map, "I would say that you zigged instead of zagged and ended up going north instead of south."

"So, what you're trying to say—which is very diplomatic of you, I might add—is that it was a simple mistake that anyone could've made, right?" she asked with a smile.

"Exactly ... well, anyone except a really great cook, that is," he teased.

"Oh! One more thing before we go," he said. As he leaned toward her to pull his billfold from his back pocket, his warm, muscular body pressed up against her arm and shoulder. The sensation was not at all unpleasant.

"This is Joe's business card," he said as he wrote on the back. "I wanna give you Logan's phone number in case you need it and my sister Annie's number in Walapai." Stammering for a second, he continued without looking up. "In case you need me or ... somethin'." He shrugged his shoulders a little as he held out the card.

Mikayla was truly touched by his concern and thoughtfulness. Their hands touched as she reached out to take the card from his fingers. She let her hand linger there as long as she could without being too obvious.

He sat there as if waiting for her to say something, playfully drumming his fingers on the table. Finally, he asked, "You're really gonna make me ask you for it, aren't you?"

"Ask me for what?" she answered honestly, a little confused, but at the same time amused by his question.

"I haven't done this in a while, but …" He winced as if saying the words were painful. "Can I have your phone number, too?"

Laughing at his expense for a change, Mikayla answered, "Sure, and if you're ever in Monterey, give me a call, and I'll make good on that dinner invitation."

"I may surprise you and do just that," he said with a quick wink and a grin. He folded the paper containing her phone number and placed it in his wallet. "Well, I guess it's time to go," he said. His words sounded remorseful as he reached out to pick up the check.

"Oh no you don't, Mr. Daulton," Mikayla declared as she quickly snatched the check from his grip. "I insist on paying for your breakfast. It's the very least I can do, so don't argue with me."

"Okay, okay. You pay the check, and I'll leave the tip," he said with a laugh as he rose from the seat.

He gathered their jackets, and followed her to the cash registers. She paid the check, and they started toward the exit door.

"Shoot," she muttered, "I forgot something on the table, I'll be right back." She scurried back to their seat to retrieve the business card he had given her. Picking it up off of the table, she noticed that he had left the waitress a twenty-dollar tip. She smiled softly at his generosity.

She returned to find him waiting to assist her into her jacket. After thanking him, he walked ahead to push the heavy glass door open for her. As Mikayla passed through the open door, Jesse lightly placed his hand in the small of her back. His touch was so gentle, she wondered if she had only imagined it.

It was 8:30, and the sun was announcing the start of a promising new day. She accompanied him to his bike and waited while he prepared to go.

A look of surprise crossed Jesse's face as he stuffed his hands in the pockets of his leather coat. Slowly, with a broad smile spreading across his face, he pulled out the canister of pepper spray. "I assume this is yours?" he asked jokingly. "I was wonderin' what you were pokin' me in the ribs with all night. I thought you were holdin' a gun on me or something."

"Oh, hush up." Mikayla laughed as she playfully grabbed the container from his hand.

"Now, seriously," he said with a grin. "Can you imagine the embarrassment? What if after twenty years of active duty—in harm's way, dodging gunfire, hand grenades, land mines, and RPGs—I was shot dead by a five foot, one hundred pound female ... on my own bike, no less." The mere idea of it seemed to strike him as hilarious.

Mikayla enjoyed the sound of his laughter, so she just stood there for a moment, letting him enjoy himself at her expense. "For your information, mister, I'm five foot four and weigh 115 pounds, thank you very much."

"Well then, that makes all the difference," he said as his laughter slowed and he regained his composure. Still wearing the most engaging grin she had ever seen, he looked into her eyes. "I'm only teasing you, Mikayla. I'm a bit of a kidder, in case you hadn't noticed."

All too quickly, his smile disappeared. Raising his hand to cover his mouth, he started to cough. At first it seemed that he was just clearing his throat, but the cough quickly became more persistent. Concerned, Mikayla walked toward him.

Signaling with an uplifted hand that he was all right, and shaking his head no, Jesse tried to feign a reassuring smile. Standing by his side, she waited with her hand resting sympathetically on his shoulder. Slowly, the severity of the coughing decreased and allowed him to catch his breath. Clearly embarrassed, he looked at her with apologetic eyes.

"Are you all right?" she asked with deep sincerity. She was surprised at how much the thought of him not being okay troubled her.

"Oh, I'm fine. Really … I'm sorry if I scared ya," he said, shrugging his shoulders as if to dismiss any seriousness. "I just got this really bad cold a few weeks back, and I can't seem to get rid of this cough." He grinned sheepishly. "Anyway, that's what I get for laughin' at ya."

"Hey," she said, "as nice as you've been to me, you're welcome to laugh at me any time you feel like it."

He looked at her for a moment. "You take care of yourself, Mikayla, and be careful," he said and turned to retrieve his helmet. There was a hint of reluctance in his tone, and a bit of sadness in his eyes.

That tugged at her heart, and for some strange reason that she couldn't quite figure out, something odd happened inside of her every time he said her name. Although she had been answering to Mikayla for twenty-nine years, whenever he spoke it, it was like she was hearing it for the first time.

"You, too, Jesse." she said with a wistful smile.

Reluctantly, she began backing away, but after only a few steps, she stopped. Watching him prepare to drive away, she had a regretful, unfinished feeling about letting him go just then. She hoped it wasn't just fatigue-induced emotion that she was feeling, but since losing Granny, she had promised herself that she would be more free and expressive with her feelings. She was tired of living with regrets, and she didn't want this to be yet another "if only" situation. For just once in her life, she decided to act on an emotional impulse. Just as he started to straddle the bike, Mikayla spoke up. "Jesse! … wait a minute." Taking a step toward him, she blurted out, "I forgot to thank you." It was the only thing she could think to say while her mind searched frantically for a better choice of words. But it wasn't so much what she wanted to say as what she wanted to do. "I can't believe how kind and considerate you've been to me—just a complete stranger you found along the highway." Taking her hands out of her pockets, she said softly, "You're one of a kind, Jesse Daulton."

Without hesitation or a single second's warning, she took a few more steps toward him and she stepped softly into his muscular frame. Wrapping both arms around his broad shoulders, she clung tightly to the man who had gone so far and beyond the call of duty to help her. She felt him tenderly return her hug as his strong arms tightened around her waist.

Wrapped in his warm, encompassing embrace, Mikayla felt more safe and protected than she had ever felt in the arms of any man. She trusted him completely. Wishing she could stay there longer, she finally loosened her hold and allowed her hands to slide leisurely down the length of his powerful arms. Standing so close that she could feel the warmth of his body and his breath against her hair, she found herself having to fight off an overwhelming urge to kiss him. She wanted to kiss him, for no other reason than just to thank him for being the wonderful man that deep down inside she knew he was. Although she released him seconds later without indulging her desire, every sensory indicator of her woman's intuition was absolutely certain of at least one thing—this man was definitely *not* just another big ol' frog.

Chapter 6

CALIFORNIA OR BUST

"A deed done in secret
is a deed from the heart."
—*Granny Mae*

The ringing of her cell phone startled Mikayla out of a deep, catatonic sleep. For a brief second, she didn't know what day it was, or for that matter, where she was. Leaning up on her elbow, she pressed the button that would put an end to the irritating noise. It was the car dealership's service department calling to inform her that her car had been repaired and was ready to be picked up. After drowsily thanking them for their courteous same-day service, she hung up the phone. A brief glance at the glowing red numbers on the bedside clock informed her that it was 4:30 PM. She knew she needed to jump out of bed and get dressed quickly if she was going to make the two-block trek to the dealership before they closed at 5:00. As tempting as a few more minutes of rest sounded, especially after the exhausting events of the previous twenty-four hours, somehow she forced herself out of the unusually comfortable motel bed.

Earlier that morning, after saying good-bye to Jesse, she had gotten a room and made arrangements to have her car checked out and repaired. True to his word, Logan Brice delivered her incapacitated vehicle to the dealership right on time. He was considerate and respectful—just the type of person she could see Jesse being friends with. After telling her that Jesse had jokingly threatened him with bodily harm if he over-charged her, Logan quoted her a more than generous price of sixty dollars as payment for his towing services. He then politely accepted her offer to buy him lunch at the fast-food restaurant next door to the dealership.

By the time Mikayla made it back to the motel and indulged in a long, hot shower, it was almost noon before she finally climbed into bed. Crawling between the sheets, she was ready and anxious for blissful sleep to arrive and render her serenely unconscious. But even though her body was willing, her mind was not. Her thoughts were racing and hell-bent on keeping her awake. Mostly, she found herself thinking about Jesse. She knew he must have been exhausted when he left this morning for his sister's house. She just hoped he had arrived there safely. Not to mention, she felt guilty that he had given her his warm jacket last night, when he was the one who was ill and had needed it much more than her. But, there was one particular thought of him that kept disrupting her attempts at sleep. She couldn't seem to put it out of her mind.

For all the kindnesses Jesse had openly shown her, there was one thing he did for her in secret that she didn't become aware of until after he had gone. She discovered it later that morning in the motel room. Having had a few extra minutes to kill while she waited for the call from Logan, she took out the map of Arizona that Jesse had bought for her at the restaurant. Since her confidence in her map-reading abilities had diminished considerably, she felt the need to take a closer look at his instructions for getting back on I-40 West and back on course for California. She wanted to make sure the route was clear in her mind.

Lingering over the map, her finger began retracing the route that she and Jesse had taken, ending up back at the location where he had found her—lost, alone, and frightened. It was then that she discovered his deception. Her breath caught in her throat when she inadvertently located Walapai on the map. When she traced back to where they stopped for gas in Santa Claus, she found that the little town, Jesse's sister's hometown and his intended destination last night, was in the complete opposite direction of Bullhead City. The big conniver had lied to her. He lied so that he could help her. He had no prior plans of going to Bullhead City last night—no plans, that is, until he decided that Bullhead City was where she needed to be. What a sneaky, underhanded, and absolutely wonderfully decent thing to do. Although Mikayla felt sure that his perception of his good deed was nothing more than a tiny sacrifice of his time, in her eyes it was nothing less than heroic. But something told her that Jesse Daulton had probably grown quite accustomed to the role of an unsung hero.

❧   ❧   ❧

By 8:30 that evening, all was well with Mikayla's world again. Her car was in the motel parking lot, repaired and good as new. All of her treasured belongings were intact and safely locked away in the trunk. She had spent over an hour on the phone with Rick and Diana regaling them with her tale of misadventure. Her story gave them a good laugh at her expense, which was followed promptly by a stern lecture from Rick instructing her to be more careful. The fact that he had assumed Granny Mae's role of worrying about her only served to endear him to her all the more.

After talking with her two best friends, Mikayla decided to go to bed early so she could begin her last day of travel bright and early, but there was one more thing she wanted to do before turning in. The idea had occurred to her in the early afternoon, and she had been mulling it over ever since then, trying to decide whether she should. She wanted to call Jesse. She came up with all of the logical and acceptable excuses for why she needed to call him, but the truth of the matter was, she just wanted to hear his voice. She wanted to talk with him one more time before they, in all probability, would lose touch forever.

She found herself in a stalemate with the phone as she attempted to gather the courage to call him. After picking up the phone at least a half dozen times, she finally allowed her finger to dial Jesse's sister's phone number. When it began to ring, she was about to snap the phone shut when she heard a pleasant-sounding female voice greeting her from the other end of the line.

"Hello."

"Umm … Hi! … is … may I speak to Jesse … if he's not busy, please?" Mikayla asked nervously.

"Yes, you may," the woman answered politely. "May I tell him who's calling, please?"

"Yes ma'am, I'm sorry. My name is Mikayla Mitchell and I …"

Cutting her off before she could finish, the woman replied cordially, "Oh, yes … Mikayla, I know who you are. I'm Jesse's sister, Annie. Jesse told us all about you when he got here this morning. Is everything okay?" She sounded sincerely concerned.

"Yes, everything's fine now, thanks to your brother." Mikayla answered, somewhat relieved at the warm reception. "I wasn't sure if I should call, but I wanted to thank him again for all his help." She knew that wasn't the real reason she called, but it sounded much more reasonable and far less pathetic than the truth.

"Oh, nonsense … he'll be glad to hear from you. We're just glad that he happened upon you when he did."

"So am I," Mikayla said honestly. "I'm so indebted to him for his generosity and his help. I truly don't know what I would've done had he not found me."

"That's our Jesse." Annie said proudly. "He's the stuff of legend around here, especially among his nieces and nephews. My husband, Taylor, teases him unmercifully about his many military awards. He says that Jesse's been decorated more times than Mom's old, artificial Christmas tree." Annie laughed pleasantly. "But you'll never hear it from Jesse. Any time you ask him about his experiences in the service, he'll give you his standard reply, 'If I tell you any more than that, I'll have to kill you,'" she said in a deep voice, comically attempting to imitate her older brother.

"Yes, actually, I've heard that already," Mikayla said, laughing along.

As though the thought had just occurred to her, Annie exclaimed apologetically, "Oh, I'm so sorry, honey. Here I am rambling on, and you called to talk to Jesse. Hold on for just a second while I walk over to the door and see if he's still out in the backyard."

Mikayla felt a fluttering in her stomach when she heard Annie in the background opening the door and asking someone to go and get Jesse because "Mikayla's on the phone."

Returning to the phone and sounding somewhat amused, Annie said, "I'm back. I sent Taylor out to rescue my patient brother. I have to tell ya, the poor guy must be exhausted. I'm afraid that my four-year-old son hasn't had much sympathy for his newfound uncle today. Corey seems to be under the impression that Uncle Jesse is his very own life-size army man."

I know how he feels, Mikayla chuckled to herself.

Annie continued, "It really amazes me how the little guy has reacted to Jesse. You know how big my brother is? Well, Corey only knew of Jesse through pictures and stories, but seconds after Jesse knelt down to meet him, Corey warmed up to him. He's been attached like Velcro to Jesse's leg ever since."

"It sure sounds like they're having a wonderful time together."

"Oh, they are. They went shopping together late this morning, just the two of them, and came back with Corey's very first motorcycle, 'just like Uncle Jesse's,' he says. They spent the rest of the afternoon putting together this adorable motorized bike, and Corey's been riding it around the backyard all evening. And, even though it has three wheels, he's afraid to ride all by himself. He'll only ride if Jesse walks alongside him. I know Jesse must be tired, but he'd never show it." Pausing for a moment, Annie's tone of amusement changed to that of pride and love for her brother. "It's funny how a heart, no matter how young or old, feels completely comfortable trusting Jesse."

"Yes, it is," Mikayla agreed softly.

After a moment of comfortable silence, Annie said, "And speaking of my wonderful big brother—here he is coming through the door. It was nice talkin' with you, Mikayla."

"Thank you, Annie," she replied. "It was nice talking with you, too. I'll try not to keep him from Corey for too long."

After a few seconds, she heard Jesse's gentle, mellow voice, sounding a little out of breath. "Hello?"

She thought she detected either shock or disappointment in his tone; it was hard for her to tell which. "Hi Jesse, it's Mikayla. I'm sorry to bother you when you're trying to visit with your family, but ..."

"Mikayla," he interjected in a shaming tone, "hearing from you brings a lot of things to mind, but I can assure you that 'bothersome' is certainly not one of them."

She could hear the smile in his voice, and his charming response pleased her immensely.

"Is everything all right?" he asked.

"Yes, everything's great. That's why I'm calling. I wanted to let you know that you were right; it was the distributor. My car's been repaired and is ready to go. I'm gonna take off first thing in the morning."

"Well, I'm glad they were able to fix it for you so quickly. I talked with Logan this afternoon to see if he had gotten your car to you all right, and he said that you seemed okay. I'm really glad that I could help you," he said with the sincerity of a lifelong friend.

"I am, too," she confessed. "Another reason I called was to ask about your cold. Are you feeling better?"

"Oh, I'm fine. Don't worry about me. I'm just a little tired," he said with a yawn.

"Did you get much sleep after you got to your sister's this morning?" Mikayla asked, still concerned about his health.

"Not yet. My little nephew has kept me hoppin' today. He's just a tiny bit excited. He got his very first motorcycle today."

"Yeah, I heard. Sounds like he thinks you're a pretty special uncle," she said, finding herself wishing that she could see them together.

"He's a great kid. I haven't been around much for the little ones in the family. That's one of my greatest regrets," he said, sounding pensive.

"Well, it sounds like you are well on your way to making up for lost time," she replied, trying to offer encouragement. "But you have to take care of yourself, too, you know. Promise me that you'll get some rest?" Mikayla was surprised that she allowed her concern to be so obvious.

"I will, but only if you promise to be careful and take care of yourself, too."

"I will," she promised. Pausing a moment longer, she could hear his soft breath on the other end. "I'd better let you go. I don't want to keep you from Corey."

"Mikayla?" he said her name suddenly, as if he thought she would hang up too soon.

"Yes, Jesse. I'm still here."

"Before you go, I'd like to say something to you."

He paused for a second, while she waited intently for him to continue.

"I just want to tell you how much I admire your courage," he said. "That's a rare trait, and one that I respect greatly."

"Courage? Me?" Mikayla replied, astonished at his compliment but extremely flattered as well.

"Yes, you," Jesse answered emphatically, with a sexy chuckle. "It takes a lot of grit to pack up and leave your family to travel clear across the country in search of your dream. But what I admire most about you is that you're not afraid to do it alone. I just think that's a very special trait … and I wanted you to know that before I let you go," he said, sounding a little more final than she would have liked.

She marveled at the compliment, especially since it came from a man who seemed to exude courage and integrity with every breath he took.

"Well, Jesse, I don't know what to say to such a flattering compliment. I've never thought of myself as having courage. And, I have to tell ya … if the compliment had come from anyone else, I would simply say 'thank you' and go on my way. But coming from you … well, I'm honored to hear those words from you. Thank you, Jesse," she said, surprised to find that she was on the verge of tears. Mikayla fought hard against the urge and successfully held them at bay. She knew that if she gave him even an inkling of how alone and frightened she was, it would shatter his admirable opinion of her.

"You're welcome, Mikayla. I meant every word," Jesse said sincerely. "And thank you, too."

"Well, I guess I'd better let you get back to your family," she said, hating that she would probably never speak with him again. She couldn't understand why she felt such an attachment to this man she had just met. Maybe Granny was right—"the heart wants what the heart wants"—but why did hers always want what she couldn't have?

"One more thing, Mikayla," he said. "I want you to know that you can call me anytime you need me. You know that, don't you?"

"Yes, somehow I do know that, Jesse," she said with an inward smile. "And I also know that when you finally get to Napa, I'll have at least one friend in California. So you give me a call when you get there, and I'll make good on that dinner I promised you."

"You bet," he said, which was far from the reassuring response of "I promise" that she was hoping to hear.

"Good-bye, Jesse."

"Good-bye, Mikayla."

After a few seconds of silence followed by the soft click in the receiver, Mikayla hung up the phone.

Climbing into bed, she curled up on her side and pulled the sheet tightly under her chin. Winding her hands securely in the crisp, cotton fabric, she wished she could somehow shield herself from the overwhelming loneliness that engulfed her each and every night. She buried her face in the overstuffed pillow, and as she had done so many times during the past few months, quietly cried herself to sleep.

The next morning, Mikayla watched through puffy eyes as the sun came creeping up and the azure blue sky gave way to a blazing pink and coral horizon. If there was one thing about Mother Nature's handiwork that she had enjoyed most on her five-day journey, it was definitely the marvelous sunrises and sunsets that she had been privy to. As far as she was concerned, they were God's most glorious displays.

She had left the motel about 5:00 that morning. After getting caught up on her sleep, she saw no reason to just lie there in bed, staring at the ceiling, so she gathered her things and got an early start on her final day of travel. With less than five hundred miles to go, she calculated that if she made minimal stops, she should arrive in California by early afternoon. This would give her plenty of time to check into a hotel and prepare for the biggest interview of her entire life—which begged the question, why wasn't she ecstatic right now? For the life of her, she couldn't stop the fantasy of Jesse from playing over and over in her mind, along with all the other "if onlys" that accompanied the impossible dream of him. She couldn't figure out how she could have gotten so attached to him so quickly. It didn't make any sense. This had never happened to her before in her life, not even during the silly and compulsive teenage years. But no matter how attracted she was to him, he hadn't sounded very enthusiastic about looking her up when he got to California. If he wasn't interested, there was really no point in her giving another minute's thought to pursuing a relationship with him. She would just have to wait and see if he called her when he got there—and that was that. Once again she found herself having to heed Granny Mae's advice: keep your focus on your future. Her only hope was that her future would be blessed with just a fraction of the happiness that had graced her past.

Chapter 7

ALESANDER DANTONI

"The best way to make God laugh
is to tell Him your plans for your future."
—*Granny Mae*

Mikayla stood motionless on the stairs leading to the entrance of the two-story, sandstone-brick office building that housed the renowned Dantoni Advertising Agency. It was 8:30 in the morning, and the promise of a late spring day lingered pleasantly in the fresh ocean air of Monterey, California. She was finally here. She could hardly believe it. Overwhelmed with excitement and apprehension, Mikayla's heart began pounding feverishly in her chest. She paused momentarily on the stairs to gather her wits and steady her fraying nerves. *Just be calm, Mikayla,* she told herself. *You didn't come all this way to get nervous and blow the interview.*

She simply had to get this internship. It was the first step toward the realization of her carefully mapped out plan. Her future happiness and fulfillment depended on it.

Summoning a fraction of the courage that Jesse was so certain she possessed, Mikayla willed her legs and feet to move. Obligingly, they carried her through the double glass doors and into the welcoming reception area, where she was promptly directed to the second-floor executive office suites of Mr. Alesander Dantoni.

Laying her purse and portfolio case on the floor next to the chair, she smoothed the back of her form-fitted, moss green dress as she took a seat in the executive's plush waiting area. The interior decor of the office complex was magnificent. Although somewhat overly masculine for Mikayla's personal taste, it conveyed a business-oriented atmosphere that inspired confidence and the assurance of quality services. The chosen palette was comprised of beiges and soft earth tones. The polished furniture and desks were dark cherry wood, with natural wheat-toned leather seating and accents.

The secretaries, whose nameplates identified them as Amy Roberts and Chloe Patterson, were kept busy by the perpetual ringing of the multiline phone system. They took messages for Mr. Dantoni and directed calls to the corresponding offices of his two top executives, Danielle Woods as Vice President of Public Relations and William Barnett as Creative Director.

While researching her perspective employer, Mikayla had discovered that Mr. Dantoni was "The Boss" and made it abundantly clear to his employees that he alone was in charge. It seemed that he had no desire to share the helm of his company with a partner. But none of that mattered to Mikayla. She didn't care how hard-nosed and controlling he was. She just wanted to be educated by one of the best CEOs in the business, a man who had climbed all the way to the top by relying only on himself.

Removing the phone receiver from her ear, Chloe informed Mikayla that Mr. Dantoni was ready to see her. The smiling secretary rose and escorted Mikayla to the boss's office, made the necessary introductions, and promptly exited the room, quietly closing the door behind her.

As Mikayla walked toward Mr. Dantoni, he politely made his way around the sizeable, but neat desk and extended his hand to her. "Please, Miss Mitchell, have a seat," he said pleasantly, motioning to a chair that was positioned just to the left of his desk. After waiting for her to be seated, he did the same.

Mikayla noted that Mr. Dantoni was an attractive man with neatly styled, short blond hair and a pleasing, but strictly businesslike smile—perhaps born more out of politeness than sincerity. His tasteful, charcoal gray business suit and plum-colored shirt and tie were immaculately tailored to fit his tall, trim, well-maintained physique.

Taking a quick glance around, she surveyed the masculine décor of his space which adhered beautifully to the earth tone color scheme of the reception area. The office was as tidy and neat as its occupant.

As he began the interview, Mikayla found him to be almost intimidatingly articulate. His deep, amiable voice conveyed considerable deliberation and intelligence. She was impressed with his courteous demeanor during the question and answer process, especially with the patience he showed when her responses were sometimes verbose and slightly less than eloquent.

After thoroughly perusing her portfolio, Mr. Dantoni leaned back in his chair and looked thoughtfully at her. "I have to say, Miss Mitchell, I am very impressed with your transcript and ranking," he told her with a polite nod and smile. "The top five percent of the graduating class is quite an accomplishment. Well done. Your portfolio and reels are superior as well."

"Thank you, Mr. Dantoni," she responded simply, thinking it best not to elaborate. She was well aware of her tendency to ramble when she was nervous, so she decided to keep the remainder of her responses short and succinct.

He continued with the interview, explaining the criteria for the internship. His generous, almost too-good-to-be-true training plan included three months of apprenticeship in all four areas of the advertising and marketing fields, which were housed in his complex. The intern would begin in the field of graphic design, with specific emphasis on Web design and print ads, and would proceed to the creative development department, then to public relations and client imaging, and finally to the television and radio production department. If Mikayla secured the internship she would receive training in every single area she had hoped for—invaluable, hands-on training as she participated in the day-to-day operations of one of the most successful firms in the industry.

Not to "kick a gift horse," as Granny would say, but she couldn't seem to stop herself from wondering, *why?* Why do this terrifically generous thing for someone? The salary he was offering was phenomenal, way above that of a typical intern position. So, the burning question was *why* offer such a rare and coveted opportunity? She couldn't imagine that it was simply a philanthropic gesture.

As if reading her mind, Mr. Dantoni asked, "I suppose you're wondering why I would choose to offer this internship opportunity."

"Yes, sir," she answered honestly. "The thought had crossed my mind."

"Well, I have my reasons," he said and paused, as if waiting for a reaction to his curt response. When Mikayla remained silent, he continued. "I'm well aware that the common misconception is that this is my way of screening possible candidates for an opening in my firm, but I want to assure you that this is not the case." He leaned up in his chair as if to emphasize the importance of what he was about to declare. "This is a one-year internship opportunity, nothing more and nothing less. I want you to be very clear on that fact—before I offer you the position," he said with a smug smile.

She was a little surprised, first by his bluntness, which she considered rather rude, and then by the instant offering of the job. She had assumed that he would need a few days to consider her credentials and references.

Smiling broadly, Mikayla responded excitedly, "Yes, sir, of course I understand. Assuming that I heard you correctly, I wholeheartedly accept the terms and would be more than honored to accept the position."

"Then, the one-year termination is of no concern to you?" he asked.

"No, sir, not at all. As a matter of fact, it fits *my plan* perfectly," she said candidly, emphasizing the words *my plan* while offering no further explanation as to the details. If he could be blunt and vague, so could she.

Mr. Dantoni opened his mouth to say something, but hesitated. For a fleeting moment he seemed somewhat intrigued as to the mysteries of "her plan." In fact, he seemed to be slightly amused. "Well, Miss Mitchell, it would seem that we share a common penchant for being mysterious, doesn't it? This should make for an interesting year," he said as he stood up, indicating that the interview was over. "The position is yours. Welcome aboard" He extended his hand to seal the deal.

"Thank you, Mr. Dantoni. I'm so appreciative of this opportunity. Thank you very much," she said, trying unsuccessfully not to gush.

Escorting her to the door, Mr. Dantoni instructed her to report on Monday morning at 8:00 to the office of Mr. William Barnett.

Moments later, Mikayla was sitting in her car, so giddy with excitement that she could barely remember Diana's two-digit speed dial number. She waited anxiously for her best friend to answer the phone. Finally, the familiar sound of Diana's voice came through the receiver.

"I got it, Diana! I got it!" she squealed, unable to contain her exhilaration.

"You did? He offered you the job already?" Diana asked with as much enthusiasm as if it were happening to her personally.

"Yes! Can you believe it?"

"What about the one-year limitation? Is he okay with giving you up at the end of the year?" Diana asked. Mikayla knew that Diana couldn't bear to think about losing her to California indefinitely.

"Yes, that's what's so great about it. He made it very clear that after my one-year internship is up, he'll be giving me the boot. Exactly what I wanted. Isn't that wonderful?" Mikayla was so elated she could barely speak.

With a note of relief in her voice, Diana said, "I'm so proud of you, Mikayla. I couldn't be happier for you. I can't wait to tell Rick. He'll be so excited."

Thinking of her two best friends and how much they meant to her, Mikayla's mood began to deflate like a water balloon spouting a pinhole leak. "I just wish I wasn't so far away from you guys. I'm sure gonna miss you all." she said, but then quickly tried to buoy both of their spirits.

"But as the old song says, 'I'll Be Home for Christmas,' and then only six months after that, I'll be home for good."

"I know. We'll just have to keep our focus on the future, as you say. But we sure are gonna miss you in the meantime." Diana told her. "Hey, by the way, when does the countdown start?"

"I start on Monday morning. That just gives me the rest of the week to find a place to live." The exact moment that those words crossed her lips, Mikayla felt an overwhelming awareness. The process had started. The fulfillment of her plan and her dream of a bright, new future had begun. As excited as she was, and as much faith as she had in herself and her carefully thought-out plan, she had a strange and sudden feeling of being ridiculed. It was odd, but she would almost swear that she could hear someone laughing from above.

Chapter 8

THE INTERNSHIP

"Lying is like overeating—it can become addictive, and
if you're not careful, you just might turn into a big, fat liar."

—Granny Mae

After only five months in the employ of Alesander Dantoni, Mikayla was convinced that his was exactly the type of small boutique company that she hoped to own and operate one day—just on a dramatically smaller scale and with a slightly more homegrown clientele. Nonetheless, she wanted to run a business in the same fashion as Mr. Dantoni ran his. He probably knew the ins and outs of advertising and marketing better than anybody else in the business, and he seemed more than eager to share his knowledge with his newfound protégé—perhaps a little too eager to suit Mikayla. She was learning more than she had ever dared hope for, so she chose to believe that the occasional glances and innuendoes from her generous benefactor were of no importance. However, she had to admit that she found his extended eye contact a bit intimidating at times. She found herself searching for excuses to release herself from his borderline flirtatious stare whenever possible.

Her three-month training segment in the graphic design department was completed and invaluably profitable. This was the area that was going to be most instrumental when she started her own company back home. Print ads and Web pages would best market most of the small, but numerous, unique mom-and-pop businesses in Guntersville. She planned to introduce the rest of the free world to the delectable goodness of Miss Lettie Mae's homemade jellies and preserves. As far as the folks of Guntersville were concerned, a biscuit just wasn't a biscuit unless it was doused with some of Miss Lettie's Georgia peach preserves or muscadine grape jelly. Mikayla could also envision Mr. Waylon's whole-leaf herbal teas and holistic remedies being distributed to the many health spas and resorts in the western states. Not to mention, with proper marketing, every baby in the U.S. would have the opportunity to grow up on Savannah Terry's wholesome and delicious organic baby food. That was the dream, anyway.

Mikayla had been working in the creative development department for only two months when Dantoni Advertising landed an enormous new account, adding yet another impressive name to Dantoni's growing list of Fortune 500 clientele. During the storyboarding process, Mikayla was permitted to voice her opinion and contribute a few minor ideas—ideas that actually ended up on the final presentation pitch to the client. As insignificant as her suggestions were, Mr. Dantoni still graced her with a generous bonus check for her efforts. To celebrate the closing of the deal and the tenth anniversary of his business, Mr. Dantoni decided to throw a formal employee/client dinner party at one of the most elegant and exclusive nightspots in Carmel.

As exciting as it sounded to everybody else, Mikayla was looking forward to this party about as much as having a tooth drilled without the aid of Novocain.

Over the course of the five months that she had been with the firm, she had spent every moment of it consumed with gathering all of the knowledge she could possibly glean from the short-lived internship. After work, she spent the better part of her evenings alone, working on projects and studying anything and everything that Mr. Dantoni felt compelled to share with her. The only exception to her strict routine was when Amy and Chloe forced her to go with them to a movie or to the mall for a little shopping. Jesse hadn't bothered to look her up when he got to his brother's home in Napa, and the congenial secretaries were the extent of her friends in California.

Still, when Mr. Dantoni approached her at the coffee bar one morning, Jesse unknowingly came to her rescue yet again.

"Mikayla, since you don't know your way around the area very well, would you like for me to pick you up and give you a ride to the party next Saturday?" her boss asked inoffensively, sounding as nonchalant as if he were addressing any one of his other employees. Maybe she was reading him incorrectly. Perhaps that was exactly the way he meant his offer, although she doubted it.

Without missing a beat, she donned a convincing smile. "Mr. Dantoni …"

"Mikayla, I've asked you repeatedly to call me Lex," he interrupted with a reassuring expression. "I keep telling you, this is an informal ship I'm trying to run here."

"Yes, well … Lex," she said, obviously uncomfortable with addressing him by his first name, "While I appreciate the offer, I've already asked my friend Jesse to accompany me." She lied through her teeth, deliberately emphasizing the words "my friend" in the hopes that he would detect the indication of a romantic interest. "You did say it was okay if we brought a companion along, didn't you?" she asked, feigning concern that she had done so without his approval.

"Yes. Yes, of course. That's fine. I was just concerned that you would have trouble finding the restaurant," he answered quickly. "I look forward to meeting your friend."

With that, he walked away, leaving Mikayla to ponder the impossible situation that she had just gotten herself into. She didn't have a single male friend within 2,400 miles that she could invite to escort her to this stupid party. Short of flying Rick down for the weekend to pose as her date, what was she going to do now? She felt like Lucy Ricardo caught up in one of her many comical and self-inflicted predicaments—a predicament usually made worse by the enlistment of help from her best friend, Ethel. Nonetheless, Mikayla made a beeline to her office. She had to make a call to Alabama to see whether her Ethel had any ideas on how she could get herself out of this ridiculous mess.

Chapter 9

THE INVITATION

"Never take life too seriously;
it goes by much too fast not to laugh at it."

—*Granny Mae*

Although armed with a well-rehearsed script that had been carefully choreographed with the help of Diana, Mikayla and the telephone in her hand were still at odds. Thinking several times that she had garnered the nerve to make the call, she would begin to dial the number only to lose her courage before pressing the very last digit of Jesse's brother's telephone number.

After savoring a second glass of her favorite red wine, Mikayla resolved to complete the call. "After all, what am I so afraid of?" she thought, as she mulled the situation over in her slightly tipsy mind. "He may not even still be in California, and even if he is, the worst that can happen is that he might say no to being my escort for the evening."

Appreciating the positive effects that the wine was having on her unraveling nerves and waning confidence, Mikayla slowly and successfully pressed the seventh digit of Joe Daulton's telephone number. After only two short rings, the phone was answered.

Hello ... Hello ... Mmm?"

That was all she allowed herself to hear before she quickly ended the call. She had immediately recognized the smooth, sexy voice coming through the receiver: it was Jesse. Oh, my God! How could something as innocuous as the sound of his voice on the phone make her knees go so weak that she had to immediately take a seat or end up on the floor? Hearing his voice for only a split second had confiscated every molecule of the false bravery she had acquired from the wine. So … she panicked and hung up on him. She hung up on the man she had been dreaming about for the past five months.

"That was real smooth, Mikayla," she said sarcastically.

Just as her subconscious mind was commencing into a firm self-scolding for the immature and cowardly act, the phone, which she was still holding in her hand, began to ring. Looking down at the display screen, Mikayla saw the caller ID information. It was the very same number she had just dialed. Oh, my God, Jesse was calling her back! At least a million thoughts passed through her mind during the four complete rings of the telephone. How could he have known it was her? Her name was always blocked out on all outgoing calls. Only her telephone number was ever revealed on caller ID screens. He was probably just calling the number back, not knowing who had made the call. He wouldn't have recognized her phone number after all this time. Could he have known it was she who had hung up on him? Whatever the reason he was calling back, she did not for one microsecond contemplate whether she was going to answer it. She knew perfectly well that she wasn't about to press that green answer button. Why would she knowingly welcome the opportunity to further embarrass herself? Mortification had already set in from her previous faux pas. The chance for a mature conversation had expired—the opportunity was lost forever—the fat lady had sung—and Elvis had left the building!

After the phone stopped ringing, Mikayla waited a few seconds before she checked her voice mail. She felt a combination of relief and dismay when she discovered that he had not left a message.

Deciding that going to bed alone would be a fitting end to her fruitless evening, Mikayla started toward the bedroom. Before she had taken two steps, the sound of the phone ringing again caused her stomach to do somersaults. After the third ring, curiosity got the better of her. As she looked down at the caller ID display, relief swept over her. It was Diana. *How does she always seem to know when I need her the most?* Mikayla wondered.

"Is he still in California? Did he say yes? Is he gonna take you to the party?" Diana began firing questions without even returning Mikayla's hello.

"I didn't talk to him," Mikayla answered shamefully.

"You didn't call him yet? You big chicken." Diana chided playfully.

"Oh, I called him all right. The problem is I hung up on him when he answered the phone."

"You did what?" Diana sounded shocked.

"Jesse himself answered the phone, and yours truly hung up on him without uttering a single word. Even though I said nothing, that single act speaks volumes about my level of maturity and sophistication, don't you think?" Mikayla asked sarcastically, as she began to laugh.

"What did you hang up for?" Diana joined in with her laughing friend. "What are you—twelve years old?"

"I don't know." Mikayla chuckled. "I guess I'm not the progressive California socialite that I thought I was." The giggles began to gradually die down as she continued. "I guess I'm still just an old-fashioned country girl at heart. Even as I was dialing the number, I could hear Granny Mae's voice in my head telling me that 'nice girls don't ask boys out on dates.'" After pausing a moment, she gave voice to the nagging thought that had been lingering in the back of her mind all evening, "Besides, if he had wanted to talk to me over the past five months, he would have called *me*."

"I'm so sorry, sweetie," Diana said compassionately. "But maybe he's had a good reason for not calling you. That's a possibility, you know."

"Yeah, I guess." Mikayla yawned. Wanting to change the subject, she asked, "How's Prince Charming, anyway?" Just the thought of what a wonderful man and devoted husband Rick was brought a smile to her face and hope to her heart. To her, he was living proof that there really were a limited number of princes still left out there in this big ol' world. They were just very few and far between. Realizing the rarity of their number, a girl with any smarts in her head would know that if by some miraculous chance she was actually lucky enough to stumble across one of those last remaining princes, it was probably not a very good idea to call him on the phone, wait for him to answer, and then hang up on him.

"Rick's working a double shift … again." The sound of Diana's disappointed voice released Mikayla's wandering thoughts and propelled her mind back on subject. "How are we ever gonna make a baby if he's never at home?" she moaned exaggeratedly.

"It'll happen for you, Diana. Don't worry," Mikayla tried to sound as reassuring as possible. "And just think how much fun the two of you are gonna have trying." With that, she successfully elicited a laugh from her dear friend.

"Well, that's wasn't a very California socialite-type thing to say, but I like the sentiment," Diana said with a giggle. "Are you gonna try calling Jesse again?"

"No way." she answered, as if her friend had just lost possession of all her faculties. "Do you remember that old saying that it's far better to just be thought a fool than to open your mouth and prove it? Well, I think I'll just heed that wise advice. Besides, I should leave the poor guy alone. He's probably got a girlfriend by now anyway."

"You're not a fool, curly top. You just got nervous, that's all. It's no big deal." Diana's attempt at downplaying Mikayla's telephone blunder was met with good-natured laughter.

"You're a really great friend but a terrible liar," Mikayla declared. "But thanks for trying." Feeling the effects of the wine, she yawned dishearteningly. "I think I'll just go to bed and try to forget the whole thing."

"By the whole thing, do you mean forget the phone call … or forget Jesse?" Diana asked solemnly.

"I guess I mean—forget Jesse," she answered quietly. "Not that there's anything to forget, really. There was never a real relationship anyway; it was just a promise of one. He just seemed so darned special." She tried to gain her composure by laughing it off, but it didn't work. "God, I sound pathetic, don't I?"

"No sweetie, you don't sound pathetic at all." Diana reassured her. "You just fell for him—that's all. There's nothing wrong with that."

"Yeah I guess ... but obviously, he didn't fall for me."

❦   ❦   ❦

After spending a restless night of interrupted slumber, Mikayla arrived at work the following morning wearing her brightest fake smile. She found it slightly amusing that people who didn't really know her could be so easily fooled by it.

Armed with even more determination than before, and vowing to succeed in at least one facet of her life, Mikayla decided to devote herself even more to her work and training. She would worry about this party situation later.

Shortly after returning from a lunch-hour work session with Miss Woods, the queen of over-achievement, Mikayla was at her desk immersed in new assignments when Chloe tapped lightly on her closed office door.

"It's open, come on in," she said without raising her eyes from the organized piles of papers on her desk.

"I just have one question," Chloe asked mischievously. "Did he do something wrong, or did you do something right?"

Perplexed by such an odd question, Mikayla looked up just as the smiling secretary set a beautiful crystal vase of fresh-cut flowers in the middle of her desk. Mikayla's mouth dropped open at the sight of the amazing bouquet of blooms in dazzling shades of her favorite color—pink. The colors ranged from baby soft pink to flaming fuchsia and every hue in between.

"Close your mouth, and open the card," Chloe teased.

Silently and with the obedience of a small child, Mikayla removed the card from the small plastic holder nestled amidst the breathtaking arrangement. Biting her bottom lip with curiosity, she opened the card.

She could have guessed until the cows came home, but she would never have guessed in a zillion years who had thought her worthy of flowers.

Reading and rereading the card several times did little to dissuade the initial shock.

As Mikayla's reaction was not in keeping with the norm of happy surprise, and sometimes even tears, Chloe questioned the somewhat unorthodox response. "Mikayla, are you okay?"

"Yes ... yes, I'm fine," Mikayla assured her perplexed friend. The sound of Mikayla's own voice seemed to break the trance she was in. An immediate and embarrassed grin possessed her face as she looked up at Chloe. "It's just ... they're from someone I haven't heard from in a while."

"Well, okay then. Enjoy your flowers," Chloe said and exited the room, softly closing the door behind her.

As if the words might have magically transformed themselves, Mikayla picked up the card again and reread the neatly handwritten message:

> *"Maybe you could give me a call to thank me for the flowers.*
> *I would love to talk to you."*
>
> —*Jesse*

Chapter 10

THE DANCE

"Being loved is as vital to the heart
as oxygen is to the lungs."

—*Granny Mae*

Mikayla twisted and turned her body nervously in front of the full-length bedroom mirror, examining and brutally critiquing the nearly perfect reflection staring back at her. Turning her head to scrutinize the view from the back, she wondered how she could have let Chloe talk her into buying such a provocative, revealing dress. It was far beyond the boundaries of her modesty comfort zone.

The icy pink, body-hugging gown of georgette silk clung snugly to her curvaceous body all the way down her torso and slightly past her hips, where the width of the slinky fabric expanded into billowy, vertical folds that created a full, sweeping hemline. The front length draped to within six inches of her ankles, gradually tapering downward in the back and ending just above the heels of her three-inch strappy sandals. The thin spaghetti straps delicately supported a slightly cowl-necked bodice that plunged just low enough to reveal a peek at her voluptuous cleavage. The back of the dress, however, was not so accommodating. Cut into a very low U shape, it plummeted all the way down her back and past her waistline by an inch or so. At that point, the fabric came together again and fell daintily into small narrow swags that folded down upon themselves. This graceful gathering of fabric at her lower back drew attention to her shapely derriere.

Wearing this gown made Mikayla feel a little exposed and self-conscious, but at the same time she had to admit that the dress certainly did boost her self-image. She felt sophisticated and temptingly sexy—transformed, in a way, from a naïve country gal into a desirable, savvy woman.

The last thing Mikayla put on was her great-grandmother's cameo necklace. The graceful, mauve-colored family heirloom complimented the dress perfectly, although that was not her main reason for wearing it. She was pleasantly surprised every time she placed the cameo around her neck. Wearing it gave her a sense of warmth and inner happiness that was impossible to explain, and even more impossible to replicate, now that Granny Mae was gone. The seemingly inanimate piece of jewelry was a comforting reminder of how it felt to be loved, the way her great-grandfather had loved his bride the day he gave her the necklace and the way that Granny Mae had loved Mikayla—completely and unconditionally. She couldn't help but wonder whether she would ever feel that kind of love again.

"I miss you, Granny Mae," she whispered as she lovingly laid her hand on the cherished pendent around her neck. *I miss being loved.*

After a deep, reminiscent sigh and one last glance in the mirror, she retreated into the living room to wait for her date.

Rearranging the throw pillows on the sofa for about the tenth time, she wondered what it would be like to see Jesse again. He had seemed somewhat tentative on the phone last week when she called to thank him for the unexpected flowers. Using his expert interrogation skills, however, he did finally pry out of her why she had called him in the first place, and then graciously agreed to escort her to the party. The conversation didn't last very long nor did it move beyond the usual pleasantries. But before they hung up, Jesse said that he needed to talk with her at length about some things, one of them being why he hadn't contacted her when he first arrived in California. Deciding that her apartment would be the best place to have uninterrupted conversation, not to mention he could collect on that home-cooked supper she had promised him, they made a date for the following Friday evening.

After hearing the distinctive sound of a slamming car door, Mikayla nervously peeked through the sheer drapery panels that covered the wide bay window in her living room. Parked in front of her apartment was a classy silver convertible, out of which Jesse had just emerged. He looked devilishly handsome in a stylish black tuxedo, white shirt, and black bow tie. His scruffy facial hair had been neatly trimmed, leaving only a precise, dark shadow of a goatee on his attractive face. His long, wavy hair had been shortened considerably but still fell just below his ears in the front and down to the bottom of his collar in the back. It was styled in a layered cut that looked naturally unkept and very sexy. Judging by the subtle golden highlights, it was obvious that he had been enjoying the California sunshine.

As Mikayla made her way to the foyer, she took one last peek in the hallway mirror. Pausing momentarily, she made a final plea to a single, stubborn curl that refused to play its part in her casually upswept hairdo.

She opened the door and quietly stepped out onto the narrow front stoop just as Jesse was mounting the stairs leading up to where she was standing. Since he was a few feet below her, she watched as his eyes leisurely trailed the length of her body, starting at the tips of her pink polished toes. She felt vulnerable under his scrutiny, but the moment his eyes met hers and he flashed her that smile that had been so effectively burned into her memory, all the uncertainty she had been feeling melted away—unfortunately, so did her knees. She found herself wishing she had paid more attention in science class. Maybe then she would understand the sudden and strange metamorphosis that possessed her body every time Jesse was within sight or earshot.

"Hello, Mikayla," he said as he topped the landing and uninhibitedly reached out and took both of her hands into his. "Wow! You look unbelievable. My memory must be failin' me 'cause it sure didn't do you justice," he told her and then bent down and planted a soft, moist kiss on her cheek.

"Well, thank you very much, Mr. Daulton," she said playfully, her cheeks burning hot from his appreciative stare and glowing compliments. "You look mighty handsome yourself." She returned his welcoming smile.

Turning her back to escort him into the apartment, she could feel his eyes as they followed the trail of bare skin beginning at the nap of her neck continuing down past her shoulders, following the delicate indentation of her spine past her waist and down to her lower back where the wispy, pink fabric appeared to cruelly put an end to his vision quest.

"Man! That's a knockout dress." he gushed.

Just as her cheeks had begun to lose the heat from moments earlier, once again they glowed crimson as she thanked him for the admiring comment.

In the living room, Jesse took a seat on the end of the sofa and she sat down in a chair to the right of him. Although he seemed a little thinner, he was every bit as good-looking as she remembered—maybe even more so.

It was he who broke the silence and initiated the conversation. "I'm glad to see I made a wise choice for the color of the flowers. I figured you for a pink gal, you know, feminine and delicate," he said, seeming to embarrass himself ever so slightly, which provoked a huge smile—a smile just large enough to reveal deep, provocative dimples on both sides of his handsome face. His face was so masculine that their appearance was surprising, although not at all unpleasant. They served only to add to his already illegal amount of charisma.

"Hey, I hadn't noticed before … you have dimples," Mikayla announced, surprised that she hadn't detected them previously.

"Yeah, I do," he admitted, as if he was sorry they had made such an early appearance. "Adorable, aren't they?" He smoothed his thumb and fingers over his face, as though nothing would please him more than if he could just wipe them away. "Now you know why I usually wear a slightly fuller beard." Leaning forward a little as if he was about to let her in on a big secret, he added, "Do ya know the worst part about these big holes in my face? The only women who seem to like them are moms and grandmothers." Clearly fishing for a compliment, he released a deep, sexy laugh.

"Oh, I don't know about that." she professed. "I happen to think they're quite attractive."

Pleased with her admission, his dimples decided to make an encore performance.

During the small talk that ensued over the next half hour, she was amazed at Jesse's unwavering composure and quiet confidence. He seemed so enviably comfortable in his own skin, while she felt as though she might jump right out of hers at any given moment. She had gotten skilled over the past few months at forging a superior level of self-assurance, but she wished it came as naturally to her as it did to him.

❦   ❦   ❦

By the time they arrived at the dinner party, Mikayla had settled into the comfortableness of Jesse's company. He was extremely easy to be with. There was no conceit or pretentiousness about him in the least. He was genuine and charming and seemingly oblivious of his affect on the opposite sex.

Arriving at the dinner party right on time, he took her by the arm and escorted her into the enormous, elegantly decorated convention area of the establishment. The room was already teeming with expensively dressed, career-building associates and clientele. She briefly introduced him to the handful of people she knew, including Lex Dantoni himself. Feeling slightly overwhelmed and a bit "above her raisin," as Granny would say, Mikayla's nerves returned with a vengeance. As though sensing her apprehension, Jesse protectively slid his arm around her waist and gently pulled her into him. Relaxing slightly in his confident embrace, she found herself grateful for his caring companionship.

"I think what we need is a drink—just a little something to knock the edge off," he suggested softly into her ear. "What can I get you?"

She didn't understand it. How could he parlay something as innocent as offering to get her a drink into something that sounded so darned sexy?

"I think you're right," she answered, trying to rise above her libido. "A Southern Suicide is my drink of choice back home, but one of those might just knock a little too much of the edge off." An ornery grin spread across her face. "So maybe I'd better settle for a white wine instead, please."

Chuckling, Jesse excused himself and headed toward the bar.

"My God, girlfriend, he's gorgeous!" Chloe's voice came out of nowhere. "No wonder you sat around for five months waiting for this guy to call. He's definitely worth the wait." She gave Mikayla a playful nudge on the shoulder. "You'd better not let him out of your sight, though. In case you haven't noticed, as far as dancing partners go, the women outnumber the men here tonight by about five to one."

Glancing over at the bar, Mikayla spotted Jesse standing with their drinks in hand, casually conversing with the bartender. Chloe was right. It seemed as though every woman in the place was practically drooling over him—like a bunch of dieting women competing for the last slice of Granny Mae's famous, low-calorie version of pecan pie.

Catching her eye, Jesse smiled at her. The way he looked at her made her feel as though he only had eyes for her.

Thankfully, she had consumed about half of her glass of wine when Mr. Dantoni decided to make a short and informal speech before dinner. After the usual niceties and thank-yous, he introduced his administrative staff to the distinguished gathering. Much to her surprise, he included her in his introductions.

Following a delectable four-course meal, Lex escorted his guests back to the convention area for a night of dancing and conversation. Only a few short songs into their first set, the four-member ensemble seamlessly segued into a classic love song, to which several couples responded favorably by taking to the floor.

"Mikayla, would you like to dance?" Jesse asked politely as he reached out to take her by the hand.

"Sure," she answered coyly, smiling up at him. "I've never danced with an Army Ranger before."

"You haven't?" he asked, pretending to be overly shocked. "Well, then, you're in for a real treat, darlin'," he said with a beguiling smile.

They joined the other couples on the dimly lit dance floor. Mikayla laid one hand on top of his broad shoulder and let the other rest lightly against his muscular bicep. As he put his arms around her narrow waist and pulled her gently into him, their bodies began to sway in unison to the music. She felt relaxed and comfortable in his grasp, but at the same time, unbelievably excited about being there. He surprised her when he removed his left hand from her waist. Slowly, he trailed his fingers up the length of her arm in search of her hand. He held it for a moment, and then tenderly brought it to his lips and kissed her fingers. Staring down into her face, he laid her hand onto his chest and held it there, covering it completely with his own.

They danced without saying a word. She felt in his arms tonight the same way she had five months earlier, the first time she was in his embrace—safer than she had ever felt with any man. Though she had known him but a short time, her instincts assured her that he was, without a doubt, one of the good guys.

With her eyes closed and her head resting against his chest, Mikayla could feel his warm, calming breath against her hair and on her cheek. His right arm was wrapped around her body. His stimulating hand rested gently against the small of her bare back. Only his thumb was in motion as he moved it leisurely up and down, gently massaging her skin. That, together with the methodical rise and fall of his chest against her face, had a pleasurable calming effect on her nerves. She indulged herself in the fantasy that they were the only two people in the room.

Seconds later, she heard him release a soft, winsome sigh that momentarily interrupted the steadiness of his breathing pattern, a disruption that she detected immediately.

Leaning back slightly, she met his stirring gaze. "Are you feeling okay, Jesse?" she questioned, with obvious concern in her voice.

"At this moment I feel like the luckiest man in the world," he said, earnestly smiling down at her. "Of all the men here tonight, I'm the lucky one who's holding in my arms the fantasy of every man and the envy of every woman in the room."

His amorous stare told her that he meant every word. "Thank you, Jesse," she said softly.

"But I think you have it backwards. I do believe I'm the lucky one here."

"Do you wanna argue about it, or do you wanna dance?" he teased.

"Dance, please." she said with a contented grin.

He pulled her close again and rested his moist lips momentarily on her forehead. Bending down, he put his moist mouth next to her ear. "Mmm ... you smell delicious," he whispered sensually.

Mikayla wasn't sure whether it was the titillating sensation of his breath in her ear, the sentiment of his compliment, or the thoughts of his soft, full lips leisurely tasting her body. Whatever the reason, his whisper instigated a noticeable shiver that started at the top of her head and traveled leisurely down the length of her body, leaving her skin covered in tiny goose bumps.

"Are you cold?" he asked sympathetically. Not waiting for an answer, he wrapped both of his arms around her body, fully encompassing her in his warm, caring embrace. "Is that better?"

"Yes," she whispered as close to his ear as she could reach, at the same time tightening her arms around his neck and shoulders, wanting nothing more than to return his show of affection and lose herself in the moment.

Unbeknownst to Jesse, the shiver that he felt course through her body was not from the chill in the air at all, but rather from the thrill of being enveloped in his arms. Mikayla decided to selfishly withhold that little secret for now.

She hated it when the slow ballad ended and the band once again picked up the tempo of the music. She wouldn't have minded staying right where she was for at least one more intimate dance.

Almost immediately after they stepped out of the magical ambiance of the dance floor, Lex appeared and whisked Mikayla away to meet and greet some of his most influential clients and associates. She knew that this was a golden opportunity for her to make acquaintances with the upper echelon of the world of advertising—individuals who could make or break a budding career—but ambition seemed to have taken a backseat to her heart this evening. While shaking hands and making small talk with an inexhaustible supply of cloned businesspeople, she kept a watchful eye on her date, catching occasional glimpses of him out on the dance floor, smiling politely and seemingly enjoying the company of several women brazen enough to ask him for a dance.

After what seemed like hours of endless introductions and courteous business banter, Lex finally placed his hand on Mikayla's elbow and led her out onto the crowded floor.

"May I have this dance, Miss Mitchell?" he asked self-assuredly, more so in the form of a directive rather than a question. Without bothering to wait for an answer, he put his arms around her and pulled her uncomfortably close to his body. Breathing heavily into her ear, he made a comical attempt at whispering, and botched an already terrible come-on line that she was sure wouldn't have worked on any female, even if it had been properly spoken. His poor manners and behavior were an obvious result of one too many California martinis.

"Lex, I'm sorry, but I really do need to go and find my date. I feel as though I've neglected him terribly," Mikayla insisted. Every muscle in her body was resisting his advances as she tried to inconspicuously push him away. His hands were on her bare back, trailing down her spine faster than she could reach around to stop them. His greedy touch disgusted her, and she let out a repulsive gasp as both of his hands shamelessly cupped her buttocks. Before she could physically react to his groping, she heard Jesse's commanding voice above the loud music.

"If you don't mind, Mr. Dantoni, I'd like to cut in," he stated simply and firmly. Removing any shred of doubt as to whether this was a request or a directive, he discreetly gripped the executive's forearm with enough muscle that Lex immediately released his lecherous hold on his reluctant dance partner.

Leading Mikayla off to the side of the dance floor, Jesse's apology was immediate. "I'm sorry if I was outta line back there. I just couldn't stand by and let someone disrespect you like that. Only a jackass treats a woman that way!" he said angrily. "But, I'm really sorry if I embarrassed you—riding in there on my white horse like that and …"

"It's okay," Mikayla said, closer to angry tears than she would have liked. Her contempt for Lex at the moment was nearly uncontainable. "I appreciate what you did, Jesse, and the subtle way you handled it. Thank you," she said quietly.

Meeting his troubled gaze, she could see the concern in his eyes. His rapid breathing bore audible witness to his anger. She felt terrible that he had been placed in such an awkward position. The compassion she felt for him quickly overshadowed her own humiliation and animosity. This rapid shift in focus allowed her to see the slightest glimmer of humor in the embarrassing situation. Hoping to diffuse his anxiety, she looped her hand through his arm and leaned into him.

As if sensing that she had something to say, Jesse bent down to allow her to speak directly into his ear.

"Actually, Lex is the one who should be thanking you," she said with a grin in her voice. "You just saved him from being bitch slapped by a short, but very angry, southern gal who doesn't take too kindly to having her fanny grabbed."

The gorgeous and dimpled expression that lit up Jesse's face was almost worth the mortification of being groped by her tipsy boss in the middle of a crowded dance floor, in the presence of all of her colleagues.

🍁　　　🍁　　　🍁

On the drive home, Mikayla and Jesse talked and laughed as though the embarrassing incident with Lex had never even occurred. It was nice to be able to just forget about it—not that her inebriated, lewd boss was going to be that lucky. He wouldn't be gaining her forgiveness or forgetfulness nearly as easily. However, she resolved to collect her just rewards from Lex on Monday. Right now she just wanted to be with Jesse.

Arriving at her apartment, she was pleased when he happily accepted her offer to come in for a cup of coffee and a dish of homemade peach cobbler. They sat on the sofa and ate and talked for well over an hour. It was hard to believe how comfortable she felt with him. She felt deeply connected to him in so many ways—in ways that she couldn't readily understand but wasn't about to stop and analyze. She tended to do that sometimes—forever overanalyzing every little thing. Yet another one of her flaming Type A personality traits that she planned on changing someday. Even so, she couldn't help but wonder if he felt the same connection.

Stretching his arms and yawning slightly, Jesse glanced at his watch. It was 3:15 in the morning.

"I'm sorry, Mikayla," he said softly as he stood to go. "I didn't realize it was so late. I'd better get going so you can get some sleep." Holding his hand out to her, he helped her up from the sofa.

For a moment he just stood there, looking at her. He looked at her as if she were the loveliest woman in the world. God, he made her feel beautiful. She couldn't recall ever being looked at with such blatant appreciation and desire. For several more moments he seemed unable to move. It was almost as if he were doing battle within himself to decide whether to take her into his arms and indulge an intimate impulse, or make a speedy exit. After releasing a deep sigh, and donning a half-hearted smile, it appeared that the latter option had triumphed. "I had a great time tonight, Mikayla," he said as he gazed into her emerald green eyes. "Thank you for inviting me."

"Thank you for accepting," she answered shyly. "I had a nice time too … well, except for … you know," she said with a shrug.

As he took a step closer, she found it difficult to breathe. She was scared to death that he was going to kiss her but even more frightened that he wasn't.

Their eyes held transfixed for a moment too long, forming an almost tangible connection that neither seemed willing to break. Hesitantly, he reached up and lovingly brushed several cascading curls away from her face. His expression, though tender and desirous, revealed an underlying reluctance. It was as though he were afraid to touch her, afraid to get too close to her, for fear of wanting more.

"You're the most beautiful thing I've ever seen," he finally professed in a voice barely above a whisper. Putting a finger beneath her chin, he gently lifted her face and slowly bent down and placed an innocent kiss on her cheek. Barely grazing the corner of her mouth, he lingered there momentarily, as if memorizing the way she felt and the fragrance of her skin.

Mikayla turned her head slightly toward him, her lips wantonly searching for his. Finding their desire, her lips met his in a tender, feminine embrace.

She felt his hands slide leisurely down the sides of her neck and come to rest delicately on her bare shoulders. Slowly, he caressed her velvety skin. His touch was smooth and gentle as he let the tips of his fingers flow softly up and down her bare arms. Finally, he surrendered and returned her kiss. His embrace was sweet and tender. Prompting her agreeable lips apart, his tongue searched timidly for hers.

Responding seductively to his probing petition, Mikayla released a pleasurable moan as the intimate connection was made. Arching her body, she wrapped her hands around his neck and pulled herself firmly against him in a strong grip of desire. She let her fingers trail up the back of his neck, burying them in his thick, wavy hair.

Inquisitively, his hands explored her bare back. As if in search of undiscovered nakedness, they slipped easily beneath the silky fabric of her dress. His touch was tender and unhurried. His breaths deepened as he repeatedly guided the tips of his fingers slowly up and down the outline of her curvaceous form.

Just as her body quivered passionately in response to his warm caresses, she felt him reluctantly begin to relinquish his hold. As he withdrew from her, their lips parted for the first time since their interlude began. She stared at him, making no attempt to hide the disappointment that she felt sure was apparent on her face.

"I'm so sorry, Mikayla. I shouldn't have done that," he declared, as if he had been caught trespassing on enemy territory.

"There's no need for you to be sorry, Jesse. I wanted you to kiss me … to touch me," she said breathlessly, trying to dissuade his apprehension. Surprised and perplexed by his actions, she continued, "I don't understand. Did I do something …?"

He interrupted her before she could finish. "No, not at all, Mikayla. You did nothing wrong. In fact, you're perfect." He gave a forced half smile as he plowed his fingers through his hair. "I just didn't mean to … lead you … give you the wrong impression." His expression grew serious again. "It's too complicated to go into tonight. Do you mind if we talk about it on Friday?"

For a moment, he looked uncharacteristically confused and disheveled. The pink blush of desire was fading swiftly from his skin, leaving his face ghostly pale. Mikayla's heart went out to him. "Of course," she answered obligingly. "Friday will be fine, but … Jesse, you don't look well. Are you okay?"

"Yes. Yes, really I'm fine," he said quickly. "I'll explain later. I'm so sorry, Mikayla." With that, followed by another profuse apology, he turned and hurriedly walked out the door.

Chapter 11

THE CONFESSION

"Always follow your heart;
it's much wiser than your brain."

—*Granny Mae*

Luckily, Mikayla returned to work the following Monday morning to find that Lex was out of town for a weeklong business meeting. *He'd better run,* she thought comically to herself. But if the truth be known, she was secretly glad for the imposed cooling-off period. If given time for her initial fury to pass, she might be able to think of more suitable words to convey her disdain for how he treated her—and at the same time allow her to hang on to her job.

She spent the majority of the long, arduous week trying to keep her mind on the mountain of work that Miss Woods kept stacking on her desk. But no matter how hard she tried, her mind was hell-bent on wondering about Jesse and what it was that he wanted to talk with her about.

Finally, Friday evening rolled around. He was due at 7:30, so Mikayla headed straight home from work to start dinner. At his request for an old-fashioned, southern-style supper, she made Granny's famous southern cottage meat loaf, buttermilk smashed potatoes, fresh sweet corn pudding, and glazed brussels sprouts. She also fried up a skillet of Granny Mae's southern fried cornbread. To drink, she brewed a pitcher of sweet Alabama iced tea with mint, and for dessert they would have old-fashioned oatmeal cake, which she baked the night before.

She set the white lace-covered table with Granny's old Victorian china and placed a petite vase of fall-colored mums in the center with a candle on either side. She had just enough time left to grab a quick shower and get dressed. After perusing the closet far longer than time allowed, she finally settled on a casual tank-style dress. The turquoise color was flattering to her skin tone and brought out the green in her eyes. It made the perfect statement—not too sexy, not too frumpy.

Moments later, the doorbell rang. Mikayla opened the door and caught her breath at the sight of Jesse's smile, as usual. He was holding a single, long-stem pink rose, which he immediately presented to her.

"Hi, Jesse. Come on in." She accepted the perfect flower from his hand. Raising it to her nose, she inhaled the sweet, intoxicating scent. "Mmmm, it smells lovely. Thank you."

"Dinner smells great, too." he proclaimed upon stepping inside the foyer.

"Well, have a seat, and it'll be on the table in just a few minutes," she said cheerfully, motioning toward the sofa.

"I would much rather follow you into the kitchen and be underfoot and in the way … if that's okay," he joked.

His gentle, mellow voice caught her off guard every time he spoke. Appreciating the way he was trying to diffuse any uneasiness between them, she happily invited him to accompany her into the kitchen to be underfoot, as he put it.

Moments later, the food was ready and waiting for them. They helped themselves from the stove and carried their plates to the table. She noticed that he served himself very small portions and couldn't help but wonder why. Was he nervous about "the talk" that was on tap for after dinner? Had the prospect of the looming conversation robbed him of his appetite, or was he not feeling well? He appeared a little thinner to her, and his face, although strikingly handsome, was slightly pale.

Nonetheless, he seemed to be enjoying the food that was on his plate. Accolades and compliments followed almost every forkful he placed into his mouth. He inquired how she made the meat loaf so moist and tasty and what made the smashed potatoes so flavorful. His interest seemed truly sincere, so she answered his questions in detail, explaining that her secrets were from Granny Mae's tried-and-true recipes. The Brussels sprouts recipe was guaranteed to convert any sprouts-hater into a lover with the first mouthful, a claim that Jesse wholeheartedly validated.

Deciding to save their oatmeal cake for later, they carried their glasses of iced tea to the living room and each took a seat on opposite ends of the short sofa.

"Well, Mikayla, you did it," he stated with a stern expression of seriousness.

"Did what?" Her eyes were wide with curiosity.

"You proved it. You really are a great cook," he said, as his face broke into a large, dimpled grin. "That was the best meal I've had in … well, that was probably the best meal I've ever had in my life. Just don't tell my mom or Annie."

Shaking her head in disbelief, she told him that she doubted she deserved such a generous compliment but that she appreciated his gratitude and flattery.

After a short silence, Jesse cleared his throat. "Mikayla, this is hard for me to do, so I may as well just get it over with," he said as he turned to face her on the sofa. She did the same, saying nothing. She waited for him to gather his thoughts.

"I've thought long and hard about what and how much to tell you." He raised his eyes to meet hers, immediately locking them in a gaze so intense she dared not even blink for fear of breaking the connection. "I guess I'll start by telling you that I wanted very much to contact you when I first arrived in Napa, but I hesitated. I hesitated for too long, and then everything started happening so fast … and then … well, then it was just too late."

Remaining silent, Mikayla waited patiently for him to continue.

"At first, I wrestled with the insignificant reasons for not calling you. You know, maybe I was too old for you, or maybe you had already met someone, not to mention the fact that you were about to embark on a brand-new, exciting career, while mine had just ended. The extent of my long-term career goal at the time we met was just to find something to do to keep myself out of trouble," he said with the hint of a smile. "But your career seemed very important to you—not that there's anything wrong with that ... in fact, I admire your ambition ... but I just didn't feel like I had much to offer a young woman as smart, beautiful, and ambitious as yourself. You seemed to have your future so planned and mapped out. I just didn't want to be a disruption ... that's all." Pausing, he reached for his glass and took a long drink of tea. Wiping the moisture from the glass onto his jeans, he continued his explanation without lifting his eyes. "Then, after wasting all that time debating the foolish reasons for not calling you, well ... then I found out ... I discovered that ... I was sick." Still looking down at his hands folded in his lap, he paused a moment before he continued. "After that, I knew I had no right to contact you. So, I just gave up on the idea of ever having you in my life." Breathing a deep sigh of regret, he finally met her gaze.

Just looking into his eyes made her feel secure. It was as though nothing bad could ever happen as long as she was staring into his protective, gentle eyes. Waiting for a moment to be sure he was finished, Mikayla spoke quietly. "What do you mean you got sick, Jesse? You're okay now ... right?" she asked, even though she knew the answer to her question before the words even left her mouth. She could tell by the expression on his face that his was not an illness that could be recovered from so quickly.

"The doctors have given me every reason to be optimistic," he answered as quietly as she had asked, "but it's serious."

They stared at each other for another moment or two, feeling a connection they neither could deny nor explain. If their relationship was measured solely on time spent together, then by all rights they would still be considered strangers. But thankfully, time means nothing to the heart.

With obvious reluctance, he finally told her. "I have cancer, Mikayla. I have lung cancer."

"Oh, Jesse—no! Not you," she uttered in disbelief, her hand automatically covering her mouth in an attempt to squelch the gasp that had already escaped. Her eyes immediately filled with tears. It wasn't fair. He was an impossibly kind man with a caring heart, a man who had unselfishly served his country for the past twenty years of his life.

"Why did God—"

"No, Mikayla, no," he said as he reached out to take her hand. "Please don't think that way. I thought the same thing at first, but God didn't give me cancer. It just happened. But I know in my heart that God will get me through this. When I first found out, I thought why me—why did this have to happen to me, but after I contemplated it for a while, I realized—*why not me*? No one deserves this disease, darlin', or any other disease for that matter, and I'm no better than anyone else."

She stared tenderly into his honorable face. Reaching up, she gently stroked his cheek. "Yes, you are," she stated softly.

As she lowered her head, the tears that had pooled in her stinging eyes began spilling down her cheeks. She repeated the words in a barely audible voice. "Yes, you are."

Moving closer to her on the sofa, Jesse lifted her chin to face him.

"After I came to terms with the disease, and quit blaming myself and the army and the doctors and God, I could focus my attention on beating this thing—and I will beat it, Mikayla. Believe me, I've faced far more formidable enemies than cancer." He looked at her with a sincere, reassuring smile.

Looking into his eyes, Mikayla drew strength from the hope and commitment she saw staring back at her. "How long have you known?" she asked.

"A little over four months, about three weeks after I got to California, but I had my suspicions a few weeks before it was confirmed."

"I wish you would have told me. I maybe could have helped you somehow," she said, sincerely regretting that he hadn't.

He shuffled his body even closer to her on the sofa, leaving no space between them; they were side by side, their thighs resting comfortably against one another. Mikayla sensed that he had more that he wanted to say. "I know that what I'm about to say to you is gonna sound extremely hokey, but I'm gonna say it anyway, 'cause it's the truth," he said, shrugging his shoulders slightly. "Believe me when I tell you … you *did* help me."

In answer to her quizzical expression, he continued. "After the surgery and diagnosis, before I started treatment, I promised myself that if God got me through the first six months of chemo and I got a clean bill of health afterwards, I would call you up and ask you out on a date. The dream of you, Mikayla, only you, got me through the worst four months of my life. I'm just thankful that God saw fit to reward me two months early. I knew it was selfish on my part, but I was really glad that you called me. And seeing as how I'm spillin' my guts, I may as well spill 'em all," he said with a chuckle. "Since the first time I saw you, through that tiny one-inch crack in your car window, when I made contact with those amazing green eyes of yours, I've felt a connection to you. I was instantly drawn to you. Then after spending time with you in the restaurant and outside when you hugged me, you were like a fantasy come true—my angel in the night—and I let you slip right through my fingers. Now that I have a second chance to tell you how I feel, I won't make that same mistake again … but that's all I can allow myself right now … to tell you how I feel about you. I can't expect more than that. I can't allow you to …"

"Can't allow me to what?" Mikayla asked. "Tell you that I feel the same way about you? That I've pined away for you for months like a smitten school girl?"

"But it's unfair to you, Mikayla. I can't allow you to settle for me like I am right now. It's hard to explain, but … it's kinda like I don't feel whole. I feel less than you deserve right now. We have to wait until I get a clean bill of health."

"Jesse, don't try to feed me that sorry excuse. You're ten times the man of any guy I've ever met in my life. You have more courage, conviction, and honesty in your pinky finger than most men have in their entire bodies. Any woman lucky enough to be a part of your life—in sickness or in health—would be anything in the world but short-changed. I can promise you that," she said in a convincing tone, hoping that it conveyed her sincerity.

"Well … although I don't agree with your high opinion of me, I do very much appreciate the sentiment," he replied as he extended his hand to gently touch her face. "Thank you. You're so sweet." His earnestness was obvious in both the tone of his voice and the look in his eyes.

She watched him study her face as if memorizing every feature. The way he looked at her never made her feel uncomfortable or uneasy. His was never a leering, "undressing with the eyes" sort of look. It was always a look of appreciation, like he was examining a priceless piece of fine art.

Moving his face to within inches of hers, he asked softly, "Have I ever told you how beautiful you are?" When he spoke in a whisper, his already seductive voice took on a low growl that excited her immensely.

"Yes … you did once, but I wouldn't mind hearing it again," she said breathlessly. The anticipation of his pending kiss had stolen her breath away. Just before his lips tenderly met hers, she heard him sigh, "You're the most beautiful thing I've ever seen."

His kisses were warm and gentle, leaving her blissfully helpless in his embrace. Her usual reserve and self-control melted at the slightest touch of his hand. She would swear that she could physically feel herself falling hopelessly in love with him. Surrendering to his magnetism, she offered up her heart. She belonged to him whether he was ready to accept her or not, leaving him more than welcome to any other part of her that he so desired. She just hoped he couldn't sense how close she was to begging.

Her physical response and delicate moan seemed to slightly lessen his reserve. As she tilted her head back, exposing the softness of her sleek, inviting neck, his desire became more evident. His lips followed suit, covering her satin skin with tender, wet tokens of affection. Slowly, he descended until he reached the hollow of her throat. He stopped.

No, Jesse, please don't stop. Once again she felt him withdraw from her. Her heart sank in her chest as he inched away from her. It hurt so much that he wouldn't let her in. For his sake, she tried to hide her disappointment, but she couldn't.

"Please don't look at me that way, Mikayla. I'm so sorry, but I can't allow this to happen. I just can't … I won't hurt you like that … please understand." Plowing his fingers through his hair, he leaned his head back against the sofa and closed his eyes.

Reaching up, Mikayla gently pushed his hands down to rest in his lap. Slowly and rhythmically she began stroking his hair with the tips of her gentle fingers, beginning at his temples and slowly trailing back through his thick, wavy hair. "I understand Jesse … I do," she whispered. And she honestly did. He had made his decision based on what he thought was best for her, putting her first. His actions spoke volumes about the man he was.

She could feel the tension slowly leaving his body with each stroke of her hand.

"God that feels nice, darlin'," he told her apologetically. "I'm so damn tired."

Her heart went out to him. She knew what a devastating effect the chemotherapy was having on his body. She felt guilty for thinking of herself and her desires when he was the one that was ill.

Releasing a contented sigh, he cracked his eyes open to look at her. "If you don't stop that, I'm liable to fall right off to sleep," he said, winking at her with one partially opened eye.

"And that would be bad because …?" she questioned cutely as she raised herself up onto her knees to kiss both of his eyes closed again.

"For one thing, it's not a great show of manhood to fall asleep in the presence of a gorgeous creature such as yourself," he explained with a smile, making no attempt to open his eyes again.

"But what if the gorgeous creature is a little sleepy herself?" she playfully cooed into his ear.

He laughed out loud at her response. "Well, that's a different story all together."

He let out an exaggerated groan as she cuddled next to his side, nudging his arm out of the way and draping it over her shoulder. Resting her bent leg across his lap, she wrapped her arm around his chest. Nestling her face against his neck, Mikayla breathed in his masculine fragrance. The familiar scent flooded her mind with the memory of being wrapped in his warm leather jacket on the back of his motorcycle—the night he rescued her.

Within moments she could tell by his rhythmic breathing that he had already fallen asleep. Kissing him lightly in the crook of his neck, she made him a silent promise. To thank him for rescuing her, she would rescue him right back.

❦   ❦   ❦

It was several hours later when Jesse awoke with Mikayla's delicate limbs entwined around his body. Her head was resting on his shoulder with her pretty face delicately pressed against his neck. Her hair smelled of fresh spring flowers. Carefully brushing aside a few strands of stray auburn curls, he pressed his lips against her forehead and hugged her, drawing her even closer to him. Sleeping blissfully, her breaths were silent and calming. He held her tightly. How he wished that his life wasn't so complicated right now. He would like nothing better than to begin an immediate and intimate relationship with this heavenly being sleeping angelically in his arms. God she was everything—everything that he never even knew he had always wanted.

Unable to resist touching her, he began softly trailing his fingers up and down her smooth, bare arm. He marveled at how soft and silky her skin felt beneath his hand.

After only several strokes, he felt her eyelashes flutter against his skin.

"Sorry, I didn't mean to wake you," he whispered quietly.

"Mmmm …" Purring happily, she stretched in his arms like a contented cat. "You make a great pillow," she told him as she began to release him from her entangling limbs.

"Glad I could oblige you, darlin' … but I'm sorry I fell asleep on ya," he confessed, deeply embarrassed that he had done so.

Seemingly to downplay his humiliation, Mikayla replied. "You didn't; I fell asleep on you, and I must say, that was the best nap I've had in a really long time."

Jesse was the first to stand up. Walking around the room to awaken his still sleeping legs, he looked down as she stretched and yawned. "Do you want me to go so you can get to bed?" he asked, but at the same time hoping she wouldn't take him up on his offer.

"No!" She answered his question so hastily that now she was the one who was obviously embarrassed. "That is, unless you want to go …?" she quickly added.

"No … I'm in no hurry for our second unofficial date to end," he answered, hoping to instigate another engaging smile. "Did you mention something earlier about cake?" He raised his eyebrows in exaggerated excitement.

"Yes, I did. Old-fashioned oatmeal cake, and it goes great with a hot cup of coffee. You likes?" she asked delightfully, donning the bright, radiant smile he had hoped for. That was one of the things he liked most about her. Even though she was an intelligent, confident career woman, she had an upbeat, carefree side to her personality, a side that he enjoyed very much.

"I likes," he responded with a laugh.

Mikayla led him to the kitchen and motioned toward a stool at the small, but convenient bar dividing the tiny dining area from the cooking area. He watched as she puttered around the kitchen in her bare feet. When she opened the door to the refrigerator, the bright light from inside the appliance illuminated her from behind, rendering her dress virtually transparent, and dramatically outlining her perfectly proportioned figure. Unable to take his eyes off of her gorgeous body, he could only hope that he was far enough away that she couldn't see that he was staring at her, or more to the point, very rudely ogling her and utterly powerless to stop.

"Leaded or unleaded?" she asked as she swung around, holding up a canister of coffee in each hand.

"Unleaded, please," he said. "Always unleaded for me since … well, I haven't had caffeine for the past four months—that is, until tonight in that delicious iced tea." He winked at her for the second time that night, mainly just to watch her reaction to it. She seemed to like it when he winked at her.

"You're on a restrictive diet that doesn't include caffeine?"

"I'm on a diet that doesn't include food, actually," he answered with a sarcastic laugh.

"You really shouldn't be eating this cake either then, should you?" she asked apologetically. "I wish I'd known."

"Just try and stop me." Laughing, Jesse reached out and retrieved the plate laden with the largest piece of cake. "It's okay if I indulge once in a while." He could tell by the look on her face that she was unconvinced. "Really … it's okay," he repeated.

He waited for her to pour the steaming hot coffee into the cups. With the first bite of cake, he exclaimed, "Wow! This cake is scrumptious."

Taking a seat across from him at the bar, Mikayla smiled at his enthusiasm. "I'm glad you enjoyed your supper, and now the cake. It's a pleasure to cook for someone so appreciative."

"My brother could use this cake on his dessert menu," Jesse beamed. "It's wonderful."

"Thank you very much. It was one of Granny's best-sellers at the church bake sales," she said proudly.

"Well, I can see why," he mumbled, shoveling another forkful into his mouth.

Mikayla waited for him to finish his dessert. "I suppose sweets aren't on your diet either?" she asked in a tone that indicated she already knew the answer.

"No," he chuckled, "not hardly." He took another sip of the steaming coffee. "I've been on a macrobiotic diet since the surgery." He could tell by her perplexed look that he would need to elaborate. "Do you wanna know what I've been up to for the past four months?" he asked nonchalantly, as if it was nothing of significance.

"Yes, I would, but I don't want to intrude on your privacy."

"No, Mikayla … I wanna tell you. Besides, you couldn't be an intrusion even if you tried," he grinned.

Taking their coffee to the living room, they seated themselves once again on opposite ends of the short sofa. They turned their bodies to face one another.

"Well, I guess the best place to start is at the beginning," he said. He explained that three weeks after he had arrived in California, the coughing spells had become more frequent. So frequent in fact, that he was coughing more than he wasn't. "I had shortness of breath and a pain in my left side and back that started out as a nagging annoyance but progressed rapidly into a sharp, burning pain that I couldn't ignore any longer. I went to the doctor, and after some X rays and scans, he discovered that I had pneumonia. At the same time, he found a very small mass on my left lung. He scheduled an immediate biopsy, which confirmed his suspicions that the mass was malignant." Stopping momentarily, he leaned forward and took a sip of coffee. "Am I going too fast for ya?" he asked considerately.

"No, I'm following along just fine ... but Jesse, if you don't feel comfortable sharing this with me ..."

He interrupted her again. "No, Mikayla. I want you to know everything."

Turning to face her once again, he smiled reassuringly and continued.

"The surgery was scheduled immediately. The doctor removed the mass and a small part of my left lung. He needed to remove enough of the surrounding tissue to be sure that he'd gotten all of the cancer ... and he believes that he did." He nodded his head optimistically. "The rest is all good news. The mass was encapsulated, which means there were no obvious roots or branches, there were no infected lymph nodes, and there was absolutely no evidence of metastasizing."

He could tell that she comprehended his rather cryptic account of events, so he proceeded.

"The surgeon referred me to an oncologist who recommended an aggressive regimen of chemotherapy intended to eradicate any remaining microscopic cancer cells. I wasn't so much opposed to a round of chemo, but I felt like his treatment plan was just a little too aggressive for me. I've never been, and am still not, an avid supporter of pumping toxic and foreign, immune-depressing chemicals into the life-sustaining bloodstream of the human body. Especially when it's my body they're pumping it into," he said with a humorless smirk. "To me it's a complete contradiction of terms, which makes it a very personal decision that absolutely no one can make for you, not even your doctor. Anyway, I did some research and located a good integrated physician that I could consult with." Pausing, he asked her jokingly, "Are you bored yet?"

"No, intrigued actually. You're doing a great job. You are much more articulate than I originally thought," she said jokingly.

He appreciated her attempt to keep the mood elevated in spite of the somber subject.

Laughing at her quick wit, he resumed his account. "The integrated doctor and I devised a plan of attack that I'm very comfortable with." Jesse went into great detail explaining the differences in an integrated doctor, conventional medicine, and alternative or holistic medicine, and how he decided on a course of treatment to battle his disease. "Anyway, we reduced my chemo down to two times a month—every other Monday—instead of four times a month. I started on a strict macrobiotic diet, which is roughly 60 percent grains, 25 percent fresh vegetables, and 15 percent fresh fruits. I drink lots of water and herbal teas. Needless to say, sugar, caffeine, alcohol, processed foods, even meats, are not a part of the diet. I've always been a strong believer in alternative medicine, so I take a few herbs and vitamins, especially those that boost the immune system and cleanse the blood."

"Wow! I'm impressed with your knowledge and determination," she said, nodding her head in approval.

"Well, having your life on the line is a fairly strong motivator. But, only time will tell if I made the right decision."

What followed was a concise account of blood work and testing that had so far indicated the he was cancer free. "Sometime during the second week in January the doctor is going to do a battery of tests—a PET scan, X rays, bone scans … all sorts of fun stuff," he teased. "They're supposed to detect any lesions or evidence of metastasis. That'll be my six-month evaluation. Then … well, then, I can feel a little more optimistic about my future." What he really wanted to say, and what he hoped she already knew, was that then he could feel confident about including her in his future. "That will be my first hurdle. But my one-year evaluation will be the most critical point in my recovery. My odds will only increase from there."

"That's a lot of information to take in. I can't even imagine what you've been going through," Mikayla said in a sympathetic tone. "All of the research and decisions you've had to make. At least you had your brother for moral support ... yes?" she questioned. "I hate the thoughts of you having gone through this all alone, Jesse."

"Oh yeah ... Joe and his wife, Sasha, have been with me every step of the way. They've been great. I stayed with them for a few weeks when I first arrived, but they've only been married for a year. Naturally, I didn't want to intrude on the newlyweds, so I got a little apartment close to the new restaurant site. That was where I was spending most of my time anyway." Shaking his head, he said with an affectionate grin, "Not to mention, I had Annie. She drove up from Arizona several times during the past four months. She even came and stayed with me when I first came home from the hospital. To say she mothered me would be a gross understatement." He laughed at the memory. "You gotta understand, I'm not used to being taken care of so ... overwhelmingly. But when I finally got it through my thick head that what she was doing, she was doing out of love for me ... and I also realized that taking care of me was helping her deal. So I finally decided to lose my macho attitude and let her go about her nursing duties. Actually, once I let go of my pride, I felt blessed to have a baby sister who loves me that much ... especially since I haven't been around for her as much as I would've liked."

It was apparent that Mikayla could sense his deep remorse. "I'm sure your family understands, Jesse."

"I hope so," he said. Glancing down at his watch, he saw that it was 3:30 in the morning. They had been talking for hours. He hoped that it had been as pleasant an evening for her as it had been for him. "Speaking of family, I'm supposed to have lunch with Joe and Sasha in a few hours. Do you wanna come?" he asked invitingly.

Her answer came without a moment's hesitation. "Sure, I'd love to."

"Well, I guess I'll get out of here and let you bed down. I'll pick you up about 1100 hours, if that's okay?" He stood and yawned sleepily, rubbing his eyes vigorously with his fists. When he opened his eyes, he noticed that she was smiling at him. Her face was glowing with a tender and affectionate expression. "What?" he asked inquisitively, as he slowly started to smile simply because she was.

"Oh, nothin," she said sweetly. "It's just … you reminded me of a little boy just then … the way you were rubbing your eyes."

Slightly shocked by her assessment, he released a deep-throated chuckle. "Well, that's not exactly the look I was shootin' for," he replied as he felt his face getting warm. He couldn't remember the last time he had blushed.

Her smile evolved into an endearing giggle. "I didn't mean to embarrass you, Jesse," she told him. Scooting to the edge of the sofa, she gazed adoringly up at him. "But you have the slightest air of innocence about you at times … it's really cute … I like it."

"Well, in that case …" he responded with a good-natured grin that he felt certain revealed those blasted dimples on his cheeks.

He held out his hand and helped her up from the couch. Pulling her up next to him, he could feel her warm breath against his chest. He watched as she slowly raised her head. He loved the way the soft, loose curls of auburn hair fell away from her flawless face as she looked up at him. Her vibrant green eyes were astonishingly beautiful in spite of the fact that she was wearing very little makeup. They were rimmed in full, dark lashes that fluttered seductively when she blinked. He wished he were at liberty to stare into her eyes to his heart's content. For a second he imagined staring into them all night long.

"Are you sure that Joe and Sasha won't mind if you bring me along?" she asked as she started walking him to the door.

He found it amusing that she was unaware of how far his mind had strayed from their conversation only moments earlier. Not only that, but the fleeting idea of an intimate interlude gave him an idea for a quid pro quos.

"No, they won't mind at all, but I'll call Sasha in the morning and ask her to set another place for lunch." He turned away from Mikayla, but not before he was sure she had caught a glimpse of him beaming mischievously.

"Okay." She giggled again. "Now what's with that ornery looking expression on your face? I haven't seen that one before."

"Oh, nothin'," he said, shrugging his shoulders. "It's just that I can't wait to tell my brother that you slept with me on our second unofficial date."

Shaking her head, she laughed out loud. "Maybe I'd better rethink that notion of you being the least bit innocent, huh?"

Lowering his chin, he raised his eyes to stare at her. "Maybe you'd better," he told her, giving her his best attempt at a dangerously sexy expression. Then he flashed her a quick wink, and walked out the door.

Chapter 12

EXCITING NEWS

"Sharing a secret with a trusted friend
is one of life's greatest pleasures."

—*Granny Mae*

A thin mist of chilly, winter moisture had quickly evolved into a steady rain as Diana exited the doctor's office and headed toward the parking lot. Checking her watch as she climbed into her SUV, it was already 5:30 PM and she still had several errands to accomplish before she could head home to start supper. Where had the afternoon gone? Mentally prioritizing the tasks in her mind, she decided everything would just have to wait until tomorrow, with the exception of running into the grocery store. She needed to pick up a couple of fresh salmon steaks, along with some tomatoes for the salad, and then she could sprint home and have supper on the table by 7:30, just in time for Rick to get home.

Even though she tried to resume the normalcy of the day, the exciting news delivered by the doctor was more than she could successfully contain. She was about to burst with jubilation. She had to tell somebody. Before starting the car, she dug through her purse in search of her cell phone. Eagerly, she dialed the number of the only person in the world she would dare divulge this news to before she shared it with Rick. Anxiously, she waited for her best friend to answer the phone. The word "hello" had barely escaped Mikayla's mouth.

"Are you sitting down?" Diana asked, with as much calmness as she could possibly muster.

"Yes, actually for the first time today. I'm in my car headed for the grocery store on my way home. It's pouring rain, I'm running late, and Jesse is coming for dinner. Other than that, things are great. Why? What's up?"

"Guess what? You'll never guess what!" Diana shrieked with joy. "I'm pregnant! I'm eight weeks pregnant. I'm going to have a baby! Can you believe it?" she asked breathlessly.

"Oh, my God! Are you sure?" Mikayla squealed with almost as much enthusiasm as the expectant mother. "I'm so happy for you! You're gonna be a mommy. I'm gonna be an aunt." As the news seemed to sink in, Mikayla let loose a flood of questions. "What'd the doctor say? Are you feeling okay? When's the baby due?"

"Whoa! Slow down, auntie. One question at a time," Diana laughed. "The doctor says mother and baby are fine. I feel wonderful, and the little one will arrive on July 22."

"Great, I'll be home in plenty of time for the blessed event." Mikayla announced happily.

"I can't wait to tell the soon-to-be daddy." Diana beamed. "I'm gonna make his favorite meal and give him the good news tonight … sort of an early Christmas present. I just had to tell you, too. Just promise that you'll act surprised when we tell you together this weekend, okay?"

"Sure thing, sis. I'll deliver an Academy Award-winning performance. I promise," Mikayla teased lovingly. "I'll see you on Thursday, just two days from now. Can you believe it's been six months since we've seen each other? I'm so anxious to see you guys."

"I know. I can't wait … Be careful, and we'll see you then."

"You, too! … Congratulations, Diana. I love you."

"I love you too, curly top."

❦　　　❦　　　❦

Even though it was only 6:30 in the evening, it was already dark outside and pouring down the rain as Diana exited the grocery store. If she hadn't been running so late, she may have had the luxury of waiting for a lull in the storm, but she didn't have the time to spare, so there was no use in even entertaining the notion. With her purse hanging from her shoulder, a grocery bag on each arm, and car keys in hand, she made a mad dash to her vehicle parked just a few hundred feet from the store entrance. Running and splashing through the water puddles, she beeped the driver's door unlocked with her keyless remote.

Breathlessly, Diana made it to her car. As she reached out for the door handle, she felt a sharp, searing pain around her right ankle, as if something sinister had simply reached out of the darkness and bitten her. Just as she was glancing down at her ankle, she felt both feet being pulled out from under her. As if in slow motion, but powerless to prevent it from happening, she felt herself falling backward toward the ground. She fell helplessly until the back of her head struck heavily against the hard pavement with a loud, sickening thud. Her purse and groceries spilled out onto the ground all around her. In the fleeting moments prior to losing consciousness, she struggled desperately to scream, to move, to get up and run away—but she couldn't. She was a prisoner in her own incapacitated body. Blinking her eyes rapidly against the cold rain that was beating down onto her face, the only audible sound was that of rushing water inside of her already violently throbbing head. Even though she tried with all of her might, she was unable to focus her blurry vision on the ominous figure standing over her. She knew that he was watching her futile struggle to escape—waiting for her inability to resist him. She tried to speak. She wanted an answer, but her mouth refused to give voice to her question. *Why are you doing this?*

Although the icy torrent continued to pour down onto her pain-ridden face, it offered little assistance in releasing her from her agonizing prison. Her world was spinning aggressively around her in a constant white circle of light, faster and faster, slowly giving way to the encroaching blackness of oblivion.

Unable to fight her way through the invading darkness that was relentlessly consuming her, Diana lost her brief but valiant battle with consciousness. As she was rapidly descending into unconsciousness, fate allowed her time for one last question—"Rick?"

Chapter 13

EXCHANGING CHRISTMAS GIFTS

"The greatest gift of all
is the one that leaves your hands empty
but your heart full."

—*Granny Mae*

Still grinning from ear to ear with the news of Diana's pregnancy, Mikayla went happily about putting the finishing touches to the dinner table. She expected Jesse to ring the doorbell at any moment. She was brimming with pride at her newfound expertise in the fine art of preparing macrobiotic meals. After researching scads of recipes, she tested only the dishes that sounded even remotely edible. Each time Jesse came to dinner, he raved at her ability to make vile green weeds and rice taste like a gourmet meal.

She marveled at his willpower and unyielding discipline in every aspect of his life, but she especially admired the way he was attacking his disease, retaliating in full force against a foe that had attacked him first. His recovery was going even better than expected. The chemotherapy was rough, but he tolerated it without complaint. His routine blood analyses and X rays were promising, giving every indication that the cancer had been completely eradicated. Yet every time Mikayla heard him cough or watched his steps slow following a chemo treatment, a wave of paralyzing fear would overtake her.

They had had seven unofficial dates since the fateful Friday night when he told her about his illness and his subsequent decision to delay the start of a serious relationship with her. Since that night, he had managed to keep intimacy at bay with the exception of a single kiss goodnight.

Although her body ached to be in his arms, his consideration and respect for what he thought was best for her invoked her deepest admiration. She found it endearing that he was attempting to prevent something from happening that had already happened. She was already hopelessly in love with him, of that she was certain. Cupid had nailed her with his arrow the morning she hugged Jesse on the parking lot outside the restaurant—the first day they met.

This would be the last night that they would see each other until after Christmas. They were both flying home the next morning to be with their families—he to his parent's home in Lawrenceburg, Tennessee, where every member of his immediate family would be gathered together for the first time in twelve years, and she to Guntersville, Alabama, to spend Christmas with Rick and Diana.

One evening, during one of their long and comfortable conversations, Mikayla was shocked when Jesse told her where he had grown up and where his parents still made their home. It was surprising to discover that they had lived the earlier parts of their lives in such close proximity; Lawrenceburg and Guntersville were separated by just a little more than a hundred miles. It truly is a small world, they concluded.

Rising from the table and thanking her for a delicious dinner, Jesse caringly took Mikayla by the hand and led her to the sofa, where he sat down close beside her.

"Merry Christmas, Mikayla," he said as he handed her an elegantly wrapped, small square box.

"For me?" she asked with a grin, accepting his gift.

"Of course, for you. You didn't think I'd forget to get my girl a Christmas present, did ya?" he teased.

That was the first time he had referred to her as "his girl." It didn't matter what was in the box; those words meant more to her than anything he could have purchased.

Carefully, she unwrapped his gift and lifted the lid. Inside were the most exquisite diamond-studded emerald earrings she had ever seen.

"Oh, Jesse, they're gorgeous," she gasped. "But, you shouldn't have …"

"I searched everywhere, but I couldn't find anything quite as pretty as you," he told her. "But these reminded me of your amazing green eyes."

Taking them out of the box, Mikayla deftly removed the gold hoop earrings she was wearing and promptly replaced them with the emerald studs.

"How can you do that without a mirror?" he asked with a smile, shaking his head.

"Years of practice," she answered. "How do they look?" She turned her head from side to side.

"They look perfect—just like you," he remarked, without even glancing at the earrings.

"Now you," she beamed as she handed him a gift.

"Mikayla, you didn't …"

"Just hush and open it," she ordered jokingly, anxious to see the look on his face when he saw what was inside.

He flashed her one of his sexiest grins. "Oooh … I think I like being ordered around by a beautiful woman."

He took hold of her delicate hands and held them for a moment. Then he accepted the package, tore off the festive Christmas paper, and peeked inside.

"Wow!" he exclaimed, clearly surprised to discover the contents of the box.

The broad smile on his face provided all the proof Mikayla needed to affirm that the surprise was indeed a pleasant one and that he genuinely liked what he saw.

Without looking up, he removed the custom-made knife from the wrappings and slid the shiny, mirror-polished blade from its perfectly fitted sheath. The distinctive scent of natural leather drifted over to her side of the sofa.

"God, what a great knife," he marveled, holding the green micarta handle of the six-inch, drop-point blade in his palm and letting it rest loosely across his fingers. "It has impeccable balance."

While intently examining the blade, Mikayla saw him notice the maker's distinctive insignia with the initials "RK." "This was made by Ranger Knives," Jesse commented. "This is handmade. I've heard great things about this guy's work, but I have never seen one of his pieces."

She watched him quietly for a moment as he inspected the craftsmanship of the knife. She liked watching him. Putting aside the fact that he was impossibly handsome, his gentle, soft-spoken demeanor made him completely irresistible. Smiling to herself, she thought, *Rick, I think you've finally met your match. This guy's an easy "10."*

"Do you like it?" she asked him, although she already knew the answer to her question.

"Yeah, I love it!" he laughed, finally taking his eyes off of the knife long enough to glance up into hers. "This is a perfect gift. How in the world did you find this?" He seemed amazed at her resourcefulness and flattered that she had gone to such lengths to please him.

"Well, I thought about what you might like, and I went snooping around on the Internet and came across the Web site www.rangerknives.com," she answered with a proud and happy expression. "Justin, the owner, helped me custom design a knife that he guaranteed any fellow Army Ranger would be proud to own."

"Well, he's right … I love it," he told her appreciatively. "You're a surprising and very cool woman, Mikayla Mitchell."

The sparkle in his hazel eyes lasted only seconds before it evolved into a smoldering, sensual stare. Connected momentarily by a mutual thought, the words "thank you" echoed from both of their mouths at the same time. Breaking his own rule of only one kiss good-night, Jesse leaned over to within inches of her face and whispered "Merry Christmas, darlin'," before tenderly planting a warm, wet kiss on her lips.

Chapter 14

MERRY CHRISTMAS

"When I am down to nothing,
I know that God is up to something."
—*Granny Mae*

Mikayla was disturbingly surprised when the plane landed at the airport and Rick and Diana were not anxiously waiting to greet her. She had left a message on their answering machine late the night before, reminding them what time her plane would arrive. She had assumed that they were out Christmas shopping at the time, but now she wasn't so sure. Nonetheless, she hailed a cab and unsuccessfully tried to dismiss the nagging sense of doom that was creeping into her subconscious.

Pulling up in front of the house, her heart began to race. Something was wrong! Something was terribly wrong. Every single Christmas since their first one as a married couple ten years ago, Rick and Diana had always decorated their home with hundreds of thousands of dazzling multicolored Christmas lights. It had become a tradition with them. Every year without fail, just a few days before Christmas, they went berserk decorating their house. Tonight, however, the only outside illumination on their front porch came from one solitary, eerily glowing bulb, its subdued presence seeming to announce the ominous situation of the occupants of the home.

Running up onto the porch with suitcases in hand, Mikayla anxiously rang the doorbell several times in a row. Finally Mrs. Gregory appeared at the door, her eyes pitifully swollen and red, an obvious result of days of bitter tears and despair.

"What is it? What's wrong?" Mikayla asked frantically, horrific scenarios already beginning to play out in her head. Had something happened to Diana? *Oh no! Not the baby?*

Helping Mikayla inside with her luggage, the despondent Mrs. Gregory hugged her tightly but said nothing. She led her guest into the living room and slowly lowered herself onto the sofa. Seeming to struggle to hold herself together, she patted the sofa cushion with the palm of her trembling hand and beckoned Mikayla to sit down next to her.

Numbly, Mikayla moved toward the sofa and sat as instructed.

Mrs. Gregory looked at her with such defeat and pain, that Mikayla knew instantly something unthinkable had happened.

"Honey," Mrs. Gregory began, "There's no easy way to say this." Shaking her head, she took a deep, labored breath. Trying unsuccessfully to maintain contact with Mikayla's eyes, she lowered her head and took hold of Mikayla's hands. "Honey … Diana's missing … she's been missing since Tuesday evening."

"What?" Mikayla asked in disbelief. "What do you mean, she's missing?"

"We can't find her … we don't know where she is," the despondent woman answered quietly.

"No! … No, that can't be! I talked with her Tuesday evening … just a day and a half ago … and she was just fine. Where is she?" Mikayla demanded as she immediately jumped up from the sofa, just as her heart seized inside her chest. "Where's Rick? Is he out looking for her?" She was struggling desperately to keep a level head, but her efforts were in vain. The unbridled fear that was consuming her was making her dizzy. "My God, why didn't somebody call and tell me? Where's Rick?" she demanded again. Painful sobs began racking her body as she paced nervously back and forth. "Oh, my God … Oh my God! What are we gonna do?"

"Mikayla," Mrs. Gregory pleaded, "Please come ... sit back down." The distraught mother was so visibly near exhaustion that she was barely coherent.

Mikayla kept pacing, this time ignoring Mrs. Gregory's plea for her to sit.

"Sweetheart, the police ... they were just here ... they just left." Mrs. Gregory looked into Mikayla's face. The love she felt for Mikayla was obvious, as was the painful dread for what she was about to tell her.

"Honey, the police took Rick ... they took him ... they arrested him ... I think they arrested him." Mrs. Gregory's resolve was fading quickly. She began rocking back and forth, as tears filled her eyes.

"What?" Mikayla reacted in horror. She could hear the sound of her own heartbeat pounding in her ears. She felt lightheaded and sick to her stomach. Her mind was in turmoil as it tried to comprehend what was happening. "Momma Gregory, what are you saying?"

"I don't know, baby. They wanted to talk ... to question Rick about Diana's ... about her disappearance. Oh My God ... they acted like he ... like he ..." She looked at Mikayla as if begging her not to make her say the words.

"Momma Gregory, what are we gonna do?" Mikayla sobbed. "We have to find Diana! But, we have to go down ... we have to get Rick first ... then we have to go out and look for Diana!" Mikayla began crying violently, her garbled words escaping her mouth only during the momentary lapses in sobs when her starving lungs demanded oxygen. "Why didn't somebody call me and tell me this had happened?"

Mrs. Gregory begged her to try to calm down. "Please Mikayla ... Rick didn't want to upset you. He ... he knew you couldn't get here any quicker than you were. Oh God! ... He was just so sure we would find her. That she just ..."

"I could've maybe gotten an earlier flight," Mikayla interjected tearfully. "Maybe I could have convinced the police ..."

"Rick's parents are with him. They've called an attorney." There's nothing else we can do ... We can't do anything!" The mother broke down. Burying her face in her hands, she released the bitter, agonizing tears that only a broken-hearted parent can shed.

Rushing to her side, Mikayla wrapped her arms around the woman who had always been like a second mother to her. "I'm so sorry, Momma Gregory … please don't cry. We'll find her … we'll get Rick and we'll find her … I promise."

The ringing cell phone in Mikayla's handbag induced a startled gasp from both women. Mikayla's hands were shaking so badly that she was barely able to press the infuriatingly small answer button.

"Hello?" she uttered faintly.

"Mikayla?" Jesse asked hesitantly, reacting as though he may have dialed a wrong number.

"Jesse," she murmured. His name was the only word she could manage to verbalize through the sobs.

"Darlin', what's the matter?" he asked tenderly.

"Jesse, I …"

"Mikayla, are you hurt?" His quiet concern was evident.

"No," she whispered tearfully, "But …"

"I'm here, baby … just calm down," he instructed, his mellow voice softening even more. "Take a deep breath, and tell me what's wrong … tell me, baby, so I can help you." He waited for her to gain her composure. "Please don't cry, darlin'."

His gentle reassurance soothed her heart. God, she needed him. She could feel his strength caressing her as though he were physically enveloping her in his arms. Finally, the sobs began to subside, slowly being replaced with the intermittent snubbing that always bears witness to a broken heart.

"It's okay, darlin'. Whatever's happened, we'll get through it together," he promised softly. "There's nothin' I wouldn't do for you, Mikayla. Just tell me where you are, and I'll be there as soon as I can."

His strong, protective voice and encouraging words reduced her fear to a somewhat manageable level. Knowing that he was there for her afforded her the slightest glimmer of hope. She didn't have to face this nightmare alone. Jesse would help her. She trusted him. He would help her in any way he could. The hope and courage she drew from him allowed her to brokenheartedly relate the horrific circumstances of her Christmas homecoming.

❧   ❧   ❧

Mikayla was amazed by how much had transpired in just a few short hours. She and Jesse were just minutes away from arriving at his parent's home in Lawrenceburg, Tennessee. It wasn't easy, but he had finally convinced her to accompany him there to retrieve some of his equipment—things he had stored with the thought that he would never have need of them again.

Within two hours of hanging up the phone with her the night before, Jesse was by her side. He accompanied her the next morning to the police station to discover that Rick had been formally arrested and charged in connection with the disappearance of Diana. Apparently, Rick was also being questioned regarding the disappearance and murder of several other women from the tri-state area, including a sixteen-year-old girl, Lacy Williams, who had been reported missing only three days prior to Diana's disappearance. Mikayla was not allowed to see or even talk to Rick. She knew he must be devastated and out of his mind with worry over his wife. She was wrought with compassion for him. His attorneys were working feverishly to get him released on bail—promising to have him out within twenty-four hours.

Afterwards, Jesse had spent the better part of the afternoon with a longtime friend, a fellow Ranger who had retired shortly before Jesse had. He was now working for the Federal Bureau of Investigations. All Mikayla knew was that his name was John and that he was assigned to the F.B.I. field office in Birmingham. He was not the agent in charge of working this case but was familiar enough to discreetly answer some of Jesse's questions. Apparently, there was one fairly viable suspect whom the authorities had questioned on more than one occasion over the past year in connection with the Night Crawler cases. The suspect was born of a very wealthy and politically influential family that had provided ironclad alibis in every instance for which their son was questioned. The prominent father was also the proprietor of a chain of notable hunting, gaming, and taxidermy stores in the surrounding states, for which his son served as C.E.O. With lack of sufficient evidence, neither the F.B.I. nor the local police department had been able to obtain authorization for any type of surveillance, phone taps or otherwise. The suspect was cleared and, therefore, completely "off-limits" to the police. A fact made abundantly clear by the family's prolific team of attorneys.

Just after dusk, Jesse and Mikayla pulled into the driveway of his parent's home—the home where he grew up. The house itself was decorated for Christmas in a simple but elegant fashion. Festive evergreen pine wreaths embellished with large, bright red bows adorned the windows, each of which was framed with rows and rows of clear, twinkling lights.

Mikayla dreaded going inside. She had been anxious and looking forward to meeting his family, but not like this, not under these circumstances. It was bad enough that she had taken Jesse away from the reunion that they had planned for months; she didn't want to dampen their Christmas spirit any more than she already had.

"Maybe I should just wait in the car," she suggested as Jesse switched off the ignition.

Turning toward her, he reached out and lovingly stroked her arm. "Mikayla," he said soothingly. "I've already explained to my family about what's happened to your friends. They know that I need to be with you now, and they understand. They know that you and I are only here to pick up some of my things. Okay?"

"I guess." She shrugged her shoulders slightly and tried unsuccessfully to force a smile.

Immediately upon entering the front door, Mikayla's ears were filled with the cheerful sounds of Christmas carols, laughter, and loud conversation. The fragrant aroma of cinnamon and pine offered further proof of the happy holiday season.

Taking her by the hand, Jesse led her toward the source of the commotion. As her apprehension increased, so did the intensity of her grip on his hand. The room quieted slightly as they entered. One by one, all heads began turning toward them.

From across the room, sitting next to the Christmas tree, a lovable, little boy with curly, blonde hair squealed with glee. "Uncle Jesse, Uncle Jesse!" Seconds later he was firmly attached to his uncle's legs.

"Hey, little man," Jesse returned the boy's enthusiastic greeting as he playfully tousled the child's curly head.

The boy looked up in bewilderment at the stranger holding his uncle's hand.

Still smiling, Jesse made the introduction. "Corey, this is my friend, Mikayla. Mikayla, this is my favorite nephew, Corey."

The little boy, clearly pleased with being introduced as the "favorite nephew," immediately donned another lovable grin.

Mikayla extended her hand to her new acquaintance, but instead of shaking her hand, he immediately transferred his embrace from Jesse's legs to hers.

"Hi, Mikawa." He tilted his blonde head back to look up at her, smiling sweetly. He had the most adorable, angelic face she had ever seen. He looked like a little porcelain doll. She was forever amazed and delighted by the innocence to be found in the eyes of a child, and Corey's were no exception. His eyes were as blue as Rick's and equally as captivating. As he loosened his grip on her legs, she bent down to meet him at his level.

"Hello, Corey. Your uncle's told me all about you," she said as she brushed her finger lightly over his round, baby-soft cheek. "You're the most handsome little boy I've ever seen," she told him.

She had an almost sacred place in her heart for children. It was an adoration that she couldn't readily explain but one that she felt awesomely blessed to have. "Children are God's most precious angels," Granny always said.

Grinning even bigger, Corey wrapped his tiny arms around Mikayla's neck and hugged her tightly with unbridled honesty and enthusiasm. She felt guilty for the smile that the child inspired. She couldn't help but think about the baby that Diana was carrying.

The little boy seemed completely content to allow Mikayla to hold him as long as she needed to.

"Thank you for the hug, angel," she whispered tenderly into his precious, little ear. "I really needed one."

He giggled cheerfully as he rubbed his shoulder up against his ear in response to the tickling sensation her soft words created.

"You're welcome," he whispered back dutifully with another melodious chuckle.

Perhaps sensing his mission was complete, Corey returned to the business of trying to figure out exactly what was in each colorfully concealed package beneath the Christmas tree.

Taking her hand again and helping her back to her feet, Jesse introduced her to his family, beginning with his mother and father who greeted her with open arms. The rest of the names and faces became confusing as the introductions were quickly made. The last to be introduced was his younger sister, Annie, and her husband, Taylor. Annie was just as sweet and congenial in person as she had been the day they talked on the phone.

"I'm leavin' her in your hands for a few minutes, Annie," Jesse told her. "I gotta go up in the attic and get some stuff." Before he had taken two steps away, he turned back toward his baby sister wearing a devilish grin. "Just keep her away from that nutty husband of yours."

"I heard that." Taylor laughed as he jokingly put his arm around Mikayla's shoulder.

Mikayla found both Annie and Taylor very easy to be around and actually began to feel herself relax a little. A few minutes into the conversation, Annie had to excuse herself to answer a "mommy yell" from Corey. Leaving just the two of them, Taylor asked Mikayla if she would like to see something that he felt sure she would find interesting. After accepting his offer, Mikayla followed him out of the room and down a small hallway adjacent to the stairs that led to the second floor of the home.

Both sides of the hallway were lined with an impressive collection of family photographs, some of which were vintage, black-and-white photographs displayed in ornate, antique frames. There were pictures of every child and grandchild at every stage of life—births, christenings, graduations, marriages, and everything in between.

Taylor drew her attention to a particular section on the wall to her left.

"This is the area I like to refer to as the 'Jesse shrine,'" he whispered with a chuckle. "I have to admit, I enjoy giving the man a rough time about his accomplishments, but I swear to you, I've never been prouder of anyone in my whole life. He's the kind of man we all wish we could be. He knows how I really feel about him … just don't tell him that I said it out loud, okay?"

Mikayla promised that she wouldn't, so he continued. "Hell, he's more like a brother to me than my own flesh and blood. It's good to know that a guy like him has your back, ya know?"

Mikayla nodded and smiled in agreement. She did know.

Turning her attention to Jesse's many accolades, she could feel her jaw slowly begin to drop open in awe. The wall was laden with citations, ribbons, certificates, and medals. There were several framed newspaper clippings, one of which boasted the headline, "Proud Soldier—Humble Man." The article began "Hometown hero and son Jesse Daulton, former first-team, all-state quarterback who led the Lawrenceburg Wildcats to a state championship in 1985, has made the transition from hometown hero to national hero. In valorous service to his country, he has …" She wanted to read the entire article, but time wouldn't allow it. She knew it wasn't going to take Jesse long to gather his things, and she knew, in fact, that he was hurrying the task for her sake. As her eyes scanned the wall, Mikayla tried urgently to take everything in. She turned her focus first to the Certificates of Specialized Training, each denoting that Jesse Paul Daulton had successfully completed specific courses in Airborne Training, RIP Training, Jumpmaster Training, Pathfinder Training, Special Forces Medical Training, Ranger School, and more.

"Wow," she uttered under her breath.

"I told ya." Taylor smiled, his pride and love for his brother-in-law clearly evident.

"Take a look at this," he said, pointing to an attractive framed display that contained a photograph, a medal, and a citation that read, "The President of the United States takes pleasure in presenting the Bronze Star Medal with 'V' device to SERGEANT JESSE P. DAULTON for heroism above and beyond the call of duty ..."

"This photograph was taken during the formal awards ceremony," Taylor interrupted, drawing her attention to the picture. Jesse looked unbelievably handsome in his dress green uniform as another distinguished-looking, uniformed gentleman pinned the medal onto the soldier's chest just above his heart. The actual Bronze Star Medal was also included in the framed display. The impressive five-pointed bronze star itself was about an inch and a half in size and was attached to a red, white, and blue ribbon.

"See the little 'V' pinned to the ribbon?" Taylor pointed again. "That's what's called the combat 'V' device. It denotes valor or heroism under fire."

"What did he do to earn that?" she asked, grateful for the opportunity to learn more about Jesse's military career.

"Hasn't he told you anything?" Taylor seemed somewhat annoyed at the notion, but at the same time all too happy to indulge her curiosity. "Jesse was a platoon medic at the time, and the mission was during Operation Just Cause in Panama. He was credited with saving the lives of multiple soldiers that night. He ran repeatedly into the line of heavy enemy fire to rescue wounded Rangers and drag them back to where he could safely work on them. He was shot twice in the process, but that didn't stop him from repeatedly running back in to tend to the wounded. I'm tellin' you, this guy's amazing," he announced with respect and admiration. "He's a legend in the special ops community."

Turning to face her again, he told her soberly, "The whole family was invited to attend the awards ceremony when Jesse was pinned, and during the reception I got to talk to one of his squad team members. His name was John. He told me that any soldier who knows Jesse will tell you that if you're ever called out into heavy combat, Doc Daulton is the medic you want watching your back. John's exact words to me were, 'If push came to shove, Jesse could keep you alive with a Leatherman's tool, duct tape, and a rubber band until he could get you evacuated out to a hospital.'"

She looked at Taylor as if he were joking, to which he replied, "I'm not kidding. It's the truth. And John was dead serious when he said it. These guys don't fool around."

Taking him at his word, a heartfelt surge of pride for Jesse passed through her heart. Although she already knew what type of man he was, it was altogether different to learn what type of soldier and medic he had been.

Returning her attention to the memorabilia, Mikayla noticed a small, wooden display case with a glass front sitting atop a petite antique stand. An American flag perfectly folded in the traditional military thirteen-fold triangle was displayed proudly beneath the glass on top of the box. The stars were folded to the top as a reminder of our nation's motto: "In God We Trust." She remembered learning that little tidbit of information from her high school history class. Perhaps seeing Mikayla's obvious interest, the beaming brother-in-law lifted the box from the table so she could have a better view of its contents. Behind the glass on the front, a blue padded background held multiple badges, medals, patches, ribbons, and tabs.

"What are all of these for?" she asked, raising her inquisitive eyes to meet Taylor's.

Starting left to right and pointing to each individual piece, Taylor began naming them with as much familiarity as if they belonged to him personally: Basic, Senior, and Master Airborne Wings; Army Achievement Medals; Meritorious Service Medals; Expert Field Medical Badges; Combat Field Medical Badges; two Purple Hearts; and last but not least, his Army Ranger Black and Gold Tab.

After Mikayla had finished examining Jesse's many accolades, Taylor carefully set the container back down onto the table. Turning back around, he took his index finger and playfully placed it beneath her chin, attempting to close her awestruck, gaping mouth.

"It's all a little overwhelming, isn't it?" he asked as he turned to face the wall again. "I knew Jesse wouldn't tell you about any of this. He's pretty tight-lipped when it comes to his military experiences and accomplishments. You know the old saying, 'heroes and humbleness go hand in hand.' Anyhoot, I thought you should know what kind of a man's man it is that you have so effectively managed to wrap around your little finger."

Surprised by his comment, Mikayla glanced over to find him grinning.

"I just tell it like I see it," he said jokingly, with a shrug of his shoulders.

Taylor had an honest, upfront quality about him, and as Mikayla returned his infectious grin, she could easily see the potential for a comfortable friendship between the two of them someday.

Hearing the stairs creak beneath his feet, they turned around to see Jesse descending the staircase with a large, black canvas bag draped over his shoulder.

Although he looked somewhat surprised when he saw the two of them standing in the hallway together, he seemed to know instantly what his brother-in-law had been up to.

"Taylor," he said, laughing out loud and shaking his head in obvious embarrassment. "Man ... one of these days I'm gonna beat the shit out of you ... and I'm gonna enjoy every single minute of it."

Chapter 15

THE CAPTIVES

"Those who do evil, have no rest."
—*Granny Mae*

The man was seated backward on the straight-back, wooden chair, his chin resting atop his folded hands with his arms stretched out leisurely across the back of the shoddy piece of furniture. The demonic smirk on his otherwise average-looking face bore witness to how deliriously happy he was with the new additions to his collection sitting bound, blindfolded, and completely helpless across from him. He reached up quietly with his right hand to wipe away the tiny stream of saliva that was trickling down his chin. His mouth watered in anticipation of adding these two perfect specimens to his growing ensemble of morbid female companions. He could hardly wait to start the next phase of their development, but he forced himself to loiter. He willed himself to adhere to his one and only hard-and-fast rule: he must refrain from haste and take his time to thoroughly enjoy each and every phase of their transformation process. He likened the process of what he did to these women to having sexual intercourse. If he rushed through it, it would be like climaxing after only two or three quick thrusts into the tight body of an untouched virgin. The way he saw it, the desired objectives were the same in both instances: to heighten and prolong the ultimate satisfaction for as long as possible.

The thrilling prospect of achieving ecstasy by way of either instance instigated an evil snicker to prematurely escape his lips before he had time to stifle it by clapping his hand over his mouth. Unfortunately, that release of pent-up excitement alerted his captives to his presence. He didn't like that. He liked watching them when they didn't know he was there. Now their bodies were tense and unnatural. His short-lived spell of demented happiness was over. He stood up and despondently shuffled across the room, his untied boots slipping up and down on his feet as he walked. He unlocked and cautiously opened the front door of the cabin. Peering out, he carefully scanned the area before he finally slipped through the small opening, closing the door securely behind him.

Only moments later, the creaking of the cabin door alerted Diana to her captor's return. She had no idea what time of day or night it was, but since he seemed to be moving rather hurriedly around the room, she hoped it was time for him to leave for a few hours. She had no idea where he went at times, and she didn't care, as long as he was gone. At least that gave her time to let down her guard and try to think—think of a way to escape. She was in excruciating pain. She was freezing cold, and her back ached terribly from days of sitting on the hard, wooden chair to which she was bound. Her hands and feet were numbly stinging from lack of circulation due to the tightly secured ropes. And her head ... God, her head was throbbing so intensely that she could hear it pulsating in her ears. She had to get away! She had to think of something—anything—she had to try to save herself and her unborn baby, and the sweet, young girl sitting next to her. *Please God ... please help us. Please give us strength,* was her silent, repetitive prayer.

Her body stiffened when she heard him walking toward her. Without warning, he forcefully removed the gag and shoved a bottle of water into her bound hands. She hastily raised the container to her lips and began emptying the contents into her parched and painful throat. The fabric he used for the gag was rough and he tied it tightly, causing the cloth to scrape and cut into the corners of her mouth. The constant half-open position of her jaws when the gag was in place caused excruciating pain and muscle spasms in her face. Desperate to be free from it for longer than it took to drink a bottle of water, Diana made the bold decision to try to communicate with her captor.

Since all she could see was the darkness invoked by the blindfold, and since he was remaining impeccably quiet, it was difficult for her to tell where he was in the room. Nervously, she directed her question straight ahead into the deadly silence—knowing that her words would reach his ears, no matter where he was.

"Why are you doing this to us?" she asked in a raspy and pathetic voice.

The cold, pungent air of the cabin hung heavy with the acrid smell of fear and death; her words seemed to hang suspended in the thickness of it.

His shock that she had the nerve to open her mouth, and raging fury that she had done so, was immediately evident.

"Did I say you could speak?" he retorted maliciously just inches from her face, his hot, rancid breath filling her nostrils.

"No, sir you didn't. But I didn't know if I would ever get the chance again. I just thought … I thought you might want to talk about it."

Diana's words were barely audible, not only due to the dryness of her throat and the paralyzing fear of what the man was going to do to her for violating his "no talking" rule, but she was also trying to sound as nonconfrontational as possible. All the while, her mind was desperately racing to unearth any shred of information she could find still buried in her memory from her one semester of Psychology 101 at Alabama State.

"Talk about what, you stupid bitch?" he demanded as he roughly grabbed the blindfold and snatched it away from her eyes, tearing out with it a measurable handful of short, blonde hair. Even though the cabin was dimly lit, the minuscule trickles of early morning sunrise streaming through the tiny cracks in the boarded-over windows forced

Diana to open her eyes slowly. She blinked rapidly—frantically prompting her dilated pupils to adjust to the light as quickly as possible.

He stood directly in front of her. Saying not a word, he glared at his frightened and vulnerable prisoner.

Diana looked up and dared to make blurry-eyed contact with her soulless captor. She wondered if Satan himself looked as average as this demon standing before her. How could something so evil, appear so normal? He had short, dark brown hair. He was cleanly shaven and neatly dressed. He looked like a neighbor someone would trust immediately, that is until one looked into his eyes. God ... his eyes were horrifying. He stared back at her as if daring her not to look away. Gripped with terror like she had never known, she fought desperately not to let him see her fear, though as close as he was, she felt sure he could hear it by way of the deafening screams roaring inside of her. Still, she maintained eye contact. Knowing this might be her and the girl's only chance to live, she gathered every ounce of courage she could muster, and in a low, even voice answered his question with one of her own. "What kind of childhood did you have?" she uttered quietly.

Quickly bending down, he pressed his face to hers as he repeated her words in a high-pitched, mocking tone, laughing loudly and hideously.

As abruptly as the laughing started, it stopped.

"Don't try to mind-fuck me, lady. Smarter people than you have tried, believe me."

Taking a step back, he sneered down at her with as much disdain as she had ever seen in another human being.

Seeing his mounting agitation, she continued with as much false compassion as she could possibly gather. "I can't imagine what devastating thing must have happened to you as a child that would make you want to hurt others as badly as you were hurt. I'm sorry ... but ... that kind of enduring pain must be terrible. I just thought that maybe ... you might wanna talk about it."

Crossing his arms in front of his body, he released another gruesome cackle. "Lady, don't make the fatal mistake of taking me for a damn fool. I know the only person you're trying to help here is yourself." Bending over, he braced his hands against his knees, once again just millimeters from her face. He glared at her with undeniable depravity. "You have no idea how fucked up I really am, do you? … 'cause if you did, you'd shut the hell up!" His breaths were coming faster and harder. It was apparent that her confrontation was fueling his anger which in turn seemed to be stimulating him sexually. She could tell by his breathing pattern, his body language, and the way he was looking at her that he was becoming aroused. She also knew that for psychopaths, anger and sexual desire are often indistinguishable and completely dependent upon one another.

"You couldn't help me even if I wanted you to … you ignorant cunt!" he blared. "Unless, of course, you want to spread those sexy legs of yours."

Still not breaking the stare between herself and the man, Diana refused to react to his despicable comment. Calmly, she lifted the bottle and swallowed the last of her water.

Her obstinacy seemed to infuriate him even further. She could almost see his mind searching for the best way to retaliate against her. Smugly, he shifted his unblinking eyes to the young girl. She was sitting perfectly still with her head bowed so low that her chin was practically touching her chest. It looked as though she was trying desperately to disappear.

"Don't you have anything to say, sweet thing?" he growled as he placed his open hand on the girl's left knee, then slowly and purposely ran it up the length of her exposed leg.

She didn't say a word, but her petite body shuddered with obvious repulsion of his filthy touch.

"The newspaper says that you're my sweet, little sixteen … my sweet little Lacy" he said, apparently pleased with that fact. He began aggressively running his hand down her right leg, crossed over, and then back up the left. With each succession, his hand moved faster and his fingernails bore down harder into her smooth, youthful flesh, leaving bright red welts on her skin. The sensation of her young, supple body beneath his hand seemed to stimulate him into a more heightened state of arousal.

"You're going to become my youngest addition tonight. Are you as excited as I am?" he asked mockingly, and then leaned over and sadistically forced his lips against her trembling and defiant mouth.

"Leave her alone, you sick bastard!" Diana screamed, straining against the ropes to stop him from hurting the girl.

Before she could blink an eye, she felt the crashing blow of the back of his powerful hand across the left side of her face. The force of the blow sent searing, hot pain radiating through her skin, into her skull, and down her neck. She lifted her bound hands to her chin in an attempt to stop the room from spinning wildly around her. Her left ear was ringing, and she could taste her own blood as it flowed freely from the sizeable cut inside her cheek. The warm liquid that quickly filled her mouth gave her a small but satisfying means of instant gratification. Waiting until she had collected a sufficient amount of blood, she spat it defiantly in his direction. The crimson fluid splattered on the sleeve of his light blue denim shirt, just as the watch on his wrist began to alarm. Cursing her belligerently, he drew his right hand back to strike her again. She closed her eyes and braced herself for another heavy blow. But instead of physically assaulting her again, he bombarded her with the vulgar rantings of a demon, at the end of which he proclaimed, "That's okay you bitch. I'll deal with you tonight." Sneering at her viciously, he raised his hand and forcefully grabbed her beneath her chin and jaw, compelling her to meet his satanic gaze. His dark brown eyes were completely void of any evidence of human emotion or conscience. They were as lifeless and cold as the fabricated plastic eyes in the sockets of an inexpensive baby doll.

"If I didn't have to wait a few days for your bruises to heal … smart ass … I'd finish you off tonight," he sneered angrily, once more just inches from her face. "That way our young little Lacy could keep me company for a few more days. I wouldn't mind having a few pieces of that squirming, tight pussy." He watched as if waiting once again for Diana to react to his vileness before he continued. "But since you felt the need to go and open up your big mouth, I think I'll just let you have the honors of satisfying me tonight … all night long. You deserve to be punished … very enthusiastically punished. Don't ya think?" His eyes grew wide with hunger as he visibly contemplated the prospect of punishing her. Maintaining a firm grasp on her chin, he pressed his face against hers. She felt his repulsive, wet tongue on her skin as he dragged it slowly up her cheek. A combination of disgust and unmitigated fear sent an uncontrollable shiver coursing through her body. As he finally released her from his grip, she watched as a devious grin possessed him, prompting the hideous laughter of moments earlier to return with a vengeance.

Diana's skin crawled in response to the unearthly sound that escaped him, a sound that was not even remotely human.

She observed him out of the corner of her eye as he made his way across the room to change his blood-spattered shirt. Before her eyes—and as instantaneously as flipping a light switch—she watched in horror as his mood reverted quickly back to rage. She wondered if he could discern the difference.

Returning to his captives, he forced the gags back into their mouths with renewed and spiteful vigor and proceeded to do the same with Diana's blindfold. He then squatted down in front of each woman and tied her hands individually to the arms of each chair.

"I'll be back tonight," he warned them gravely. "And as for you," he said as he roughly grabbed and squeezed Diana's thigh, "you *will* do everything I want you to do. I promise you that … sooner or later, you will. It's just a matter of how much pain you're willing to endure before you do. What the hell do I care? You're already bruised … what's a few more gonna hurt?" Emitting another evil snicker, he ran his hand force-fully up between her legs and whispered snidely, "By the way, sexy … thanks for the foreplay."

With that, he rose and sauntered triumphantly out of the cabin, leaving the women alone to silently contemplate their terrifying fate.

Chapter 16

THE STAKEOUT

"America without her soldiers
would be like God without His angels."

—*Granny Mae*

It had been a little over twenty-four hours since Mikayla had returned home to the news of her best friend's disappearance.

She was once again in the living room of Rick and Diana's home, where she sullenly observed Jesse plan his strategy and ready his equipment. His nimble fingers expertly and speedily loaded rounds into half a dozen empty ammo clips and inserted batteries into several electronic devices that she could not readily identify.

Glancing up, he must have noticed the turmoil of emotions churning behind the large green eyes staring back at him.

"Mikayla, darlin'," he said as he sucked in and released a deep breath. "I'm sorry ... but there's no way in hell I'm lettin' you go in there with me. That option is nonnegotiable, and that's the bottom line," he stated gruffly.

This was the first time he had ever spoken to her so abruptly and condescendingly. She could tell by the look in his eyes that it hurt him to do so, but still it made her angry.

"You can't do it all by yourself, Jesse," she retaliated heatedly. "Don't be so bullheaded." She was growing angrier by the minute. Who did he think he was telling her what she could or could not do?

"I think I'm a little more qualified to judge my own capabilities and lack of limitations than you are, sweetheart," he told her sarcastically. "I fully intend to do this on my own, and contrary to what you may think, I'm completely capable of doing so." He looked at her for a long moment; his stoic, hazel eyes reflected absolute certainty of success, forged from twenty years of achieving just that. "I would hope that you'd have a little more faith in my abilities," he added as though he was insulted and hurt that she didn't.

It wasn't that she didn't have faith in him, or that she didn't trust him, it was just that she was worried about him. She didn't want him to have to do this thing all alone.

The hurt in his eyes readily melted her resolve. *Darnit'!* She wished that he'd just let her stay angry—it hurt much less to feel the anger than to feel the other painful emotions lurking so closely beneath it. Nonetheless, she felt the frustration at him slowly begin to diminish, being replaced with defeat, fear and bitter sadness.

He stared into her eyes as they welled with tears. His voice softened slightly. "Mikayla, darlin' … I'm sorry. I didn't mean to speak to you like that, but I'm not gonna let you win this one. I just can't." Jesse laid the gun and clips down on the coffee table in front of him and turned his body to face her. "I wish you could understand. It's just so far out of the realm of possibility that I would take you in there with me, that I can't even find the words." Shaking his head in frustration, he persisted. "You should be considerin' yourself lucky that I'm gonna let you come along to keep an eye on the tracking monitor. I can't believe I'm actually allowing you to do that, but I really don't have much of a choice, now do I?"

He seemed to be waiting for a response to further the argument, but Mikayla said nothing.

She was hesitant to say anything more. She was twenty-nine years old. She didn't need his permission to do anything she damned well pleased. But she was also smart enough to realize that this was his mission, and if she wanted to be even the minutest part of it, she had to abide by his rules. Any further comments on her part would be futile and detrimental.

"Okay, Jesse," she finally muttered, throwing her hands up in defeat.

Seemingly pleased that this battle was over, he made an effort to console her. "If you'll just trust me on this, Mikayla, I promise you on my life, I'll bring Diana back home." His voice took on a much more amicable tone as he reached for the tracking monitor. "Now," he asked, "are you ready to learn how to operate this thing?"

"Yes," she answered cooperatively, "but I thought you said it was illegal for the police to put any kind of surveillance on this guy."

"It is," he volunteered nonchalantly, flashing her a quick wink. "They didn't tag him—I did."

Her mood elevated slightly as a result of the wink. "How'd you manage to do that, Ranger Daulton?

"Simple," he said as he fidgeted with the device, "John gave me the intel on the target; I tailed the guy this afternoon and waited for him to leave his car unattended." Jesse continued his explanation without looking up, recounting his actions as if there was nothing to them. "When the guy parked his vehicle outside of his daddy's hunting store, I wheeled into the lot several spaces away. I watched him exit his vehicle and waited till he walked into the store. Then I got out of my car and began walking in the same direction. Clumsy me," he said, grinning slyly as he raised his eyes to meet hers, "I accidentally dropped my keys right next to the rear of his car. As I bent down to pick 'em up, I palmed the small magnetic tracker and stashed it quickly beneath his back bumper."

Impressed by his cunningness and his endearing grin, but mainly because she simply couldn't help herself, she leaned over and planted an affectionate kiss on his surprised mouth. She hated that she had hurt his feelings. He had such a tender heart beneath that tough Ranger exterior. She felt so lucky to have him in her life. She'd never known a heart like his—so giving and selfless—driven by a deep, abiding need to protect and help others. He wanted so much to help these women that he didn't even know.

They smiled at each other, taking full advantage of their newly discovered ability to speak without words.

"Jesse?"

"Yes, darlin'?"

How can you be so sure that this is the guy?"

"Well … that's just it … we're not sure," he said, shaking his head. "John and I spent all afternoon going over the case files, and the truth is … there's no real hard evidence to link this guy to the murders. If there was, the police would have him locked up by now."

"So, why are you and John so convinced he's the one?"

"Gut, darlin' … just a gut feelin', and it's almost always right," he told her with a tired sigh. He went on to explain that out of all the possible suspects involved, he and John kept coming back to this one. "But, his family's very influential." he said, showing obvious disappointment. "Not that that would cut any ice if the police had any hard and fast evidence, but they don't. And with his team of attorneys breathing down their necks and scrutinizing every little thing they do, the police have to be extra careful not to step on his rights."

"So naturally then, you can't go to the police for help?"

"No way," he replied with a bit of a chuckle. "They'd lock me up if they knew what I was up to."

"Can't John help?" she asked with a bit of desperation in her voice. "Can't he go in there with you, Jesse?" she pleaded as the tears welled up again. Her fear seemed to be returning with a vengeance. She was so scared about Diana, and worried about Rick, and now Jesse too. He was so ill, she felt so badly that she had gotten him involved in this. If something happened to him, she would never forgive herself. She could feel herself trembling inside. She was so physically exhausted and emotionally drained that her emotions were as ready to spill over as her tears.

Jesse looked over at her with such honest compassion that it melted her heart. He laid the tracking device down on the table. "No, Mikayla … John can't do that … I can't let him do that … but I'll be okay. Everything's gonna be okay," he told her as he scooted over next to her and gathered her into his arms. "John and I have it all worked out. We're pretty sure we know where he's holding the women. We trailed him this afternoon with the tracking device. Everything's gonna be okay, baby. Just trust me."

God, it felt good to be in his arms. With her head against his chest, she could hear the gentle beating of his valiant heart. "I do trust you, Jesse … I do," she cried. "But … what if he catches you … what if he hurts you too … what if Diana's already dead? Oh my God! What if he's already killed her, Jesse?" Mikayla couldn't suppress the tears another second. Jesse rocked her in his arms, as the feeling of overwhelming sadness engulfed her. A flood of tears poured down her face. The salty release flowed over her lips. She had assumed that after Granny Mae's passing, she would never taste tears that bitter ever again. She was wrong.

Jesse didn't try to suppress her tears. He just held her … he held her tightly, and let her cry.

❧   ❧   ❧

It was 4:00 AM and still very dark outside. Only the golden beams of the black SUV's parking lights lit the densely wooded, country road. Jesse was driving very slowly as he alternately monitored the woods to the right of the road and the flashing red dot on the screen of the tracking monitor. Mikayla kept quiet, knowing he was far from thrilled with her presence.

Even though she was going to be hidden away safely in the woods and wouldn't be stepping one foot out of the vehicle, she knew that he would have preferred her to be safe at home in a warm bed. It would have been one less thing on his mind at the moment. But still, in spite of his druthers, he was making a gallant attempt at being cordial.

Jesse's hushed voice cut through the eerie silence. "According to the tracking device, our man is holed about three miles ahead and to the east, which is deep into the woods to the right, just outside your window." He pointed in the direction with his right hand, explaining that he needed to find a clearing in the trees that would conceal Mikayla and the vehicle and get him closer to the target.

"How close to the target do you want to get?" Mikayla asked softly, for no other reason than simply to keep him talking. The sound of his rich, baritone voice was comforting. It seemed to ward off the uninvited fear that kept tickling the back of her neck.

"I'd like to get to within a mile or a mile and a half of the site, if I can. If, in fact, the women are still being held there, I don't know what condition they'll be in when I reach them. I may have to carry one or both of them out, depending on their injuries. So the closer I can get to them, the better. But I don't want to get any closer than a mile."

"Why not get as close as you can?" she asked timidly.

"Well, I have to keep the SUV—and its stowaway—tucked away at a safe distance."

He looked over at Mikayla for the first time since they had gotten into the car. The lighting was so dim that she couldn't be sure but thought she detected the slightest hint of a smile on his attractive face.

"Besides, I don't know for sure that this man is working alone. Even if the monitor shows him leaving the site, that doesn't mean that there isn't someone else in there guarding the captives. I can't just pull up into the driveway and knock on the front door, now can I?" he teased.

"I guess not," she responded sheepishly.

"Mikayla ..." He spoke her name apologetically yet seriously. "I hate to have to ask you this. I should have asked you sooner, but ... but I gotta know for sure before I go in there. I trust your judgment explicitly, so I'll accept your answer as fact and go on from there."

Though unable to see the remorse on his face, she could hear it in the tone of his voice.

"Are you absolutely certain of Rick's innocence?" he asked. Is there the slightest doubt in your mind that he had anything to do with Diana's disappearance or the abduction of those other women?"

Slightly taken aback by his question, but with absolute conviction, Mikayla stated simply, "I've never been more certain of anything in my life."

Nodding, he continued as though he hadn't even asked the question.

"I wish I'd had more time to trail this guy a little longer to gather some more intelligence on him and his habits. I would've been better able to prepare, but ..." Tapping on the brakes, Jesse pointed ahead to a narrow, single-lane, dirt road. He stopped when he reached it and checked the monitor again. "This is the road he uses to get in and out," he said with unwavering conviction.

To Mikayla, it looked more like a carved out path than a road. But whatever it was, Jesse wheeled the vehicle slowly onto it. Barely creeping forward, he kept his eyes on the left side of the road, hoping for a clearing in the trees in which to safely conceal the SUV and its occupant.

After a few tense moments of searching, Jesse finally spotted a slight opening amidst the dense woods to the left. Steering the vehicle into the narrow space in the trees, they were instantly swallowed up by the overgrowth of foliage. The roughness of the forest floor made for quite a bumpy ride, jostling the passengers back and forth in their seats and making Mikayla terribly nauseous. She closed her eyes and laid her head back against the seat in hopes of quelling the ever-increasing threat of the expulsion of her stomach's contents. Finally, the vehicle came to a stop. Mikayla opened her eyes and could see that their makeshift road had come to an end. They were stopped in a small, circular clearing in the trees about twenty feet in circumference, which left no way out but the way they came in. Alternating the gearshift from reverse to forward, Jesse began maneuvering the vehicle so that it would be facing the opposite direction for a quick exit when the time came. Finally, after successfully turning the SUV around, he switched off the engine and the parking lights. Mikayla was thankful for the sweet lack of motion, and so was her stomach.

Except for the faint glow of light radiating from the tracking monitor, the darkness was completely engulfing, both inside and out.

"Gosh, I can't even see my hand in front of my face," she whispered.

"Don't tell me that my girl's afraid of the dark?" he teased as he snapped a small, green chemical glow light and laid it down on the floor of the passenger's side.

"I know this isn't much light, but it's all we can afford. I don't want us to stand out like a beacon in the night. Your eyes will adjust to the darkness in just a few minutes, and you'll be able to see a little better," he told her encouragingly.

"What do we do now?" she asked.

"We wait. We wait for him to make the first move. Waiting is sometimes the hardest part."

Sitting there in the eerie glow of green florescence, she felt the need to barely whisper. "Jesse?"

"Yeah?"

"Are you scared?"

"Well, darlin'," he said with a hint of levity in his voice, "I'd love to sound like the big, brave Ranger here and tell you that I'm not feelin' a little bit of fear startin' to creep in, combined with a heavy dose of adrenaline." Growing more serious, he continued. "But I won't say that—not to you." He glanced over and met her gaze. "There's this old army saying about admitting fear in a combat situation. It states that if you say you're not scared, then you're either a fool or a liar."

He must have seen the nervous expression on her face because he quickly added, "Not that this is combat. I don't plan to go charging in there with guns ablazin' or anything." He smiled. "Most people think that fear is a sign of weakness, and in some instances, it is; but in a situation like this, if you control it properly, it can actually work to your advantage by keeping you sharp and on your toes. Controlled fear can keep you alive ... do ya know what I mean?"

Mikayla nodded her head solemnly. "I think so."

"I'll be fine, Mikayla," he told her as he reached over and stroked her hand tenderly. "I'll do what I've been trained to do, follow the plan, and everything will be fine."

"Okay," she replied softly, feeling somewhat relieved. "What exactly is your plan, Jesse?" she asked as she wrapped herself in a small blanket that she was thankful she had remembered to bring. She was already beginning to feel the chill of the forty-degree outside temperature.

"Well, this is strictly a rescue operation … 'easy in and easy out' … carried out as quickly as possible. As soon as that bastard leaves them alone in there, I'm gonna go in and take back what he had no right to take in the first place."

"You make it sound so simple."

"It is simple," he said with a wink. "Nothin' to it."

God, she wanted to believe him. She wanted to believe that he was just going to waltz in there without incident and get her best friend and that little sixteen-year old girl out of there, safe and sound.

"I keep praying that they're both okay—that Diana's okay," she whispered tearfully. "Nobody knows this except me, Jesse, but I think you should know … Diana's pregnant. She's eight weeks pregnant. She was planning to tell Rick the night she disappeared."

Mikayla watched his reaction to her news. He ran his fingers through his hair in frustration, and she could tell that he took her words to heart. If he wasn't motivated and fired up enough already, that added tidbit of information was apparently all the stoking he needed.

"Don't worry, Mikayla; we'll get 'em out of there." He stared straight ahead.

Studying his face in the dim light, she could see the tense movement in his jaw. She knew that he wanted nothing more than to rescue these women from their nightmarish ordeal. She also knew that it made no difference to him whether they were friends or strangers. He would do the same for both.

"Jesse?"

"Yes, Mikayla?" He turned to face her again.

"I know you don't like to talk about it much, but why did you choose to become a soldier? I mean, how did you know that the army was what you wanted to do with your life?"

He looked at her questioningly, as if wondering why she chose a time like this to ask about his career choice.

"We've got nothing but time at the moment," she argued with a shrug of her shoulders. "And, I'd be real interested to hear how Ranger Daulton came to be."

"You would, would you?" He chuckled pleasantly, then paused for a moment and looked at her as if waiting for her to take back the request and get him off the hook. "Well okay," he said finally, "if you wanna know. When I was a senior in high school, I thought I had it made. I had a full ride to the University of Tennessee on a football scholarship. Being the star quarterback of the team, I was really full of myself and way too cocky for my own good." A mischievous grin lit up his handsome face. "Other than playing football and chasing girls, I really had no idea what I wanted to do with the rest of my life. Then one day the school held a Career and College Fair for the senior class. Me and a few of my smart-ass friends decided we would spend a little time at the U.S. Army career booth. I'll never forget it. There was this Army Ranger medic there and he was talking to some other guys about having direction for your life and finding your place in the world." After a moment's pause, Jesse continued reflectively. "Well, that guy impressed the hell out of me. It was just like a light came on inside of me that day, and it has been burning there ever since. Being a soldier, especially a Ranger ... it's not just what I did, it defined who I was, who I am, and who I'll always be."

"Did you ever regret enlisting?"

He laughed pleasantly. She loved the sound of his sexy, manly laugh, and she was sorry when he had to stop to continue his story.

"Regret that I joined up? Never in a million years." He shook his head back and forth decisively. "It was the best decision I've ever made in my life. But I have to say, there were times, especially during Ranger School, that my poor body wondered if it was such a great idea."

Mikayla smiled. It made her happy that he was finally letting her in. "Tell me about the process. Did you know going in that you wanted to make the military your career?"

He laughed again as if to protest her prodding. "Darlin', that's a very long story."

"You got someplace else to be?" she teased.

Relenting to her request to hear more, he proceeded. "When I initially enlisted, in May of '85, I enlisted into the army as a medic with a unit choice of Ranger assignment. I spent six weeks in basic training at

Ft. Jackson, South Carolina. Then to MOS—that's Military Occupational Skills—for eight weeks of medic training at Ft. Sam Houston, Texas. From there to Ft. Benning, Georgia, for airborne training for three weeks and then into the RIP—Ranger Indoctrine Program—for three weeks. RIP is where the recruits are what we called 'grilled and smoked' to see who has the intestinal fortitude to become a Ranger." He stopped to pour himself a cup of hot coffee from the thermos. "Are you bored yet?" he asked. "Want some coffee?"

"Nope to both questions. I'm quite fascinated, actually. Continue please," she urged.

"After RIP, I was assigned to the Third Battalion 75th Ranger Regiment at Ft. Benning, Georgia, where I spent eighteen months as platoon medic. I also took some EMT courses during that time. Then in late spring of '87, I volunteered for Ranger School at Ft. Benning, where I spent fifty-eight days of pure mental and physical torture. It was the hardest thing I've ever done in my life. It was during Ranger School that my body wondered if I'd made the right decision to enlist." Stopping for a moment, he smiled at her again. "But after some strategically placed stitches and some minor internal injuries, I made it through and graduated on July 30, 1987."

"What is Ranger School, exactly?" she asked, trying her hardest to keep up with the barrage of information he was relaying.

Jesse explained that Ranger School is divided into four phases designed to train soldiers to fight in all types of differing environments. The first phase being held at Ft. Benning, Georgia, where a soldier develops the military skills and the mental and physical endurance necessary for combat situations. "This is the phase where they try to kill you while testing your resilience," he said with a laugh. He then elaborated on the second, or mountain phase of training at Camp Frank D. Merrill in Dahlonega, Georgia, where soldiers learn techniques for combat in mountainous areas. "The third phase," he continued, "used to be the desert phase at Dugway Proving Grounds in Utah. It was done away with in '95, which doesn't make much sense to me, but anyway, Dugway was where a soldier was taught techniques for combat in desert environments. Then, finally, the fourth phase is at Camp Rudder at Eglin Air Force Base in Florida, where soldiers are taught techniques for combat in jungle or swamplike environments."

"Wow! I assume that not everybody makes it through that grueling process …?" she asked, immensely impressed and proud of the fact that he had.

"No way … generally, only a little more than half of the guys that sign up make it through to graduation. Like I said, Ranger training was the hardest thing I've ever done in my life. Actually, Dugway was the most difficult phase for me, personally."

"Why? What made it any harder than the rest?"

"Well, it was just physically tough for me. The conditions were awful. I hated the sand, and it was cold. You gotta understand, the major objective of all phases of Ranger School is to test your stamina and ability to think under the most extreme mental and physical conditions. A recruit is subjected to sleep and food deprivation on a daily basis. So, you are always sleepy and hungry, but you are expected to react and perform as you are being trained to do—as one of the most elite group of fighting soldiers in the U.S. military. Anyway, I felt like a POW after I finally completed the course and got my hard-earned Black and Gold Ranger Tab," he said with another laugh.

"After Ranger School, I was reassigned back to the Third Battalion. I got my first promotion to sergeant in the fall of '88, and in '89, I made the decision to reenlist. Then I decided to go for HALO training at Ft. Bragg, North Carolina, and from there to Ft. Sam Houston, Texas, for further medic training. Then I went back to Ft. Benning for Jumpmaster and Pathfinder Training.

"What's all that specialized training for … I mean, what's HALO, Jumpmaster and Pathfinder for?"

"Well, HALO is High Altitude Low Opening freefalling, or kind of like skydiving," he explained. "Jumpmaster training teaches a parachutist how to become the one who ensures that all conditions are safe for all jumpers in his assigned aircraft. And Pathfinders are specially trained leaders that set up drop zones and landing zones for soldiers and equipment."

Not willing to let him off the hook just yet, Mikayla probed for more details. "Well then, would it be too intrusive if I ask about your combat experiences?" She winced when she asked the question. She felt bad for being nosey, but her hunger to get to know him better seemed to have outweighed her good manners.

He smiled faintly. "No … if you wanna know, I don't mind tellin' ya. I just can't believe you're interested in all of this stuff." He glanced over at her. "And don't tell Taylor any of this either; that nut already has enough ammunition to use against me," he teased. After taking another sip of coffee, Jesse continued. "My first combat was during Operation Just Cause in Panama on December 20, 1989. We had to go over there when Noriega started showing his butt declaring war against us, and harassing U.S. citizens and our military personnel stationed in Panama. The Rangers had three targets to secure that night, the Torrijos-Tocumen International Airport and Airfield, the Rio Hato Military Airfield, and then Noriega's beach house. The Second Battalion, Company A and B of the Third Battalion, my Batt at the time, and a Regimental command team launched a parachute assault on the Rio Hato Airfield. Before we were dropped in at 0100 hours, two F-117 stealth fighters went before us and dropped a couple of 2,000-pound bombs to pave the way. The bombs were intended to stun the Panamanian Defense Force—you know, to take the fight out of 'em."

She nodded her head to indicate that she understood.

"Our jump was a low-level jump from only 500 feet in altitude, and we were being shot at while still in the air. When we jumped from the C-130s, the skies were dark except for the flashes of antiaircraft and small weapons fire from the ground. Actually, some guys were shot while still in the aircraft waiting to jump. I was just praying that no one else would get hit on the way down. Since 500 feet didn't allow much time, some of the guys didn't check their mains and drop their rucksacks first, so there were immediate injuries and guys yelling for help as soon as we hit the ground. I was scrambling as soon as my feet touched down, stabilizing broken legs and ankles and bandaging the more serious lacerations."

He paused for a moment. She could tell that it was difficult for him to find the words. A part of her regretted that she had asked, but she waited. Finally, Jesse continued.

"It took a few hours before the airfield was relatively secure for the MEDEVAC helicopters to begin landing with supplies and to start evacuating the casualties. During those two hours, we lost four Rangers and forty-four more were wounded."

"Wasn't that the mission that earned you your Bronze Star?"

"Yeah," he said pensively as he refilled his coffee cup. "There was this one guy who was new to our unit. His name was Jackson Murfey. For some reason, on his first day, we all started calling him 'Jax.'" Jesse shook his head and laughed, as if the nickname conjured up a pleasant but distant memory. "Even though I was just a few years older than him, he always reminded me of a big ol' kid. He spoke with a real slow, southern drawl, and he was always asking questions, just like an oversized curious kid, and he was a real practical joker. Anyway, about thirty minutes after we had made the jump, I was about halfway to the mark when I heard someone in between the gunfire hollering for 'Doc Daulton.' That's what the guys called me most of the time in the barracks, but that night most of the injured were yelling 'Medic' like they're supposed to. Anyway, here's this kid, Jax, all shot up and lying out in the open on the runway, yelling for me to help him. A couple of Rangers close by laid down some cover fire for me, so I hunkered down and went out there to get him. I could hear the bullets whizzing past my head, so I grabbed him under his arms and dragged him by the shoulders back to where I could work on him out of the line of fire." He paused again and turned to look at Mikayla. His warm hazel eyes relayed the vividness of the recollection and the admiration he had for the wounded man. "This guy had four gunshot wounds—one in his arm, two in the leg, and one that had grazed him on the side of his neck. I couldn't see very well. It was dark, and I was working from my red lens light, which I was holdin' in my mouth. Here I am trying to check for exit wounds and trying to keep him from bleeding out, and he keeps asking me if I can patch him up and get him back on his feet so he can complete the mission. I'll never forget that kid," he said fondly.

"Oh God, did he …?"

"No … he didn't die," Jesse said with a thankful smile. "After just a few months of convalescent leave, he was back with us in the Third Battalion. In 1991, he was reassigned to the First Battalion and was deployed to Desert Storm where he was wounded again. When it came time for him to reenlist in 1992, he decided it was time to go back home, and I haven't seen or heard from him since then."

"What happened in your career after that?" she asked, hoping that he would finish.

"Lord, woman," Jesse protested. "Give it a rest. Aren't you tired of hearing about me for a while?"

"Negative, First Sergeant … keep going."

Laughing at her response, Jesse complied. "In January of '91, I got a little burned out. The Ranger lifestyle's very difficult. The constant training and deployments take their toll on the old body, so I took a break for a while. I served as a senior instructor at Ft. Benning for a couple of years. In January of '93, I went back to B Company with the Third Battalion and was deployed to Somalia, as part of Operation Restore Hope. On October 3, 1993, I participated in what was supposed to be a short 'in and out' mission. The mission was actually a daylight raid to capture key leaders of the civil war in and around Mogadishu. The short raid, which had been estimated to take no more than thirty minutes, escalated into a fierce eighteen-hour fight. Seventeen men died during that mission—six of whom were Rangers—and sixty-nine were wounded." Turning his body toward her, his tone changed dramatically to that of reverence and remorse. "A buddy of mine, Matthew Myles, was awarded the Congressional Medal of Honor for his actions during that mission. I don't know if you know about the Army Ranger Creed, but one of the vows embraced by the creed is that we'll never leave behind a fallen comrade—never. Many Rangers have lived up to that vow over the years, and on that particular day, Matthew was one of 'em.

He paid the ultimate price when he refused to leave behind an incapacitated, and about to be captured, fellow Ranger." Jesse paused, and took a sip of coffee. He was quiet for several seconds, and she wondered if he was going to continue. She remained silent.

"In order for Matthew to get to this guy," he began again solemnly. "He had to cross this intersection that some of the soldiers had dubbed 'the funnel of death' because enemy fire was so tremendously fierce there. Matthew didn't even hesitate; he ran head on into the heavy bursts of AK-47 fire from the Somalis to get to this guy. The Ranger's leg had been shot up pretty bad, so Matthew picked him up and practically carried him back across the bullet-riddled street while his squad members and some Delta Force guys did their best to lay down enough fire for them to get back across safely. They made it, but Matthew sustained several hits in the process." Jesse took a long pause before finally resuming his account. "My buddy died in the helicopter while they were being evacuated out. The Ranger he saved that day was a medic. The medic did what he could to stop the bleeding, but Matthew had too many critical wounds; he'd lost too much blood." Pausing again, he stared into Mikayla's eyes. His saddened expression revealed the vastness of his pain and sorrow. Hesitantly, he started to say something else, but he stopped.

She could see the uncertainty on his face, so she waited patiently for his decision to continue. It would have to be his decision to tell her what was on his heart; hers told her not to ask.

Finally, still staring into her eyes, he told her solemnly, "Mikayla, the Ranger medic Matthew saved that day ..." He shook his head and released a troubled sigh. "It was me. He died saving my life."

As he said the words, Mikayla's breath caught in her throat. Leaning toward him, she reached out and took hold of his hand. Although her words felt grossly inadequate, she said them anyway. She didn't know what else to say. "Oh Jesse, I'm so sorry ... God, I'm so sorry."

He nodded his head and forced a faint smile of gratitude. Taking in another deep breath, and after a few quiet moments of reflection and respect, he set out to hurriedly bring an end to his storytelling. "Anyway, I stayed with the Third Batt until 1997. Then from '97 to 2000, I was a

Ranger instructor at the Troop Medical Clinic at Ft. Benning, and I was platoon sergeant at Ft. Drum, New York, for two years after that. Finally, I was assigned to the First Battalion as a senior battalion medical sergeant/NCO and was deployed to Iraq as part of Operation Iraqi Freedom from April to August in 2003. While in Iraq, I was promoted to master sergeant." He paused again and drank the last of the coffee in his cup. "After Iraq, I worked as the Non-Commissioned Officer in Charge at the Womack Army Hospital Emergency Room at Fort Bragg, North Carolina, for the remainder of my enlistment until the day I retired on May 1, 2005, after twenty years of active service."

She waited a second to make sure he had finished. "Wow, that was quite a distinguished career you had, Jesse. I'm very impressed ... and for what it's worth ... I'm very proud of you."

"It's worth a lot," he said sweetly, "And thank you, Mikayla. But, I swear, I've never in my life talked that much about myself." He glanced over at her and grinned mischievously. "It's dawn already. What'd you do? ... drug my coffee?"

"You haven't seen me drinking any of it, have you?" Mikayla said with a smug expression that quickly evolved into a tender smile.

Their eyes held transfixed for the longest moment.

The first to grow self-conscious from the stare, Mikayla commented, "It sounds like you didn't have much time for a social life."

Jesse seemed reluctant, but he finally broke eye contact and returned his attention to the conversation. "Well, it seems to work out for a lot of guys, but still it's not the ideal career to have if you want a normal home life. It's very difficult being a soldier's girlfriend, much less a wife. I did get close to marriage once, though. We were getting pretty serious just before I was deployed to Somalia, and well, I guess those circumstances and that experience made the decision for her. She ended it." He paused a moment. "How about you? You ever been married or close to it?"

"Yes, I was married once. We were together for a little over four years before we divorced," she admitted. Looking back at him, she saw that he seemed amused.

"Really?" he said rather surprisingly.

On the verge of becoming insulted, but starting to laugh because he was laughing, Mikayla replied, "What is it? Do you find it hard to believe that someone would actually marry me?"

"Not hardly, darlin'," he said with an impish and dimpled grin. "I find it hard to believe that someone actually had you and was stupid enough to let you get away."

A slight movement on the tracking monitor caught Jesse's eye and quickly severed the levity of the moment. "Our guy's on the move," he said as he straightened up in the seat and checked his watch. "It's 7:30. He must be leaving for work at daddy's hunting store. I guess that's his sorry attempt at pretending to be a normal human being."

Mikayla's body language and facial expression must have given her away, because Jesse's focus shifted quickly back to her. "Mikayla, let's go over the rules one more time." Waiting for her complete attention, he began sternly barking out his orders. "Do not get out of the SUV for any reason. Do not open the window or the door for any reason. If I tell you to go—you get the hell out of here. If you see or even sense anything suspicious—you get the hell out of here. Just drive straight out of the woods, turn to the right onto the dirt road, and then left on the black-top. Do you understand?" he demanded harshly.

"Yes," she answered, looking directly into his intensely focused eyes. It was like a switch had been turned on inside of him. He was no longer Jesse; he was a soldier—a soldier committed to successfully accomplishing the mission that had been set before him.

"We'll be able to stay in constant contact with the ear communicator and the receiver. I can hear you and you can hear me at all times, but don't talk unless it's absolutely necessary or unless I ask you a question. I'll keep you informed as much as I can. You understand?"

She nodded her head in the affirmative.

"Don't take your eyes off of the tracking monitor. It'll track him within twenty-five miles of here. Let me know immediately should he start back this way." He waited until she nodded again and gave him a hint of a smile, indicating that she understood and that she was okay.

"Mikayla," he said hesitantly but firmly while staring directly into her eyes, "there's a .38 revolver in the glove box just in case you need it. All you gotta do is point and shoot ... can you do that?"

Her faint smile of seconds earlier had quickly disappeared, and although somewhat shocked at his unexpected question, she answered with the response that she knew he needed to hear. "Yes, Jesse ... I can."

He seemed satisfied that she would be safe during his absence, so he took a deep breath and began gathering his gear together. Taking his eyes off of the monitor for only seconds at a time, he watched until the blinking red light disappeared off of the edge of the screen.

"Okay, Mikayla." He reached over and took hold of her trembling hand. "It's time to get this thing done. Are you all right?" he prodded gently as he gently squeezed her hand.

"Yes ... yes, I'm fine," she answered. Her voice was weak and low as she fought hard against the urge to cry. "You'll be careful, won't you?" Her eyes were wide with the need for assurance.

"Yes, darlin', I'll be careful, and I'll be back with Diana and Lacy. I promise." He stared at her with such blatant self-confidence that she believed every word he said. He was as composed as if he were simply going off to work. She guessed that in a sense—he was.

He raised her hand to his lips and kissed her fingers. After a quick wink, he was out the door. As he motioned Mikayla around to the driver's side of the car, he began looping his arms through the straps of his backpack. After placing the earpiece into his left ear, he tucked his girl safely away behind the steering wheel.

"Mikayla," he said seriously, "I want you to reach over and get that .38 out of the glove box and lay it in the seat next to you."

His directive came as a surprise. She didn't want him to know, but she'd never touched a gun in her entire life. The fact that it was there if she needed it was one thing, but to actually handle it was entirely different. But, for his sake, she did as he asked. Mechanically, she reached in the box and retrieved the cold, heavy pistol and laid it in the seat about twelve inches from her thigh.

"Mikayla?"

"Yes, Jesse," she whispered, still staring at the gun.

He waited for her to make eye contact before he continued. "Don't touch it again, unless you have to use it … okay?" The focus and confidence reflected in his eyes was amazing. "You never pick up a gun, Mikayla … unless you intend to use it."

"Okay," she assured him with a slight nod. "I understand."

He pressed the automatic door lock button, and closed the door. Through the glass between them, he gazed intently into her eyes one last time. Fluidly, he removed the 92 Beretta pistol from the shoulder holster beneath his jacket and within seconds had turned and headed southeast into the woods. Mikayla watched as the man she adored stealthily disappeared into the darkness of the thicket.

Chapter 17

THE RESCUE ATTEMPT

*"A true hero is defined not by his words
but by his actions."*

—Granny Mae

Jesse made his way expertly through the first half-mile of his trek, navigating the nearly impenetrable section of the woods by keeping a keen eye on the obstacle-ridden terrain that lay before him. Carefully, but swiftly, he chose the path of least resistance in order to keep his presence known only to himself.

Flourishing with lush, massive evergreen and longleaf pines, parts of the winter forest were as green as if it were springtime. The ground was strewn with brittle plants and bushes, along with plenty of rocks, thick beds of fallen pine needles, and downed decaying trees, all of which made walking at a steady pace a definite challenge. Stopping to check his GPS for the final time, Jesse was approximately three hundred meters from his intended objective, the location where he believed the women were being held. If his estimations were correct, he should reach them in about thirty more minutes.

As his objective grew closer, his steps grew slower. Uncertain of the enemy's level of intelligence or degree of paranoia, Jesse followed his instincts and years of tactical training in choosing his path. He watched for any possible early warning defense devices that, if activated, would reveal not only his presence but also his exact location.

Pausing momentarily, he could hear the methodical and reassuring sound of Mikayla's soft breath in his ear. Magnified by the small speaker buried deep inside his ear canal, it was almost an intimate connection; he could practically feel her breath on his skin. But most importantly, he knew she was safe as long as he could hear that gentle, steady pattern. In keeping with his promise, he quietly spoke her name.

"Mikayla?"

"Yes, Jesse. I'm here."

"Are you all right?"

"Yes, I'm fine," she whispered. "Don't worry about me. Are you okay?" The concern in her voice was obvious. "You sound a little out of breath."

"Never better," he replied, although that wasn't entirely true. After only a forty-minute hike he was already beginning to feel slightly winded and fatigued. He knew his body well—more so than most—and this definitely wasn't his body, at least not the one that had endured years of thirty-mile road marches without so much as a sore muscle. The reality of his physical limitations was proving difficult for him to accept. He was angry with his weakened body for failing his resilient spirit, a spirit that vowed to complete this particular mission or die in the process.

"Listen," he told Mikayla intently. "I'm about twenty minutes from the objective. I'll speak to you when I can, and let you know what's going on. Just stay alert and maintain silence on your end. Don't ask any questions, okay?"

"Yes, I understand."

"All right then, here we go." His forward progress became painstakingly deliberate. He continued to choose his steps stealthily, producing nonexistent proof of his presence. After advancing less than sixty meters, he spied a barely visible strand of thin wire stretching out across his path about six inches above the ground. Looking from left to right, he was unable to readily see where the wire ended in either direction.

Tracing the strand off to the left, he found the end of the pressure-type, trip wire. It was attached to a homemade detonation device, which was rigged with a trip flare and boom maker. Holstering his gun, Jesse pulled a six-inch serrated blade from the sheath attached to his belt and his Leatherman tool from his jacket pocket. Seconds later he had successfully disarmed the makeshift burglar alarm. Rolling the wire as he went, he followed it to where it was anchored to a tree in the opposite direction. Kneeling down, he clipped the wire, finished rolling it up, and shoved it into his pocket.

As he was preparing to continue on, he detected a quiet rustling in the dry brush directly in front of him. Staying in his crouched-down position, he peered through the bushes in the direction of the sound. Cowered to the ground about forty meters away and inching its way toward him was an enormous black guard dog. It was obvious by the way it moved and its apparent sharp listening skills that it had been well trained in the duties of guarding and protecting to the death.

When the animal had crept to within thirty-five meters of Jesse's position, it spotted the intruder to its domain. Stopping dead in its tracks, its dark and lifeless eyes made immediate contact with the unwavering stare of its prey. Immediately the dog's ears flattened out as it lowered its massive head, baring a mouthful of razor-sharp teeth. Foamy saliva dripped from its powerful, quivering jaws.

Anticipating the pending attack, Jesse quickly slipped his right arm out of his jacket sleeve and swung the garment smoothly around the back of his body and off of his left shoulder.

Responding to the movement of its prey, the dog released a low, rumbling growl just seconds before it pounced into action. Rapidly, it began closing the distance between the two.

Keeping an eye on the approaching animal, Jesse used his right hand to quickly grab the jacket and wind it repeatedly around his left forearm, hoping to provide a minimal amount of protection against the vicious bite he was about to receive.

Reaching its intended victim in several vigorous bounds, the dog made one final and swift lunge at its prey.

With a firm grip on the knife clutched in his right fist, Jesse held up his padded, nonfighting arm, as he steadied himself against the force of the animal's momentum. Viciously, it latched its powerful jaws onto his outstretched limb. Feeling the unyielding pressure of the dog's death grip on his arm, Jesse quickly rose to his feet. Unwilling to relinquish its hold, the ferocious animal hung from Jesse's forearm as its hind legs were being lifted off the ground. With a combination of strength and adrenaline, Jesse held the fifty-pound, gyrating and struggling animal in the air as he plunged the knife deep into its exposed underbelly. Starting between its hind legs, he dragged the blade up the entire length of its body and into its rib cage. One short yelp and a few seconds later, the animal's powerful jaws relaxed and released. Heavily, it fell to the ground—dead at the feet of the victor.

Undaunted, Jesse hastily wiped the blood from his knife and hand, slipped his jacket back on, and continued on his mission.

Relying strictly on instinctual awareness and tactics from this point on, he estimated that he was a little more than a hundred meters from reaching his objective. Forward progress was minimal as he paused every ten to fifteen meters to stop, look, listen, and smell. His senses were on high alert as he made slow and premeditated advancement toward his target.

Seconds later he spotted the cabin, covertly concealed by dense foliage not more than sixty meters to the south. Closing the distance, but taking advantage of the convenient cover of Mother Nature, he circled the small, wooden structure, checking for any signs of activity in and around the building. Scouring the woods, he investigated any dead space where someone could be hiding.

The cabin was a simple, unrefined dwelling that revealed evidence of many years of existence but absolutely no indication of occupancy. The windows were heavily boarded up, as was the east-facing back door. Haphazardly stacked on the north side was a generous pile of weathered firewood, to the left of which was a large, fuel-powered electric generator. The door to the front was padlocked as well. Other than that, the perimeter around the cabin was clear. Satisfied that the target was unguarded from the outside, Jesse quickly relayed the news of its discovery to an anxiously awaiting Mikayla. After swiftly choosing his best approach and escape routes, Jesse crept silently up to the backside of the building.

Putting his ear to the crack between the door and the facing, he listened for proof of life. Hearing none, he removed his backpack and placed it on the ground at his feet. Quickly, he retrieved a mini, infrared fiber-optic camera from his pack. Inserting the flexible surveillance end of the device between the cracks in the door, he fed it through the opening. The room was lit solely by the minimal illumination of the morning sun streaming through the thin spaces between the crudely boarded-up windows. Peering through the viewfinder, Jesse could see the entire contents of the nearly vacant living space of the dwelling, which he estimated to be a little less than a seven-by-seven-meter area. On the north side of the room was a small, circular wooden table with one decrepit chair tucked beneath it. To the left of the table was a counter, neatly arranged with a coffee pot, a hot plate, and a small, countertop refrigerator. One other smaller room was located to the right of the front entrance. The door leading to that space was closed and padlocked as well. Scanning to the opposite side of the area, he found the objects of his mission—the restrained captives: two women bound, gagged, and blindfolded. But, most importantly, they were still alive. The younger woman matched Lacy's description. She was petite with long blonde hair. The other was taller and had short blonde hair. He recognized her from a photograph; it was Diana.

Both captives sat motionless in wooden chairs, spaced less than two meters apart. Their hands and bare feet were individually tied to the corresponding arms and legs of their chair, and they were each scantily dressed in nothing but a man's short-sleeved shirt. Jesse felt a twinge of anger course through his body. Since the only source of heat in the room at the time was a small, propane space heater located about four meters from where they sat, he knew the women must be insufferably cold. He also knew that the captor had stripped them of their clothes and shoes not only for the torture and degradation it provided, but also to squelch any thoughts they might have of trying to escape.

Withdrawing the camera from the space, he weighed his options for gaining entrance to the cabin. Since the rear door was heavily boarded and padlocked, the quickest choice would be to enter through the only window on the backside of the structure. Pausing momentarily, he relayed the good news to Mikayla that the women were very much alive. Then, after removing a crowbar from his backpack, he began prying the boards away from the window. Forcefully, he rammed the bar in and ripped away the barriers, exposing what was left of the fragile window-pane as a final deterrent. Using the crowbar, he shattered the glass. The loud sound of the breaking and falling shards produced muffled screams from both women. After nimbly climbing through the opening, he was finally inside. The temperature in the room felt even cooler than the forty degrees outside. There was a foul smell in the air, an odor Jesse readily associated with death. Purposefully, he made his way across the gritty, wooden floor, the boards creaking eerily beneath his feet. He approached Diana first. Her body language told him that she was consumed with fear. Her body was stiff and shivering. The knuckles of her tightly clenched hands were inhumanly white from nervously gripping the arms of the chair.

Attempting to trick her mind into listening to his words instead of her fear, Jesse spoke barely above a whisper, forcing her to focus and listen intently to what he had to say.

"Diana, listen to me carefully," he instructed. "I'm a friend of Mikayla's. My name is Jesse, and I'm here to get the two of you out of here. Do you understand me?"

Neither woman made a sound, but Diana responded favorably by nodding her head, prompting Jesse to continue. Raising his voice slightly so that both women would be able to hear him, he told them, "I don't want either of you to be afraid, but we need to move as quickly as we can to get you both untied. Then we'll get you outta here."

This time both women nodded their heads.

"Now, I'm gonna move around behind each of you and remove your blindfolds first and then the gags," he told them in a calming, monotonous voice. "But I need both of you to do something for me. I need for you to stay as quiet as you possibly can when I remove the gags. Can you do that for me?" He watched for an affirmative response.

Once again, both women gave him a silent nod of understanding.

Moving behind Diana first, he noticed the large laceration on the back of her skull. Her short, blonde hair was stained and matted with dark red clumps of dried blood. A soiled, bloody bandage lay on the floor behind her. She cringed when he tenderly touched her injured head.

"I'm sorry, Diana, but you're gonna be okay," he told her reassuringly. "I'm just gonna take the blindfold off first, and then I'll remove the gag."

Taking hold of the knot of the blindfold, he carefully slid it off the top of her head. Seeing that the knot on the gag was pulled extremely tight, he decided not to waste time struggling with it. He pulled his knife from the sheath and carefully sliced through the fabric that was covering her mouth. Although she didn't say a word, he could hear her inhale a deep breath of freedom.

Under Diana's watchful eye, he moved over to where Lacy sat nervously awaiting her turn.

"I'm gonna remove your blindfold and gag now, Lacy," he told her quietly. "I'm gonna touch your head, but don't be afraid."

When he removed the cloth from her eyes, she squinted painfully against the morning sun beaming through the broken window.

Carefully, Jesse cut through the fabric of the gag. Returning the knife to the sheath, he walked back around to face the women. He kept enough of a distance so as not to further frighten them, but stood close enough that they could easily see him. He tried to obtain a quick read of their mental and physical status. Of the two horrified females staring back at him, it was blatantly obvious that Lacy was teetering dangerously close to hysteria. Her body language and the depth of terror he saw in her large blue eyes revealed the fragility of her mental state. Giving

Diana the faintest smile and nod, Jesse cautiously moved toward the younger girl and stooped down in front of her.

He felt Diana's watchful eyes upon him as he spoke softly to her fellow captive.

"Lacy, I want you to listen to me carefully, sweetheart," he instructed, staring reassuringly into her frightened face. He fought the urge to reach out and touch her trembling hands. "I'm not gonna hurt you. I swear. You believe me, don't ya?" he asked, in hopes of dissuading her fears.

The young girl nodded as a single, cascading tear rolled down her colorless cheek and dropped onto her lap.

The terrified child touched Jesse's heart.

"I'm gonna release your feet first, and then your hands, okay?"

"Okay," she whispered in a barely audible tone.

Jesse gave her an encouraging smile. "Now, don't be afraid. I'm gonna use my knife to cut through the ropes, but I won't cut you. I promise."

He maintained eye contact with her as he slowly retrieved the blade from his belt. Gently, he cut through the ropes around each of her small feet. Due to the lack of adequate clothing and the frigid temperature of the room, her skin had taken on the unnatural tone of the glittery, blue nail polish painted on her toenails. Once again anger flashed through him when he observed the rope burns and scrapes around her ankles, telltale signs of a painfully desperate struggle to free herself. Her right ankle was badly swollen. There was a thin, but deep laceration around its entire circumference. The tissue around the cut was inflamed and red with infection. Jesse recalled seeing this same type of injury on the other victims in the case files that he and John had studied the day before. The authorities had surmised that at the time of the abduction, the killer had positioned himself beneath his intended victim's automobile, where he lay in waiting. He waited until they were standing directly next to the driver's door—just inches from his evil hands—then he quickly reached out and wrapped a thin wire around their ankle. Using a combination of loss of balance and the infliction of pain, he brought them down.

This guy's very existence made Jesse's blood flow hot in his veins. Jesse saw him as nothing more than a predator ... an animal whose useless life meant that others would die. Innocent women would continue to fall prey until somebody caged this animal or killed him, one or the other. At the moment, Jesse preferred the latter.

Moving up to unbind Lacy's hands, he noticed the same rope burns on her wrists as he had seen around her ankles. His eyes were drawn to the fresh, blood-streaked scratches on her thighs. Smiling sympathetically at her once more, he cut through the ropes that finally released her from her hellish bondage to the chair. The moment her hands were free, she lunged forward and immediately wrapped her arms around Jesse's neck, holding on for dear life.

He could feel her petite, chilled body shudder as the intense sobs of relief escaped her. Momentarily holding her in his arms, he let her cry, comforting her with assurance that she was safe now and that he was going to take her home. Unsuccessful, however, in persuading her to sit back down in the chair—knowing that they were pressed for time—he promptly abandoned the attempt. Instead, he allowed her to cling desperately to his arm as he moved over toward Diana.

Jesse glanced into Diana's misty eyes. She shifted her gaze from his face, to the girl, and then back again, after which a tearful smile took possession of her swollen and bruised face.

Crouching down in front of the best friend of the woman he loved, he affectionately addressed Mikayla on their wireless lifeline. He could hear her crying happily as he spoke. "I think somebody here may need to hear your voice, darlin'. He took the earpiece out of his ear and placed it into Diana's.

Jesse listened quietly to Diana's tearful end of the joyous reunion of the two best friends. As he cut through the ropes that were holding Diana captive to the chair, he observed her legs and body shivering uncontrollably, a likely result of a combination of borderline hypothermia and the eager anticipation of freedom.

Still holding on tightly to the security of her rescuer's muscular arm, Lacy pointed to the video camera suspended from the ceiling in the corner of the opposing wall, informing Jesse that the kidnapper might be watching.

"I know," he told her, nodding his head, "but we'll be long gone before he can get back here. Don't worry."

For the first time, he saw a slight but brief smile on the pretty face of his new friend, offering a tale-tell glimpse into the amazing resiliency of youth.

Taking the earpiece from Diana's extended hand, he returned it to his ear.

Staring into his reassuring eyes, Diana forced a wavering smile. "Thank you, Jesse," she whispered. As she cautiously attempted to stand for the first time in days, he took her by the arm and assisted her to her feet. "Thank you," she uttered numbly as she summoned the strength to stand on her own. Placing her hand on her tummy, several broken-hearted tears rolled down her cheeks.

"It's gonna be all right, Diana," Jesse told her, squeezing her arm gently. "Everybody's gonna be fine."

Smiling faintly in response to his emphasis on the word "everybody," she began rubbing her hands quickly up and down her freezing arms in a futile attempt to generate warmth from the friction.

"Why don't you ladies go and check out that refrigerator to see if you can you find something to eat or drink? I'll see if I can find where he may have hidden your clothes and shoes."

Using the temptation of food and water as lure, Diana took Lacy by the hand and finally coaxed her away from Jesse's protective presence.

Picking up his backpack and crowbar, Jesse walked over to the small, padlocked room. Glancing up, he noticed that Diana was observing him intently as he retrieved an intimidating .40-caliber automatic Glock pistol from the bag.

"You're not going to need that gun in there," she said. Her brown eyes were wide with fear. "Don't go in there, Jesse," she pleaded desperately.

"I'll be fine, Diana," he told her calmly. "I have to make sure there are no other victims. Someone in there may need my help."

"It's too late," she responded tearfully. "There's no one in there." Her final thought was barely above a whisper and, therefore, audible only to herself, "You can't save them, Jesse … they're gone."

Giving her a nod of understanding, but still determined in spite of her objections, Jesse resumed his efforts to gain access to the room. He hoped to at least find some warm clothes and shoes for the two women. Checking his watch he saw that he had been inside the cabin for six minutes. He felt an uneasy urgency to get this escape underway, an urgency that was growing stronger by the minute. Wedging the end of the bar behind the hasp of the lock, he began applying forceful pressure. After several vigorous flexes of his ample biceps, the lock finally relinquished its stubborn hold.

Turning back to face the watchful and terrified victims, he issued specific instructions. "You ladies stay put. Don't come in here." he stated firmly. "I'll be back in just a minute."

Although he was reasonably sure that this was a nonthreatening entry, for precautionary measures he positioned his body behind the wall to the left of the door opening. Holding the Glock firmly in his right hand, he used the end of the barrel to give the door a gentle shove. As it slowly swung open, the hinges creaked loudly as if sounding a warning, ceasing only after the door knob had tapped lightly against the wall where the door finally came to rest.

Adhering to years of strict tactical procedures, Jesse prepared to "pie" the room by efficiently sectioning off and securing one area of the room at a time. With the tip of his index finger, he switched on the illuminator mounted beneath the barrel of his weapon. Extending his right arm, his finger poised and resting lightly on the hair trigger of the Glock, he peered defensively inside the darkened space. As dark as the midnight sky on a moonless winter evening, the impenetrable blackness in the windowless room was pierced brightly by the intermittent, thin white beam radiating from the barrel of his gun as he rapidly and efficiently secured the area.

Although Jesse had been prepared for the possibility of a physical assault from something lurking in the darkness, he was not quite as prepared for the nauseating attack on his senses as he stepped inside the menacing room.

The repulsive stench of death and decomposing human flesh instantly invaded his nostrils and filled his lungs to capacity with the ghastly odor—the vileness of which challenged his chemo-heightened gag reflexes to their limit.

Successfully ignoring his queasy stomach, he swiftly scanned the room again with the limited beam of his gun light. Thankfully, he spied two large, battery-operated lanterns, one on a makeshift table against the left wall in the back of the room and one suspended by a piece of rope that had been draped over a ceiling beam a few feet directly in front of him. After taking a few cautious steps forward, he was able to reach up and switch on the lantern hanging overhead. The minimal wattage it provided served only to illuminate the center of the room, leaving the corners and outer walls eerily muted. Directly beneath the glowing lantern sat a six-foot wooden butcher's table; beneath it he noticed a small, motorized pump with several feet of coiled, clear plastic tubing extending from one end of the apparatus. Perplexed by the odd device, his eyes followed the pump's power cord across the floor to the right side of the room. Aiming the light on his weapon in the same direction, he discovered a small, chest-type freezer. Directly to the right of the freezer stood an odd and ominous-looking piece of stainless steel equipment flush against the wall. Being an avid hunter and fisherman himself, Jesse readily identified the apparatus as a freeze-dry machine commonly used in taxidermy. The peculiar-looking, three-foot circular chamber, sitting atop and to the right of the motor, made the piece of equipment easily recognizable. The knowledge that this unique method of taxidermy was especially useful if a specimen has scales or skin as opposed to fur, piqued Jesse's interest. And since the kidnapper had all of this same equipment at his disposal at any one of the multiple hunting stores owned by his father, Jesse wondered why he had this makeshift shop set up out here in the middle of nowhere. What was he preserving? Glancing around, Jesse noticed that there was not a single mounted trophy in sight.

In response to a gloomy intuition, a sickening feeling of dread washed over him, coming to rest once again in the pit of his vulnerable stomach.

Stepping cautiously around the table, he made his way to the left side of the space and switched on the second battery-operated lantern. Initially thinking that the increased lighting would be a blessing, he would soon discover otherwise.

The additional illumination revealed that the entire back wall of the room had been covertly concealed by a nearly invisible covering of heavy, black fabric—smooth and gatherless—hanging from a large, wooden dowel rod that extended from one side of the room to the other. Instinctively, Jesse raised his Glock to the firing position as he walked toward the center of the drapery, readily locating the barely visible split in the middle that separated the material into two equal halves. Taking hold of the foreboding ebony fabric with his left hand, he thought he was prepared for anything that he might find concealed behind the curtain. Slowly, he pulled the drapery to the side. As he slid it across the rod, it gathered into long, vertical folds—first to the left and then to the right. With each inch of darkness brought to light by the faintly glowing lanterns, Jesse became more and more shocked and outraged. It was like raising the curtain on a macabre stage show. Unable to fully comprehend, or mentally accept the visual images that his eyes were conveying to his brain, he took several stumbling steps backward. He had absolutely no time to squelch the revolting reaction his gut was having to the unthinkable scene before him. His body's physical retaliation to the mental picture was instantaneous as the contents of his stomach spewed forcefully from his mouth.

Through the earpiece he heard Mikayla inhale quickly as if preparing to say something, but she refrained—remaining silent, just as she had promised.

"I'm okay, Mikayla," he lied. "We're all okay."

Wiping his mouth on the back of his shirtsleeve, he regretfully turned back to the heinously inhuman display—incarnated evidence of what pure evil could do if given a mind to possess and a body with which to carry out unearthly deeds.

Good God! How could any human being commit such a gruesome act against humanity, not only once, but seven times over?

Stunned and saddened, he slowly raised his eyes to meet the gaze of the seven haunting and lifeless female faces staring back at him. They varied greatly in appearance, by nationality and age, but each one undeniably lovely in life. The realism was uncanny. The ethereal expression on their faces was that of an awakened dream state. Their hair was painstakingly styled, and their makeup expertly applied. Their spiritless eyes stared back at him as if longing for a savior who never came.

Taking a cautious step closer, Jesse desperately hoped against hope that he was wrong, that they were not real. He examined their features and the texture of their skin—so lifelike and temptingly touchable. He knew instantly they had not been artificially fabricated. These were once living, breathing, vibrantly beautiful human beings, women whose lives had been tragically cut short by a madman's diabolical fantasy. He could almost hear their screams for help emanating from the walls of this room.

Compassion and remorse gripped his aching heart. He wished he could have somehow known, somehow been able to help them. God, he wished he had been there to save them from suffering this fate. He wished for a world free of predators who were capable of doing things like this, something so cruelly sadistic—an act made even worse by the obvious pride and demented pleasure with which it had been so meticulously carried out.

Unable to stand the accusatory look in the women's eyes a second longer, Jesse lowered his gaze.

The startling realism of the professionally preserved heads was in sharp contrast to the unnaturally stiff bodies of molded plaster to which they were appallingly attached. Although it was obvious that great pains had been taken to appropriately dress and pose the improvised trophy stands, the attempt at artificially imitating the female body had failed miserably. The limbs of the unpliable mannequins were unrealistically bent and awkward. Their icy, smooth fingers were stiff and unfeminine, void of a female's soft and delicate nature that makes a man lust for her tender touch. The inanimate legs were straight and shapeless, lacking the supple muscles and definitive curves of a woman's provocative form.

It was apparent that although this madman had succeeded in taking the lives of seven gorgeous and innocent women, he had failed miserably in his attempt to re-create them for himself.

As much carnage and evil as Jesse had beheld in his life, even he was uncharacteristically shocked by the evidence of the unspeakable torture and mutilation that had transpired in this tiny, makeshift hell. And though he knew in his heart that his guilt was unfounded, he was still deeply remorseful that he hadn't been there to prevent their suffering.

Despondently, he turned away. He couldn't help these women now, but by God, he would see to it that Diana and Lacy didn't suffer the same terrible fate. He was going to get them out of there.

Adhering to his original objective, which was to find them some warm clothing, Jesse quickly scanned the room with his gun light. His eyes were drawn to a cardboard box sitting atop a rudimentary table to the left.

According to the business label on the box, it had been shipped from Germany. Lifting the flaps, Jesse peered inside. Once again his stomach turned over inside of him. The box contained a dozen or more small, clear plastic cases. Each case contained a disturbingly authentic-looking pair of prosthetic eyes, varying in color from the lightest shade of blue to the darkest brown, providing concrete proof that this psychopath had no intentions of stopping with only seven women in his collection. Jesse hurriedly folded the flaps down on the gruesome container.

Rapidly surveying the table, he took notice of the killer's vast collection of scalpels, crafting implements, and molding clays. The table was orderly littered with an abundance of cosmetics. Spread out on a piece of thin, white cloth were ten perfectly polished fingernails, as if ready and waiting to be applied.

Shaking his head in disgust, Jesse shined the light toward the front of the room and spotted a small pile of clothing and shoes stacked neatly on the floor in the far right corner of the space. Relieved that he had at least found what he came in there for, he gathered the garments in his arms.

Preparing to exit the killer's macabre trophy room, he paused momentarily at the door. After issuing a silent and heartfelt apology to the unfortunate victims, Jesse wished fervently for the opportunity to personally "tag" the toe of their murderer. Nothing would please him more. Mentally placing that burning desire at the top of his short, one-item wish list, he walked out and closed the door behind him.

He returned to find Diana and Lacy standing in front of the tiny propane heater, sharing a bottle of water and a candy bar. In an effort to conceal the turmoil of emotions churning inside of him, he gave them a courteous nod as he started across the floor.

Still, he knew they would sense a change in his demeanor.

He walked solemnly to the other side of the room and laid their clothes and shoes on the table. "I'm gonna step outside for a minute while you ladies get dressed," he said as he headed toward the open window. "Get ready as fast as you can, and give me a yell when you're done. I need to have a quick look at your injuries, and then we need to get the hell out of here."

He was relieved, however briefly, to step out into the fresh air and sunlight. Inhaling deeply, he tried desperately to rid his lungs of the hideous stench of death.

In a definite rush to make their escape, it took only moments for the women to get dressed. They promptly called Jesse back inside.

He checked Diana's head wound first. From what he could tell beneath the matted hair and dried blood, it was a rather large laceration, but fortunately the bleeding had stopped on its own, which cinched his decision not to take the time to clean and bandage the wound. His main priority was getting them safely out of there as swiftly as possible. Lacy's wound, however, was a different matter. She was barely able to stand on her injured right foot. It was swollen so badly that it wouldn't fit inside her shoe. Jesse worked as tenderly as he could to clean and bandage the infected wound. The young girl winced in pain as he worked but never made a sound. He glanced up at her once and gave her a quick wink of apology and support, which prompted another glimmer of a smile. After wrapping her ankle snuggly, he slid a sock over her petite foot. Pulling the shoestrings out of her sneaker, he cut the sides of the shoe with his knife and slid it easily over her foot. Using the white, cloth tape from his first-aid kit, he wrapped it several times around the outside of her shoe to attach it securely in place. Standing up to test it out, Lacy was clearly relieved that she could at least stand and hobble on it with far less discomfort.

Checking his watch for the last time, Jesse found that sixteen minutes had elapsed since he had arrived on the scene. Exiting through the window first, he checked carefully for any signs of impending danger before assisting the ladies past the broken shards of glass still imbedded in the framework of the window. With the relieved escapees close on his heels, he led the way back into the woods in the direction of the SUV.

Without pausing, he spoke quietly through the communicator. "We're on our way out, Mikayla. We shouldn't be more than forty-five minutes away." He finally allowed himself to breathe a premature sigh of relief.

"Thank God," she whispered. "Is everybody okay?"

"Yeah, everybody's fine. Lacy's ankle's injured pretty bad. It's very painful, I'm sure, but she's a real trooper." Glancing back, he found the girl's innocent face beaming with pride at his compliment. "Is there any activity on the tracking monitor?"

"No. Nothing at all." She sounded extremely glad to relay that bit of good news.

"Great. Stay in the SUV, Mikayla. Wait for us there, okay?" he insisted seriously.

"Roger that," she answered lightheartedly, inducing a slight grin and a shake of his head in response. He found that uplifting facet of her personality very endearing.

The women trudged behind their rescuer with very little conversation. Lacy was the first of the two behind Jesse in their journey out of the woods. Repeatedly, she refused his offer to lean on him for support, seemingly determined to live up to his glowing praise of her physical toughness.

When they were finally within about fifteen minutes of Mikayla's position, and the comforting assurance of a safe getaway, Jesse gave himself permission to relax a bit. He sighed deeply and felt a tiny measure of tension drain from his tired body. Unfortunately, his reprieve was very short lived.

Concentrating on the gentle rhythm of Mikayla's breaths through the earpiece, the deafening sounds of shattering glass, and Mikayla's desperate scream, came as a tremendous shock. He stopped dead in his tracks, causing Lacy and Diana to almost topple into him like tumbling dominos.

"Mikayla! … What the hell's going on?"

A second helpless and heart-wrenching scream from Mikayla traveled through the earpiece, followed by the muffled sounds of a violent scuffle.

"Mikayla, answer me!" he directed authoritatively. Listening helplessly to sounds of her terrifying struggle, he felt as though his heart was being ripped from his chest. "Mikayla!" he shouted. "Mikayla! … don't … I'm coming, Mikayla. I'm comin'!"

"Jesse!" was the last panic-stricken word to pass through the small, black receiver box, followed promptly by disconnected silence.

"Son of a bitch!" Jesse bellowed, as he angrily yanked on the wire to the earpiece and jerked it swiftly out of his ear. Raking his fingers repeatedly through his hair, he tried to calm his racing thoughts. The heavy weight of guilt for bringing Mikayla along was already bearing down hard. Dammit, he knew better. Yet he allowed her to persuade him otherwise. Shaking his head, he tried to clear his mind. There would be plenty of time for blaming himself later. Right now he had to formulate a plan of recourse.

One glance at Diana and Lacy told him that they were both keenly aware that something terrible had just happened to Mikayla. On the verge of hysterics, they watched as if waiting for him to take control of the situation and tell them what to do.

They didn't have long to wait. Jesse quickly regained his composure and was ready to do whatever was necessary to help Mikayla.

"Ladies, we gotta get movin', and we gotta move quick." As he continued his instructions, he ripped the backpack off of his shoulders and handed it to Diana. Leaning down, he directed Lacy to climb onto his back in the typical "fireman's carry."

"We can move faster if I carry you."

She did as he instructed without a breath of argument. He hoisted her up onto his back, she wrapped her arms around his neck, and they took off in the direction of the SUV.

"I'll get the two of you within a few minutes of the vehicle, then I'll stash you out of site while I find out what the hell's going on," he told them calmly as he strode quickly forward, totally unhindered by the added weight of the teenage girl clinging desperately to his back.

Chapter 18

A TIME TO DIE

*"Saying I love you
is not half as important as showing it."*

—*Granny Mae*

The assailant pulled Mikayla barbarically to her feet by way of a hefty handful of her long, thick hair. She was terrified and screaming at the top of her lungs, both arms and legs flailing wildly in a futile attempt to free herself from his grasp.

How did this happen? The last thing she remembered was waiting anxiously in the car, staring at the reassuring blank screen of the tracking monitor, and listening to Jesse's comforting breaths through the communicator. She was elated that he, Diana, and Lacy were only fifteen minutes away. How did she go from the euphoric anticipation of their reunion, to the sheer terror that she was feeling now?

She recalled the sudden blast of what she thought was a gunshot, followed by hundreds of tiny pellets of glass that exploded into the interior of the vehicle, bombarding the left side of her face and body with sharp, stinging pain.

Her horror intensified at the realization that the hands and arms that had reached through that broken window, attempting to lay claim to her body, were the very ones that possessed her now.

She had tried to get away. She remembered scooting across the seat, as she tried feverishly to escape the clutching hands. Using the gun didn't even register as an option. *Run to Jesse—run into the woods towards Jesse*—was the only thought in her mind. She pulled on the handle to the passenger side door. She felt the door give way, and felt her body tumble out of the vehicle and onto the ground. The last thing she remembered was watching the communicator receiver—her lifeline to Jesse—being crushed under the heavy heel of a man's boot. Her heart sank as the shattered pieces—still shouting out her name—were driven deeply into the red, clay dirt.

Almost immediately, the assailant had her by her hair. And try as she might, she couldn't get away. It seemed the more she struggled, the better he liked it.

Holding a large hunting knife in his right hand, he extended it intimidatingly in front of her face. "If you stop struggling and screaming, I won't have to hurt you. Do you understand me?" he fumed impatiently.

Although overwhelmed with terror, Mikayla knew that she had to keep her wits about her if she wanted to stay alive. Temporarily abandoning the attempt to liberate herself, she quieted her grappling arms and legs. Although his hand was still deeply entangled in her hair, she painfully nodded her head slightly to indicate that she understood.

"Okay, then," he said in an eerily pleasant, composed tone as he placed the knife next to her throat. Slowly, he began walking them backward, away from the clearing, coaxing her along with the threat of the sharp blade against her skin. "You and I are just gonna go right back here and wait patiently for that thieving son of a bitch who just broke into my cabin and stole my personal belongings. I feel sure he's racing valiantly to your rescue. He's the one you were crying out to, correct?" he asked in the same deceivingly amiable voice. "I assume you mean a great deal to him—yes?"

Once again she shook her head slightly in the affirmative, trying desperately to think of how she was going to warn Jesse.

The man paced them back into the woods about twenty feet, to where he seemed to feel confident of their concealment amidst the trees.

"Now then," he told her as he tightened his grip on her hair and removed the knife from her throat, "just stay calm and don't move. I would hate to have to kill you before your knight in shining armor arrives, but I gotta put this knife away and get my pistol out," he laughed snidely. "I don't want to be caught bringing a knife to a gunfight, now do I?"

Thinking this might be her only chance, Mikayla twisted her body fiercely in a vigorous attempt to free herself. She cried out in pain from the excruciating torment of her hair being savagely ripped from her scalp, but her painful efforts were worth it when she sensed liberation from his evil grasp. Stumbling forward, she felt his hands graze the back of her jacket as he tried to regain his hold on her fleeing body. She began running as fast as she could toward the edge of the woods in the direction of the SUV. Her legs felt heavy, but she forced them to carry her toward the clearing. She was flooded with a temporary wave of relief when, after several quick seconds, she emerged from the trees and out into the opening. God, if she could only make it to the SUV, although instinctively, she knew she couldn't. She knew that her reprieve would be short-lived, that her captor was going to catch up to her at any moment. He was so close behind her that she could almost feel his foul breath on the back of her neck. So, with no time to spare, she began yelling out as loudly as she could, shouting out a warning to Jesse that the man had a gun and that he was going to kill him. She couldn't see Jesse anywhere, but she prayed that he could hear her voice. That was all that mattered to her at the moment: that he be forewarned.

Catching up to her, the assailant viciously grabbed her by her right upper arm and stopped her in her tracks. His fingers dug deeply into her soft flesh. He gripped her arm with the tenacity of a ferocious animal, causing her to scream out in pain.

He clutched the deadly hunting knife firmly in his right hand and held it poised in front of him. With one brutal yank of his powerful arm, he spun her entire body around and pulled her toward him. He stared wickedly into her eyes as the sharp blade easily pierced her supple skin and plunged deep into the soft tissue of her upper abdomen. What she could only assume was his desire to prolong her agony, he twisted the weapon inside of her quivering body, and then leisurely pulled it back out. Her pitiful moan of torment offered audible witness that he had succeeded in increasing her suffering.

It took a moment for Mikayla to realize what had just happened. She felt the pain and pressure of the stabbing, but somehow it hadn't yet registered that it could be life-threatening. Her left hand moved intuitively to the area of the burning pain. Immediately she felt the warm and sticky sensation of blood as it oozed through her fingers and down her stomach. Looking down at her hand, she saw the vivid, scarlet evidence of the gravity of her injury. She began to feel faint and weak from the pain and the sight of the blood draining from her body. Her weakening legs wouldn't be able to keep her standing for much longer, much less assist her in escaping her attacker, she knew that; but she kept fighting. As much as she loathed her arms for betraying her, still they clung to her captor for the support of her failing body.

Moments later, her useless legs began to buckle beneath her. As she began slumping toward the ground, the man reached out and put his arm around her waist. His support alone was the only thing that kept her on her feet. "You can't give up just yet," he told her. "You're all I've got left to bargain with."

Slowly, she turned her head away from him; she refused to allow this horrible man's face to be the last thing she would see on this earth before she lost consciousness. She struggled to maintain her focus on the trees on the opposite side of the clearing; the direction from which she knew Jesse was running to help her. She knew in her heart that he was trying to get to her as quickly as he could. God, she didn't want to die. But if it was her appointed time to go, she wanted it to be while staring into the eyes of the man she loved. She wanted his loving face to be the last thing she would see in this life. As much as she wanted that, it took only seconds for her to succumb to the debilitating fatigue. She closed her eyes. Trapped in a body that was unable to fight back, she felt her attacker stick the barrel of a gun against her right temple. He held it there firmly in place.

❈   ❈   ❈

Jesse swiftly and secretly exited the woods, his Beretta clutched securely in his hand. Holding his weapon primed and ready in front of his body, he made his way undetected over to where the SUV was parked. He glanced quickly into the vehicle, confirming what he already knew in his gut—the seat was empty, and Mikayla was gone. *Dammit,* he mouthed silently.

Hunkering down, and using the car for cover, he slowly crept toward the rear of the SUV, a vantage point from which he could covertly scour the area for signs of Mikayla. As he reached the rear bumper, he heard a slight disturbance in the clearing just on the edge of the woods to the west. Quickly he darted his head in and out from behind the vehicle to assess the situation.

At a glance, he saw a man holding a gun pointed at Mikayla's head. He noticed that he had his arm around her waist, holding her in position. Her eyes were closed and her body was hanging limply, supported solely by the strength of her assailant. But it was the massive, glaring crimson stain on her pale pink jacket and white shirt that caused his heart to race and his temper to flare. God! She was wounded, and it looked bad. She was losing a lot of blood. There wasn't time to play around with this lunatic. If he was going to save Mikayla, he was going to have to act quickly.

Deciding that a hard and fast confrontation was his best option, he rose swiftly to his feet from behind the vehicle, instantaneously taking aim at the head of his enemy.

The coward was using Mikayla's frail and injured body as a shield from Jesse's looming assault. The only parts of his gutless body that were not concealed behind hers was a small part of his head, his hand that was holding the gun, and a tiny portion of his right shoulder.

With both hands on his weapon, Jesse steadily and confidently sustained a perfect aim on the small portion of the man's head. He was dead certain he could make the shot from fifteen feet. It was an easy kill. All Rangers know their assigned weapons like the back of their hand,

and Jesse was no exception. He excelled at the qualification range every time out with his particular assigned weapon, a 92 Beretta 9mm. He was familiar and competent with many different weapons, U.S. and foreign alike, but with his Beretta he knew he could put a bullet through this man's defective brain in a millisecond. His one and only concern was that, from a possible reflexive action, the killer could also pump one into Mikayla's. He had to wait for the perfect moment. He had to catch him off guard. Saving the life of the woman he loved was his top priority. The sweet taste of revenge would have to come second.

While maintaining his deadly aim on the soon-to-be dead man, Jesse called out loudly to the woman he loved.

"I'm here now, Mikayla. Open your eyes and look at me!" he demanded authoritatively. "Open your eyes right now, Mikayla! I want you to look at me."

He saw her muscles tense and her head move slightly. He knew she was attempting to do as he requested. *Please baby, just look at me. Let me give you strength*, he pleaded silently. For one wavering moment, he watched as she raised her head high enough and opened her eyes wide enough to stare in the direction of his voice.

At the sight of his beautiful Mikayla, her expression wrought with agonizing pain, Jesse's heart began racing with uncontrollable anguish and anger. It was obvious to him that she was barely hanging onto consciousness. He waited until she locked onto his eyes, then he spoke slowly and firmly, directly to her, as if they were the only two people present.

"I'm here, darlin'," he told her protectively. "I'm here, and I'm not gonna let you die. Just trust me, Mikayla." Pleading with her not to die, he wished that his words could somehow give her the strength she needed to hold on.

Her expression remained unchanged. Her eyes were fixed and unblinking. He knew that he was watching her life ebb away—he knew because he'd seen the same expression many times before.

"Do you hear me, Mikayla?" he begged. "Just hang on for me. Please! Hang on for a few more minutes."

His heart ached inside of him with the thought that she might die not knowing how much she meant to him. As much as he had fought against it, she had gained full possession of his heart. *What if I never get to tell her that I'm completely consumed with love for her?*

With that thought fueling his anger, Jesse turned his attention to the man unfortunate enough to be the recipient of his impending wrath. "You made a big mistake, asshole," he snarled vehemently. "You never should've hurt her."

The man reacted nervously to Jesse's piercing stare and smoldering fury. He stammered for words. "If … if you don't back off, I'm going to finish her off right now," he threatened, shaking the gun for emphasis.

For the first time in his life, Jesse was inwardly furious beyond all control. But outwardly, he maintained complete restraint, putting his years of discipline and determination to the ultimate test. Not flinching in the slightest, and holding the gun with unyielding steadiness, he spoke calmly but loudly. "I'm gonna give you one chance to live … only one. Take the gun away from her head, and then slowly lay both the girl and the gun down on the ground. If you do that … if you do that right now … I swear I'll allow you to live as long as *she* does." Jesse nodded his head in Mikayla's direction, indicating that *her* life was the man's only hope of survival. "If she dies, you die … It's that fuckin' simple."

Jesse's face was deadly pale with rage. He paused momentarily to emphasize his intentions. "You can live—or you can die—right here, right now. You got thirty seconds to decide. And make no mistake, asshole—I *will* kill you."

Five seconds later, the man shifted his weight ever so slightly, exposing just enough of his vulnerable right shoulder to his opponent's deadly aim. With a split second reaction to the target's hostile intent, Jesse's impeccably aimed shot pierced the silence. The bullet ripped through the captor's shoulder, yet still he managed to swing the gun around in Jesse's direction as he released his grip on Mikayla. Jesse pumped two more well-placed shots that struck his target dead in the center of his heartless chest, sending him reeling backward before he stumbled motionless to the dirt. That quickly, the man's murderous rampage was over.

Mikayla's lifeless body lay slumped on the ground. Running to her side, Jesse yelled for Diana and Lacy, who were still hiding where he had stashed them—safely concealed and armed with his Glock—amidst a dense clump of trees and brush. He instructed Diana to bring him some blankets from the car and the black bag from his pack. Tenderly he turned his love's crumpled body over onto her back. Quickly checking her vital signs, he found her pulse weak and thready. Her breathing was shallow and labored. He tore open her blood-soaked shirt to expose the knife wound in her upper abdomen. He winced at the gravity of her injury. The blade had entered her body off center and a few inches to the right. From the location of the ominous wound and the massive amount of bleeding and variation in color, he surmised that the knife had lacerated her liver. He prayed that the vital organ had received only insignificant damage.

Mikayla's face was ashen. Her skin was cold and clammy to the touch. These symptoms, combined with a possible liver injury, told Jesse that she was suffering from hemorrhagic shock due to the extreme loss of blood.

Diana ran to his side with the black bag and positioned herself on the ground on the opposite side of Mikayla. She was crying uncontrollably as she covered her best friend's fragile body with blankets and folded one to form a pillow that she placed gently beneath Mikayla's head. She watched as Jesse ripped open the black bag and quickly emptied its contents onto the blanket. Tearing off the paper wrapping, he grabbed a large handful of gauze, placed it over the freely bleeding wound, and pressed down firmly with the weight of his body trying desperately to stop the bleeding.

He had been watching Mikayla's chest for evidence that she was still breathing and had become quickly aware of the timing and the weakening rhythm. When he saw her chest fall with the exhalation of an old breath but not rise from the intake of a new one, he knew immediately that her breathing had stopped completely.

Jesse's calm and determined voice broke into the sound of Diana's unrelenting, heartbroken sobs. "Listen to me carefully, Diana. I need your help." Shifting his attention momentarily from Mikayla, he stared into the tear-streaked face of her distraught friend.

"Diana, I need your help to control the bleeding. I gotta start CPR now!"

She silently followed his quickly issued instructions. Grabbing a handful of fresh gauze, she resumed his vigil of applying pressure to the unforgiving wound, as Jesse swiftly and expertly began his efforts to resuscitate Mikayla's unresponsive body.

Ignoring his directive to stay in the car, Jesse heard Lacy restlessly shifting her weight directly behind him.

"Lacy, I need you to do something," he instructed loudly. "Go back and look in the car for my cell phone. Call 911 and tell them we need an ambulance and the police. Tell them to hurry."

Already turning toward the car to do as he asked, Lacy yelled back to him in a tear-filled voice. "But I don't know how to tell them where we are."

"The cell phone is equipped with GPS. They'll find us. Just tell them to hurry."

Obediently, Lacy made her way slowly to the car. Moments later, Jesse impatiently turned his head in search of his young accomplice. He spotted Lacy sifting frantically through the weeds on the passenger side of the car, and watched as her face lit up with excitement as she retrieved the phone from the tall grass. Hobbling back to Jesse, he heard her make the 911 call.

"The ambulance is on the way!" she shouted happily to Jesse as soon the phone snapped closed in her hand.

"Good girl, Lacy," he yelled back over his shoulder as he continued to administer CPR, trying desperately to restart Mikayla's lifeless heart.

"One, two, three, four, five ..." Jesse counted as he applied forceful compressions to her chest. "Breathe, darlin', breathe," he whispered quickly between each breath that he forced into her empty lungs.

He stopped momentarily for the fourth time to check for a pulse. Not able to find one, he grew more and more concerned that she had gone too far. He couldn't bear the thoughts of losing her. Leaning over her, he placed his hands beneath her shoulders and pulled her limp body close to him and held her tightly. His words poured straight from his heart. "Please don't give up, Mikayla. Please don't leave me."

Feeling immediately guilty for revealing his loss of hope, he heard Diana and Lacy's heartbroken reactions. They both were crying inconsolably.

For the past twenty years, Jesse had lived his life in accordance with the doctrines of the U.S. Army Ranger Creed—statements of belief and faith that had not only defined who he was during his time of service, but also molded him into the man he would always be. The creed denounced the very existence of the word "surrender." Surrendering wasn't an option then, and Jesse saw no reason to succumb to it now.

"No, Mikayla, no! Don't you dare quit on me." Jesse tenderly laid her back down on the ground. "I won't let you quit." He defiantly resumed CPR.

"One, two, three, four, five ..." His bitter tears spilled down onto Mikayla's face as he once more forced life-sustaining oxygen into her lungs. Removing his lips from her mouth, he turned his ear to listen for signs of breathing. His heart sank in his chest as he heard nothing—nothing but the sound of his own blood raging through his veins.

"Please God, don't take her away from me," he pleaded under his breath.

Although there was every indication that his efforts were in vain, still Jesse was unwilling to give up hope. Despondently, he placed his palms on her chest and administered another thirty compressions to her heart, manually pumping blood to her vital organs. Then, lowering his mouth to hers, he filled her lungs with two more loving breaths. Hoping against hope, once again he checked for breathing. "Please, baby ... breathe for me," he begged quietly, but still Mikayla showed no response.

Unwilling to give up, Jesse resumed his efforts. Pausing momentarily, he placed a soft, tender kiss on her colorless lips. As he started to raise himself back up, he felt against his face what he thought was a soft, faint exhalation of air coming from her mouth. He prayed that the sensation was real and not just a fabrication of his consuming desire for her to live. Lowering his ear closer to her lips, he watched her chest intently for movement. His eyes were blurry from the pooled tears. He closed them tightly, forcing the salty collection of moisture to find an escape route out of the corners of his eyes. Overwhelming relief consumed him as he saw her chest begin to gently rise and fall. He could feel her delicate breath against his ear. He was momentarily speechless as words of untold thankfulness traveled the distance from his eternally grateful heart to God's always listening ears.

"She's breathing," he whispered. "She's breathing."

Releasing a guarded sigh of relief, he tenderly picked up her listless hand and brought it to his lips. He stared down into her beautiful face. With the tip of his finger he gently touched a deep bruise on the side of her cheek—regretful that he had not been there to protect her, longing to take away her pain. God, how he loved her. So much more than he ever thought possible. He knew that he could never fully express the depth of his love for her, but he vowed that as soon as she opened her eyes, he would somehow find the words.

The sound of the blaring sirens preceded the two ambulances that arrived on the scene just seconds ahead of the police. Jesse stood as two paramedics rushed toward the victim on the ground.

Waiting until they were within earshot, he began shouting out Mikayla's vital information. "She has a penetrating abdominal injury from a knife puncture in the thoracoabdominal area. I believe her liver's been lacerated. She's in hemorrhagic Class III shock. At one point, her vitals stopped at which time I administered CPR and successfully resuscitated her. She's been breathing on her own for the past couple of minutes."

One of the paramedics started an IV and covered Mikayla's mouth and nose with an oxygen mask, while the second paramedic applied a pressure bandage to the bleeding stab wound. Moments later, Mikayla was placed on a gurney and was ready to be transported to the hospital.

In response to Jesse's request to ride along with her in the ambulance, the attendants hurriedly, but politely, cited the codes and regulations that prohibited him from doing so. Respectful of their rules, he backed down, but not before quickly leaning over and placing a tender kiss on Mikayla's cool, damp forehead.

Diana and Lacy were being attended to as well. When Diana saw them moving her best friend toward the ambulance, she insisted on being transported in the same vehicle. Climbing into the back of the ambulance, she promised Jesse that she would take care of Mikayla until he could get there.

Weak from fatigue and emotion, Jesse watched as the ambulance sped away with the love of his life inside. He was helplessly unsure of whether she would live or die.

"Jesse!" Lacy yelled as she wrenched herself away from the paramedics and limped over to his side. Taking hold of his arm, she looked up at him reassuringly. "Mikayla will be okay Jesse," she told him tearfully. "She has to be okay." With that, she wrapped both of her arms around his waist and buried her face into his chest.

Returning her childlike embrace, Jesse stroked her hair as she cried compassionately.

With a choice in timing that he would soon live to regret, the police officer in charge of the crime scene walked over to confront and question Jesse.

"Mister ... you've got some serious explaining to do for your part in this," he demanded indignantly, his arms folded in front of him. "What in the name of heaven went on here this morning?"

Hearing this, Lacy swiftly relinquished her hold on her rescuer and snapped her petite body angrily around to face the officer. "Jesse saved our lives here this morning—that's what happened!" she yelled furiously, her pretty, young face streaked with tears and dirt. The volume of her high-pitched voice drew the attention of everyone on the scene. "You're the one who should be doing the explaining!" she shouted accusingly. "Where were you when he came in there and rescued us all by himself, risking his own life?" Trembling with a combination of fury and contempt, she glared up at the towering officer that she had just so effectively rendered speechless.

Jesse was sincerely touched by Lacy's rabid defense of his actions but wanted no part in causing her any further anguish.

"Lacy, honey … it's okay. I'll be fine," he reassured her. Laying his hands on her shoulders, he turned her around to face him. "They just need me to answer some questions, that's all. Trust me, Lacy." He smiled and looked squarely into her enraged blue eyes. "You go ahead with the paramedics. I'll see you at the hospital … I promise." Motioning to the paramedics that she was ready, he placed his hand gently on her back, prompting her toward the waiting ambulance. He watched as she took two hesitant steps on her own before she stopped. Turning back around to face him, her expression revealed a varied array of tumultuous emotions. Nodding his head to indicate that he understood, he gave her a quick wink.

Smiling faintly, she tearfully mouthed the words, "Thank you, Jesse."

Chapter 19

A REUNION OF FRIENDS

"The heart will remember a friend
that time has long forgotten."

—Granny Mae

Jesse waited impatiently for the automatic double doors to slowly creep open. Finally they allowed him access to the lobby of the hospital emergency room. Rushing inside, he obtained directions from the receptionist on how to find Mikayla and then purposefully he made his way through the endless, stark white hallways of the Alabama medical facility. Finally, reaching the end of a maze of identical corridors, he spotted Mrs. Gregory and Rick standing at the end of the hallway. They were just outside the door of the waiting area, which was filled to capacity with people keeping vigil for their loved ones in surgery.

Rick met him halfway down the long hallway, his hand outstretched in gratitude. His red-rimmed eyes bore witness to the despairing tears he had shed on behalf of his beloved wife and Mikayla, his dearest friend in the world.

"Man, I don't know how I can ever thank you," Rick said appreciatively shaking Jesse's hand. His smile was obviously forced and he looked emotionally drained. He was unshaven and disheveled, but unashamedly thankful to the man who had successfully brought an end to a most horrific nightmare.

"No thanks necessary, Rick," Jesse told him sincerely, looking him directly in the eye and firmly returning his handshake. "What's going on? Is Mikayla still in surgery?"

"Yeah, after they pumped four units of blood into her and got her stabilized, they rushed her straight into surgery from the ER. They're trying to repair her liver and are doin' an exploratory to check for any further internal damages. She's been in there for over two hours." He gave a tired and worried sigh, looking dangerously close to tears. "She's gonna be okay, though," he said to nobody in particular.

They turned and continued down the hallway toward Mrs. Gregory. "Hey, are the police done questioning you?" Rick inquired. "They kept you long enough," he added sarcastically, obviously disgusted with the local men in blue at the moment.

"Yeah … they're satisfied with my account of what happened." Jesse gave him a congenial pat on the back. "They're not gonna press any charges."

The two men stopped when they came to where Mrs. Gregory was standing. She appeared exhausted but guardedly relieved and thankful for the safe return of her girls.

"Thank you, Jesse," she cried softly, wrapping her arms around him in a warm, caring hug. He returned her embrace, grateful to her for the many years of motherly love she had shown to Mikayla.

"You don't need to thank me, Mrs. Gregory," he replied modestly. "You being here for our girl is thanks enough."

He felt her reluctance to release him. Smiling softly, she reached down and took hold of his large hand. "I'm not willing to let my gratitude be dismissed so easily." she told him as she looked deeply into his eyes, and tightened her tender grip on his hand.

Gently squeezing hers in return, he was comfortably willing to hold onto her for as long as she would allow him to. He could see why Mikayla loved this woman so much. She had the heart of a mother—he could see it in her eyes.

"How are Diana and the baby?" Jesse asked softly.

Rick's face brightened slightly at the mention of his love and her delicate condition. "Believe it or not, the doctors say they are both doing remarkably well. Diana's suffering from dehydration and some cuts and bruises, and ... she'll need some counseling they think, but thankfully ... she'll recover in time. And according to the ultrasounds," he said with a hint of a grin, "Our baby seems to be doing just fine, too."

"Speaking of Diana and my grandbaby," Mrs. Gregory interjected, "I believe I'll mosey back up and check on them and leave the two of you here—standing guard for our Mikayla." She gave Jesse's hand one last squeeze and a pat before she released it. "As long as one of you promises to come and give me an update the minute you hear something," she insisted sweetly while pointing her finger at the two grown men.

Rick's affection and concern for his mother-in-law was evident as he bent down and kissed her on the cheek. "We promise, Mom. As soon as they finish with Mikayla, I'll be up to join ya."

Mrs. Gregory nodded wearily and patted the side of Rick's smiling face. "I hope my grandbaby has that smile," she teased affectionately, causing Rick's slight smile to grow even larger.

Turning back to Jesse, tears of happiness and gratitude found their way down her cheeks. As she reached up to hug him once again, she whispered softly into his ear, "We love you, Jesse. Welcome to our little family ... son." She removed a tissue from the sleeve of her blouse, and wiped away her tears. "A mother can't have too many children, you know," she said with a tender smile.

It was almost midnight, and Jesse's tired but determined eyes remained focused on the two large, stainless steel doors that led to the recovery room of the hospital surgical unit. His heart skipped a beat each time a gurney pushed its way through the swinging metal barricade, carrying yet another patient that wasn't Mikayla.

He was trying hard to be tolerant—trying to just be thankful that she had survived the attack and the grueling five-hour surgery—but he desperately needed to see her. He needed to bear his stubborn, old heart to her before it burst inside of his chest. He just prayed that God would give him the opportunity to do so.

The surgeon who had worked tirelessly for hours, tediously repairing the damage done to her body from the brutal knife wound, was guardedly optimistic about her recovery—or so his assistant said. Out of consideration for his patient's anxiously waiting family, the surgeon had sent his assistant out to the waiting area to give Jesse and Rick periodic updates on her condition, twice during the surgery and then once afterward, while he was sutchering the incision. The damage to her liver was more extensive than the doctor had anticipated, but there seemed to be no further internal damages. Considering the severity of her liver injury, the painstaking surgery had gone very well. He fully expected Mikayla to pull through and believed that her liver would regenerate itself without any further intervention. Jesse appreciated the doctor's optimism and consideration, but until he could see her with his own eyes, touch her perfect face, hear the gentle sound of her breath in his ear, and taste her sweet lips for himself, he wasn't going anywhere.

Mikayla groggily opened her eyes to a darkened and unfamiliar room that was dimly lit by a small, fluorescent light fixture mounted directly over the head of her hospital bed. The soft, humming noise emitted by the glowing tube was the only source of sound in the room. Glancing around at her surroundings through unfocused eyes, Mikayla's attention was drawn to a large vase of fresh-cut flowers sitting on a table at the foot of her bed. She kept her eyes trained on the bouquet, waiting patiently as her focus grew gradually sharper and sharper, until it was as clear as the tall crystal container that held the arrangement. It was a stunning selection of pink long-stem roses and fuchsia daylilies, delicately accented with baby's breath and greenery. It was absolutely lovely and brought back peaceful and pleasant memories of Granny Mae's exquisite flower gardens.

As Mikayla's eyes regained their sharpness, her mind followed suit. And as it did, a thin bead of sweat erupted over her upper lip as the terrifying memory of the attack came creeping back into her consciousness. It returned slowly but with vivid clarity, as if she were momentarily reliving it. She lifted her left hand and lightly touched the place where the knife had entered her abdomen. She felt the thick, soft bandage beneath her fingers. A nauseating wave of panic consumed her as the reality of the horrific scene came vengefully rushing back. She recalled the ear-piercing sound of the gunshots.

"*Oh my God!*" she thought as she raised her hand to her spinning head. "*Where's Jesse? Did the kidnapper shoot him? God, please don't let him be dead.*"

Determined to find answers, she tried desperately to raise her upper body in a futile attempt to get up. Oddly, her body felt slightly numb all over except for the excruciating pain in her torso which prevented her from lifting any part of her body with the exception of her head. The agonizing effort was well worth the discomfort, however, when she looked down and found what she was looking for—Jesse, sitting all alone by the side of her bed. Barely visible in the dim lighting, he was seated in a chair as physically close to her as he could possibly get. His upper body was bent forward onto the bed, with his head resting lightly on her upper thigh. He had her right hand encompassed in both of his, cradling hers in the middle like a precious gem. He was sleeping quietly—looking exhausted and ill himself—but, nonetheless, keeping watch over her and protecting her with everything he had left.

Her eyes filled instantly with tears. God, how she loved him. She felt as though her heart would burst with love for him—a kind of love for a man that she never knew existed. Reaching down, she lightly touched his hair and smoothed it away from his kind, handsome face. She watched him as he slept. Trying not to wake him, she tenderly stroked his hair, all the while praying that God would restore his health and bless him with a long and happy life. He deserved that more than anyone she had ever known.

"I love you, Jesse," she whispered faintly. "I love you all the way up to God's house and back down again." It felt good to speak those words to him. It was the best way she knew to convey the immeasurable infinity of her love.

She wondered how he could have possibly heard her almost silent confession, but he did. His warm hazel eyes fluttered open and made instant contact with hers. Lovingly gazing at her, he breathed a contented sigh. Smiling affectionately, he whispered back, "I love you, too, darlin'. Somehow, I think I always have."

Slowly raising himself up, he watched her face closely as he carefully transferred his body from the chair onto the side of her bed. Tenderly, he leaned toward her. "Is this okay? I'm not hurting you, am I?" he asked quietly. She shook her head no. He took her hands into his and kissed her fingers. She watched as he closed his eyes for a second, as if saying a silent prayer.

"I'm not very good at this kind of thing," he said with a nervous sigh. "But I'm not about to tempt fate." Pausing for a second, he stared into her misty eyes before he began his heartfelt confession. "I love you, Mikayla. I'm completely and hopelessly in love with you," he declared openly. "I've loved you since the second I saw you, and I'll love you till the day I die. I'm just ..." He lowered his head regretfully. "I'm just sorry that it's taken me so long to tell you. I hope you can forgive me."

Placing her hand beneath his chin, she lovingly lifted his face to hers. Pausing for a moment, she looked into his guilt-ridden eyes.

"I love you, too, my knight in shining armor," she said, revealing a hint of an adoring smile. "And you have nothing to be sorry for, Jesse," she told him compassionately, "nothing at all."

She knew beyond any shred of doubt that she wouldn't be alive if not for him. "Thank you for saving my life," she whispered sincerely.

"I ... I shouldn't have allowed you to come along. I let that bastard get to you, Mikayla. I'm so sorry. He had a gun to your head. I just ... reacted." Jesse shook his head and lowered his eyes once again. "I'm so sorry."

She knew him well enough to know that he was shouldering every ounce of the blame for her getting hurt. The unfounded guilt was written all over his heartbroken face. But she knew the truth.

"Not the first time you saved my life," she explained quietly, smiling sweetly. "The second time."

He looked up at her quizzically—his eyes filled with tears on the verge of spilling over.

Her smile slowly diminished as she began to explain. "I remember I was lying on the ground. It felt really cold against my back … like I was lying on a sheet of ice," she described softly. "You were kneeling over me, and I began … kind of like falling downward, as if the ground had split open and was swallowing me up. I tried so hard to reach up to you." Her heart began to beat faster as she recalled the frightening experience. "I was so scared. It was like I was in a deep hole surrounded by freezing water. I could feel the icy coldness weighing down my body. As I gasped for air, it began filling my lungs." She put her hand to her chest, pausing momentarily to catch her breath. The memory was so vivid in her mind that she felt herself deprived of oxygen all over again. "I could hear the water rushing into my ears as it was consuming me. I was so lost," she said breathlessly, "And I was drowning, Jesse, I was drowning in death." Her eyes grew wide with the stark realization of how close she had come to dying.

Jesse opened his mouth to say something, but she interjected, the tone of her voice softening, reflective of the dissipating fear. "But I remember, through the roar of the raging water, I could hear your voice. I could hear you repeating my name over and over." She stared into his caring eyes. "You were begging me not to go—begging God not to take me away from you." A rush of tears began streaming down her face as she fought against the painful tightness constricting her throat. Determinedly, she forced her words through. "I was so lost in the darkness," she said faintly. "I couldn't find my way back on my own. Then I heard your voice … and I followed it. I followed the sound of your voice, Jesse." Her chin quivered with emotion as she tried to smile. "I found my way back because of you, baby. You saved my life." She cupped his loving face in her hands. "You didn't leave me, Jesse," she sobbed softly. "Thank you for not leaving me." She was barely able to finish her words before he covered her mouth with a kiss.

❧   ❧   ❧

The gentle morning sun was peeking through the sparkling, clean windows in Mikayla's serene hospital room. Closing her eyes, she delighted in the sensation of the warm glow on her face, encouraged by its awesome strength and ability to provide light, even through her tightly closed eyelids. Smiling inwardly, she could hear Granny's loving voice reminding her not to look back, reminding her that this bright new day marked the beginning of a whole new life for her—for her and Jesse.

Tapping lightly at the door, the love of her life entered the room with Diana, Rick, and Mrs. Gregory close on his heels. Instantly, the air was filled with the sounds of thankful laughter and happy tears. Mikayla noticed that Jesse lagged a few steps behind, seemingly to afford the devoted family some private time together. He was standing with his back to the door when her surgeon stealthily entered the room. Engrossed in watching the joyous reunion, Jesse was obviously startled by the sound of the man's deep voice directly behind him.

"Howdy, Doc Daulton. How ya been?"

Jesse's expression revealed that the slow southern drawl of the voice sounded distantly familiar. As the man stepped forward, Jesse's eyes flashed quickly from the name tag on the white coat to the huge smile on the doctor's face. Pinned to the pocket of the perfectly starched jacket, the black cursive lettering on the gold ID badge identified the physician as "Dr. Murfey."

"Jax? Oh my God, man! Is that you?" Jesse asked joyously, wrapping the doctor in a huge bear hug and slapping him enthusiastically on the back with both hands. "I would've recognized that goofy grin even without your name tag," Jesse announced jokingly.

"Yeah, can you believe it after all these years?" the doctor asked, still smiling. "I was havin' a cup of coffee in the doctor's lounge last night after the surgery, and I caught a glimpse of the news on the TV. Lo and behold, there you were, big as life and up to your old tricks."

"Don't tell me you are the amazingly gifted surgeon that I've been hearing so much about," Jesse asked appreciatively, "the one who saved my Mikayla's life yesterday?"

"That would be me," the doctor answered, patting his Ranger brother on the shoulder. "I stuck my head in the door last night, but you were both resting and I didn't want to disturb you. I knew you'd be here this morning. Besides, I told the nurses to tackle you if you tried to get away before I got to talk with ya," he teased. "It's really good to see ya, buddy." His voice conveyed his obvious sincerity.

"You, too, Doc Murfey," Jesse said with obvious pride at saying the word "Doc." "I can't tell you how many times I've wondered about you and how you were doing. I hated that we lost track of each other." Returning the friendly pat on the shoulder, he continued seriously, "I'm really proud of you, Jax. You're a dedicated and caring surgeon. Thank you for fighting so hard to save Mikayla."

"You're welcome, Doc," he answered, uncharacteristically serious for a moment. "I had a pretty awesome role model, ya know." It took only seconds for him to don his trademark grin once again. "What do you say after we check on our patient, we go down to the hospital cafeteria and grab a cup of mud and catch up?"

"Sure, if you don't mind stopping off with me for a minute while I check on Lacy. I promised her I'd stop by to see her again this morning. She's gettin' sprung today."

"No, I don't mind at all. I'm off duty in five minutes, so I'll catch up with you in her room. Then you and me gotta talk privately. I gotta hear the scoop on what went down out there yesterday morning … lone ranger," the doctor laughed heartily. "Hey, the next time you're gonna try a stunt like that, give me a call first. I'll tag along and cover your back."

Chapter 20

ANOTHER GOOD-BYE

"Sometimes an enemy can be like an artichoke;
if you peel away the prickly outer layers,
you may discover a sweet, tender heart hidden inside."

—*Granny Mae*

(Six Months Later)

Mikayla had returned to work only five short weeks following the attack, and had been back on the job for going on five months now. Her body was slowly healing both physically and mentally. The nightmares were tapering off in number, but still as terrifying as ever when they came. And, although, she and Jesse had still not become sexually intimate—on rare occasions, as if he could somehow sense her need—he would spend the night with her. After waiting for her to slip comfortably into bed, he would lie down next to her and gather her into his safe, strong arms. Following a meaningful goodnight kiss, he would hold her close and softly caress her—smoothing his warm hands up and down her arms and shoulders, and up and down her back. Over and over he stroked her until she drifted off to sleep. Then, he held her securely up next to his warm body all through the night while they slept.

His love and caring was instrumental in her battle to heal and over-come her injuries—both the seen and the unseen. Jesse had the soul of a medic in every sense of the word. She hoped he would pursue his calling in the field of medicine someday—maybe as an EMT or a nurse. That's what God had designed him to be, she was sure of it. It seemed that his touch alone was healing; it was as though one could feel Jesse's heart in his fingertips. He had a gift, and she planned to do everything in her power to see that he used it. What he saw as a career that had just ended, she saw as one just beginning.

But, today was a milestone in Mikayla's career, as it marked the one-year anniversary of when she had originally stepped through the doors of Dantoni Advertising for the very first time—a heartbroken dreamer driven by the pursuit of happiness that she had hoped a successful career would bring. How foolish she had been. This practical concept may work for some, but not for a woman like Mikayla—not for someone who had tasted how it felt to be truly loved. She was left with a heart so dependent on that gift of unconditional acceptance that survival without it was simply the act of existing—a poor substitution for the joy of living.

She was a lucky woman. In the end, she had gotten what she came for, just not in the way she had planned.

In the months following his embarrassing impropriety at the office dinner party, not to mention his slightly inappropriate behavior since day one, Lex had been the definition of discretion. As his intern, she couldn't have asked for a more considerate boss or brilliant mentor. She had the impression that he had forgotten more about the business of advertising than she ever hoped to learn. And late one evening when the opportunity presented itself, she told him so. She found it amusing that this was the only time in the twelve months they had worked together that she had ever seen him blush.

Her admirable compliment was born out of observing him excel in a situation where most others would have failed—and failed miserably. It was during an impossible, last-minute bid to land a brand-new, multi-million dollar account—a venture that most would have viewed as a laughable exercise in futility. To Lex it was a welcome and invigorating challenge, one that he triumphantly met head on.

After humbly accepting her compliment, Lex issued one of his own. He told her that the reason he hired her on the spot last year was because he had seen in her not only a burning desire for her own success, but also a rare, elemental ingredient imperative to becoming a successful advertising exec: she had a strong passion to help others succeed as well. Having not only met his expectations, she had exceeded them by leaps and bounds.

On this, Mikayla's last day in his employ, he surprised her with a small going-away party and a very generous bonus. But the greatest shock came in the form of a permanent job offer, a newly created position as his vice president of marketing.

Ushering her into his office for a few private moments together, he waited for her to take a seat, then he sat down in a chair next to her and promptly offered her the job.

"Now, Lex," she said teasingly, "you made it very clear during my interview last year that there was no chance whatsoever that this internship would lead to a job offer."

"I know, but that was before I realized what a valuable asset you would become around here," Lex answered with a sincere smile. "And not just an asset, but, I think in time, a good friend as well. If you refuse … I'm really going to miss you, Mikayla."

"I'll miss you too, Lex," she said genuinely.

"You don't have to decide right now," he told her thoughtfully. "I know things with Jesse are a little … unsettled. Let's just consider the job offer open-ended for now, shall we? Just in case you change your mind." He looked at her with the compassion of a long-time friend.

"Thank you, Lex. I appreciate that," she said honestly.

Grateful for his kind gesture, she wrapped her arms around his shoulders and hugged him tightly. She thought to herself how ironic it is that sometimes our most formidable enemies can make the dearest of friends.

"I'll just hold off on posting a new intern position for now," he told her matter-of-factly.

Pulling back to look at him, she saw that his face was adorned with a sneaky grin.

"I knew it. I knew it all along," she lied with a laugh.

❦   ❦   ❦

Mikayla had always hated good-byes, and today was no exception. One by one her co-workers and friends of the past year stopped by her office to wish her good luck and give her a good-bye hug or kiss or both.

Chloe was the last of the well-wishers. "I'm going to miss you," she said, trying to be cheerful but not very successful in the attempt.

"Oh, Chloe," Mikayla replied sadly. "I'll miss you, too, honey. You've become such a good friend. I so much appreciate how quick you were to take me in, making me feel welcome and comfortable when I first arrived out here. I won't ever forget that. Thank you." Mikayla rounded the desk to seal her words of appreciation with a heartfelt hug. That's the one thing she felt best about bequeathing these "stand-offish western-ers," as she jokingly called them: the fine art of a good ol' southern hug. Most of her co-workers were unaware of the fact, until Mikayla came along, that southerners love to hug and will do so at the drop of a hat for almost any occasion, sad or happy. But she finally did it. It wasn't an easy task, and it took almost a year to accomplish, but she finally broke the taboo of innocently embracing a co-worker. She felt good about leaving behind a company full of huggers in her wake.

"Are you in a hurry? Got a second to sit down and talk?" Mikayla asked, not quite ready to say good-bye to her special friend just yet.

"Sure, but don't you have a date with Jesse tonight?" Chloe inquired, seemingly happy at the prospect of having some extra time to spend with her departing friend.

"No, we don't tonight, actually," Mikayla answered, her smile instantly disappearing. "But we do have a date of sorts in the morning. I'm going with Jesse to the hospital in the morning for his one-year checkup. He's scheduled for a battery of tests and procedures bright and early. Then we'll meet with his oncologist in the afternoon to get the test results. The doctor will be able to tell us right then and there if the cancer is in remission or if it has, God forbid, metastasized."

Chloe reached out for her friend's trembling hand. "I'm sure he's going to be okay, sweetie," she said encouragingly.

"I know, but …"

"No buts about it, Mikayla. Jesse's going to be healthy and good-looking forever," Chloe announced with a grin. "You guys are going to get married, buy a house, have beautiful babies, get rich with your advertising agency, and live happily ever after," Chloe told her convincingly. Giving her head a definitive nod, she added, "And that's all there is to it."

"Well, I certainly hope you're right," Mikayla said, thankful for her friend's speedy reversal of a quickly downward spiraling mood. "I just wish you'd try to be a little more optimistic about it." She returned the bright and contagious smile that was facing her. "Chloe … have you ever considered relocating a little farther south?" she asked in an exaggerated Alabama drawl. "I do declare, I believe I detect the soul of a true Southerner in you, girl."

Chapter 21

THE DAY OF RECKONING

"A house is where you live,
but home is where you're loved."

—*Granny Mae*

Mikayla was standing on the stoop in front of her apartment trying in vain to enjoy the warmth of the early morning sunshine, along with the invigorating fragrance of the recently rain-washed air. But she was far too engrossed in the daunting day ahead to partake in such simple pleasures of the senses.

She had just gotten off of the phone with Diana after a two-hour conversation. They had had a lot of those lengthy and meaningful talks since their horrific ordeal over six months ago. Mikayla was pleased with the progress of her friend's recovery. Diana's sessions with her counselor seemed to be helping her come to terms with what had happened to her, but oddly enough, not nearly as therapeutic as sharing her feelings with her lifelong friend. As painful as it was to hear, Mikayla listened sympathetically when Diana needed an ear—and offered encouragement when she needed a lift. The only thing they didn't talk about was the possibility that Mikayla may have to break her pinky promise to be home in time for the birth of Diana and Rick's baby. Little Richard Paul was due to arrive in less than one month. Mikayla prayed that she would be home in time to welcome him.

She found it odd how everything important in her life was precariously hinged on the outcome of one single doctor's appointment.

Just like clockwork, Jesse arrived promptly at 0700 hours to pick her up. She liked that about her military man. He was always right on time, if not early. On this particular day, however, she wouldn't have minded at all if he had been late—very late. She had dreaded this day for weeks and was certain that he had too, though he hadn't complained or even mentioned it a single time.

She hated what he was going to have to endure today—the endless battery of tests and X rays, being poked and prodded with needles, and having radioactive chemicals pumped into his veins in preparation for the scans. But at the end of the day, if the doctor blessed them with good news, then all the pain and suffering would have been well worth it. Remission, or better yet, cured, was the word they longed to hear. She thought it strange the almost tangible power that one little word could wield. Remission had been her constant prayer since the day he had told her about his illness. She wanted nothing more in life than for Jesse to be okay. She wanted him to be healthy and happy more than she wanted her own health and happiness. Nothing mattered to her more than Jesse.

Walking down the sidewalk toward the open car door, she noticed his unexpected, but greatly appreciated, jovial expression.

"Good mornin', darlin'," he said cheerfully as soon as she was within earshot.

"Howdy, handsome," she reciprocated in kind, wondering how he could be so jolly in the face of the torturous events looming over him like a dark and fateful storm cloud.

"You look wonderful," he told her appreciatively. "I love it when you wear pink." He helped her into the car and scurried around to the driver's side.

Turning to face her in the seat, he stared into her eyes for a moment without saying a word. She watched as the endearing smile she loved so much gradually dissipated from his gorgeous face.

"Do you trust me, Mikayla?" he asked solemnly.

Without a moment's hesitation, she answered his rather odd question. "Of course, I trust you, Jesse," she said, wondering why he had suddenly turned so serious. "What's going on?" She began to feel a little anxious. "Are you okay?"

"Darlin', what I'm about to ask you to do will be very difficult, I know that, but I really need for you to trust me on this, okay?" He continued, as somber-faced as she had ever seen him. "Can you just go along with me today without asking any questions—not even about the tests and the consultation with the doctor? Just pretend we didn't even have the appointments." He stared at her pleadingly as he took her hand. "Can you do that for me? Please?"

After all these months, he apparently still had no idea of the emotional and physical effect he had on her. When he looked at her with those intensely focused, yet dreamy, hazel eyes, she would do anything he asked—anything, anytime, anywhere.

"Yes, I can do that," she answered honestly, although fearfully.

"Good." His dimpled smile returned with a vengeance. "And don't look so scared. This is a good thing, I promise."

"Okay," she said, shrugging her shoulders in bewilderment but bidding herself to follow his lead. She truly did trust him. It wasn't just something she said to appease him. She trusted him from the very depths of her heart and soul, and strangely enough, deep down inside, she knew she had from the first moment she looked into his eyes on that deserted Arizona back road—the very same eyes she was so hopelessly lost in now.

"I love you," she whispered seriously.

"I sure hope so," he said with an impish chuckle.

Less than an hour later, Jesse wheeled the car into an open space in front of a charming, old beachfront business. With the magnificent, blue Pacific Ocean as a backdrop, even the obviously long-lived structure had an appealing attractiveness about it. The sand and weather-beaten building was supported by ten-foot wooden stilts and seemed anchored to the beach by a long pier that extended out into the slightly calmer part of the water, well past the white-crested waves that swelled up to eight feet or more before crashing violently down onto the pristine, white beach.

The dark blue paint on the weathered, old hut was in sharp contrast to the white-shuttered windows and oversized white letters announcing the purpose of its existence—"Monterey Bay Whale-Watching Tours."

"Have you ever been whale watching, Mikayla?" Jesse asked excitedly. Once again the anxiousness in his eyes reminded her of the curious, little boy lurking playfully within the man.

"In Alabama? I don't think so," she answered cutely.

"Come on, you big nut," he laughed.

❧   ❧   ❧

Leaning against the railing of the powerful fifty-five-foot boat, Mikayla could see that Jesse took great pleasure in explaining every little detail of whale watching to her.

"What kinds of whales will we most likely see today?" she asked, munching on a handful of popcorn.

"Probably, if we're really lucky, we'll see a humpback or a killer whale. But I hope you get to see a blue. They're my favorite. They're absolutely magnificent."

"I take it you've done this before," she said, stating the obvious. She was glad that he was enjoying himself so much, but she couldn't help but wonder what they were doing here whale watching instead of at the hospital where they were supposed to be.

"Yeah … Joe and Sasha brought me out when I first got here last year. It's one of the most awesome things I've ever seen. To see these majestic animals in their own habitat, well, it's just somethin' I'll never forget … and I wanted to share it with my girl." He turned around and looked at her with wide-eyed wonderment. "I bet you didn't know that the blue whale is the largest creature that has ever lived on the face of the earth, did ya? … even bigger than dinosaurs."

"No, I didn't, but I sure hope that's one of them right out there!" she exclaimed, pointing directly behind Jesse, "because if they get any bigger than that, I don't want to see one." She shrieked, dropping her bag of popcorn and spilling kernels all over the deck. She was exhilarated and terror-stricken all at the same time.

Jesse spun around in the direction of Mikayla's pointing finger. Blindly reaching behind him, he grabbed her around the waist and pulled her protectively into him.

Neither said another word as they watched the nearly seventy-foot gentle giant gracefully breach the surface of the ocean. The sound of the spray being exhaled from the animal's blowhole was astounding as the impressive spew of water shot thirty feet up into the air. The enormous animal floated elegantly on the surface with only a fraction of its massive body exposed to the cool ocean breeze. It lingered there lazily for a moment, taking in several life-sustaining breaths before diving back into the water and lifting its massive tail high into the air, making a weighty and rapid descent into the deep, blue sea.

"Wow! Did you see that?" she gushed gleefully. "That thing's almost twice as big as this boat, and it really is blue."

"I told ya," he said with an excited laugh. "That was a blue whale, and believe it or not, that fella can grow twenty or thirty feet longer than that—if he eats enough shrimp, that is."

"That's the coolest thing I've ever seen in my life. Does he live in these waters all the time?"

"No, he just comes up for the summer," Jesse explained, growing somewhat thoughtful. "They usually start turning up about the first of June every year. Scientists say the blues come here for the krill fish, but I like to believe they think of this place as home. I think every living creature has an innate desire to go home," he told her sentimentally. "How about you, Mikayla, do you wanna go home?"

"Yeah, if you want to, I'm ready. Are you tired, Jesse?" she asked, her expression of awe changing immediately to one of concern.

"No, silly girl, I don't mean home here in California; I mean home to Alabama."

"Oh," she said with an embarrassed giggle. "Sure, I wanna go home someday, but we have to wait until we find out if …"

"We don't have to wait, darlin'," he told her lovingly. "We can leave today if that's what your sweet, little Southern heart desires."

"No, we can't, Jesse." Holding up both hands, she took several steps away from him. "We have to wait and see what the doctor has to say about you … your health," she stammered hesitatingly. *Why was he doing this?* He knew they had to wait for his test results before they could make any future plans.

"Wait … wait, Mikayla," he repeated, reaching out for her as she continued to back away. "That's what I brought you all the way out here to tell you."

She stopped and just stood there, staring into his eyes and waiting for an explanation.

"Actually, I brought you out on this boat for two reasons—one, so that we could share this awesome display of Mother Nature together, and two, so that you couldn't get angry and run away from me when I tell you what I have to tell you." Taking in a deep breath, he released it slowly and deliberately. "You can't get away from me on this boat," he offered with a nervous chuckle. "Not until I have time to explain myself."

Her mouth was gaping open from mounting shock and apprehension, but she uttered not a word.

Running his fingers nervously through his hair, he returned her intense stare. "God, this is hard," he muttered. Stalling for time, he tried desperately to recall the speech he had so effectively rehearsed over and over again the night before. Deciding it best just to come clean and then beg for forgiveness, he began. "Mikayla, darlin' … I wasn't quite honest with you about my appointments at the hospital. The appointments were originally scheduled for today—but the hospital called me a few days ago and rescheduled them for yesterday. I went to the hospital for the tests and doctor consultation yesterday. I went without you … I went alone," he told her point-blank. He winced as he said the words, as if it pained him physically to tell her of his deception. "Please understand, darlin'. I didn't want to put you through that nerve-racking ordeal. It's bad enough to go through it myself, much less put you through the mental torture and anguish as well. Can you forgive me? Please, Mikayla … say you forgive me," he begged sincerely.

She continued to stare at him for a moment longer. How could he do that? What gave him the right to decide what was best for her? She had planned to go to the hospital with him, to comfort him and be there for him. She wanted to show him how much she loved him. And right this minute, she wanted to be very angry with him for denying her that opportunity, not to mention for betraying her as well. But yet … here he was, standing before her, begging her for forgiveness. Dammit! How could she possibly be mad at him? He was the most precious and considerate man she'd ever met, willing to do anything and everything in his power to save her a moment's worth of pain. She couldn't bring herself to be angry with him. Her heart simply wouldn't allow it—not for a second.

Sighing heavily, she walked back toward him. Reaching out, she smoothed her hand over his gentle face. "Jesse … baby … you've gotta stop doing that," she pleaded. "You can't shield me from every possible pain and hurt for the rest of my life."

"I can try," he told her lovingly. "I gotta' try, darlin'."

That caring response brought immediate forgiveness, not only because it was the sweetest sentiment she had ever heard in her life, but because she knew that he honestly intended to do just that—protect her, both physically and emotionally, with every fiber of his being.

"God, Jesse … I love you," she declared as she stepped into his arms.

"I love you, too, Mikayla."

He held her close, expelling a deep sigh of contentment. "And according to the doctor, I'm gonna be around to love you for a long, long time."

"You are? Oh my God, Jesse, I was so afraid to ask," she said anxiously, stepping back to face him. "What did the doctor say?" She desperately wanted to know, and even though it appeared to be good news, she was still frozen with fear of the answer.

"Well, in a nutshell," Jesse told her with a grin, "the doctor said my future was so bright that I was gonna need to buy a new pair of sunglasses. My cancer's in total remission."

"It is?" she shrieked gleefully, leaping back into his arms and kissing every inch of his face. "Is he sure, Jesse, is he sure?"

"Yes, he's certain," he proclaimed happily, hugging her tightly and laughing out loud, not caring in the least that the other thirty or so passengers on the ship were now watching the two of them rather than the whales. "There's no mistaking the test results. The doctor couldn't use the word 'cured' yet, but he said that the reports from the scans and stuff were better than he ever could've hoped for."

"So, it's over? No more tests or chemo or horrible food?" she questioned gleefully.

"Yes, Mikayla, it's over. And since you've yet to answer my original question, I'll ask it again. Do you want to go home—to Alabama?"

Her reply came without a second's hesitation. "Yes, I do." She grinned sweetly. "How about you, handsome? Do you want to go home?"

"Yeah." He answered both her question and her grin with a charming smile. "Yeah, I do."

Taking his hand, she looked into his eyes. "Where *is* home for you, Jesse?"

"Wherever you are, darlin'," he stated simply … "wherever you are."

Chapter 22

THE DREAM REALIZED

"Don't go in search of love;
let love find you."

—*Granny Mae*

Mikayla's darkened bedroom glowed ethereally with the soft glimmer of candles and the brilliant iridescence of a full moon shining through the window. The sheer, white draperies billowed gently in the breeze from the open pane. As if Mother Nature were doing her part to set the scene, a gentle rain had begun to fall, filling the room with cool, clean air.

Standing beside the bed, Mikayla lifted her arms and slipped a sinfully seductive nightgown over her head. The silky, gossamer fabric fell weightlessly into place, covering her curvaceous figure in a veil of red sensuality. Smoothing her hands down her body, the slinky material felt nonexistent beneath her fingers, revealing her form beneath it as though she were completely unclothed.

She had been fantasizing about this moment for months—her first time with Jesse. In anticipation of the event, she had fully expected to be nervous and inhibited, but she wasn't in the least. The more time she spent with Jesse, the more appreciative she became of the even keel with which he faced the unevenness of everyday life. Be it in good times or in bad, experiencing anything with Jesse was always a treat, never a tribulation.

The sound of the wine glasses clinking together announced his return to the bedroom. Seconds later, she felt his warm, strong hands slide seductively around her waist from behind her. God, she loved the way his hands felt on her body. His touch was electrifying. Every part of her responded to him in every imaginable way.

She closed her eyes and enjoyed the sensation as his hands slid across her stomach, caressing her skin through the silky fabric of the gown. Pulling her into him, he hugged her tenderly.

"I've wanted you for so long, Mikayla," he whispered into her ear. He then proceeded to deposit slow, lazy kisses on her neck and shoulders. Shivers of arousal possessed her as his soft, wet lips made contact with her skin.

She felt his hands creep slowly up her torso, massaging her body as they went, leaving behind a blazing trail of heat. She placed her hands on top of his arms and began gently stroking his skin with the tips of her fingers, erotically dragging her fingernails back and forth across his flesh.

He continued to explore her body, tormenting her into mounting anticipation. Finally, as his hands lay claim to her breasts, she sighed gratefully. It was as though she had waited forever for him to touch her this way.

Gently, he caressed her ample breasts. Slowly and deliberately, he squeezed and released them in a tantalizing motion—kneading her firm but giving flesh in his insatiable hands. His thumbs masterfully manipulated her nipples to immediate response. As her nipples rose eagerly to meet his touch, so did the intensity of her desire.

He groaned in appreciation of her breasts as they filled his palms to overflowing.

"I love the way you feel in my hands," he told her, his voice taking on a husky growl.

She felt his breath begin to quicken against her neck as she pressed her body against his bare chest. His hungry moan of desire filled her with passion.

Reluctantly releasing her breasts, he slid his hands up her silky body. Guiding her by the shoulders, he gently turned her around to face him. Staring down at her, the smoldering look in her eyes melted him like butter. He watched as she placed her dainty hands on his chest.

She felt her way from one side of his sculpted upper body to the other, inspecting each defined and hardened muscle. She ran her fingers through the abundance of dark, manly hair on his chest, pausing only to tease his nipples with the end of her finger. Stealing intermittent upward glances at him, she planted moist feminine kisses on his muscular body.

The sensation of her passionate touch served only to fuel his desire, motivating his hands to travel urgently down her back in search of her buttocks. Gently, he smoothed his hands up and down her firm, round derriere. The silky fabric covering her skin proved not a hindrance but an enhancement to the pleasurable awareness of her stimulating curves beneath his fingers. Yearning to feel her closer, he grasped her bottom with both hands and pulled her tightly against his hot, aroused body.

Reflexively, she arched herself into him. Wrapping her arms around his shoulders, she pulled him into her as well. The titillation of his hard chest against her stimulated breasts urgently increased her greed for him.

"Make love to me, Jesse," she groaned desirously. "Please."

His passion flamed out of control at her seductive request. Sliding his hands quickly up her body, he located the thin spaghetti straps of her gown. Placing his fingers beneath the meager means of support, he slid them to the side and off her shoulders, prompting the slippery piece of clothing to slide quickly down her form and come to rest in a silken heap around her ankles.

Staring into his eyes, she let her hands glide smoothly down his firm, impressive form, her fingers rising and falling as they rode the ripples of his toned and chiseled physique. Coming to rest on the waist of his form-fitting jeans, she inserted her index fingers between the rough denim fabric and his soft, warm skin. Sliding her hands around to the front, and without breaking her stare, she nimbly undid the button. The sound of the zipper being undone seemed to send a shiver of excitement coursing through him. She felt him inhale sharply as she slowly slipped her hand beneath the fabric, finally coming in contact with his anxious, bare body. It was blissful to touch him so intimately after all these months. The sensation of him in her hand, the feel of him gliding beneath her fingers, gratified her as much as it did him. The sound of him moaning her name as she began gently caressing and stroking his hard, excited anatomy, fueled her burning desire to please him and to be pleased by him.

Lowering her face to his chest, she nibbled his skin gently.

"Don't make me beg, Jesse," she pleaded.

Driven by her sultry petition, he quickly stepped out of his jeans. Bending down, he scooped her nude, voluptuous body effortlessly up into his arms and laid her tenderly down on the bed. She watched as his eyes unhurriedly and appreciatively surveyed her nakedness.

Lying down on his side next to her, he leaned up on his elbow. Looking into her face, he smiled tenderly. Stroking her hair with the backs of his fingers, he confessed softly, "You are so beautiful, Mikayla."

She returned his tender, adoring smile.

His hand moved skillfully up and down her body, his gentle fingers touching and exploring her at will. She quivered uncontrollably at the stirring awareness of his touch.

Lingering momentarily at the right side of her abdomen; he gently touched the prominent scar, the permanent reminder of how close she had come to death. She tensed slightly, and closed her eyes. The scar made her feel unattractive. She wondered if it bothered him; if perhaps he thought her less sexy because of it. The uncertainty faded quickly as she felt his moist lips on her skin; gently he began kissing every inch of the imperfection. "You're so perfect," he whispered.

Once again she felt his warm, groping hand move purposefully down the length of her body, not stopping this time until it reached her thighs. Resting there momentarily, he massaged her silky, soft skin, so very close to the place she longed for him to touch. At last, he slid his hand deep between her willing legs, timidly parting them ever so slightly.

She eagerly offered herself to him, giving him access to any part of her he so desired. She quivered in anticipation as his warm hand slid slowly up the inside of her thigh. Pressing his palm against her anxious feminine anatomy, his tantalizing fingers began to explore her.

"Jesse ..." she moaned breathlessly.

Continuing to plant soft, wet kisses on her tummy, his breath was heavy against her skin. "I wanna please you so much, baby," he whispered as he inched his finger inside of her wet, slippery body. Masterfully, he moved his hand and finger in a gentle back and forth motion ... massaging her ... enticing her ... not stopping until waves of passionate release coursed through her. Moaning his name, she felt herself pulsating in his hand.

Raising his head, he looked into her eyes. It was apparent that being the instrument of her pleasure had aroused him even more. Pinning her to the bed with his sensual stare, he carefully placed his knee in the space he had created between her legs. She watched the stimulating flexing motion of his impressive biceps as he gingerly lowered his warm, hard body onto her.

His intense, hazel eyes burned dark with passion as he stared deeply into hers—gazing through to the heart of her.

"I love you, Mikayla," he whispered, his voice wrought with raw emotion.

"I love you, too, Jesse," she echoed, as she reached up to touch his handsome face. Smiling faintly, she delicately traced the outline of his lips with the tip of her index finger.

She wanted to touch him, every part of him. Lovingly, she began running her hands up and down his strong, muscular outstretched arms.

Her breath caught in her throat as he brought his face closer and closer to hers. She wanted to close her eyes, but she didn't want to stop looking at him. He stopped, lingering only inches from her mouth as they breathed in each other's breath. Sighing deeply, she inhaled the sensual aroma of beer from his slightly parted lips. He backed away from her just a bit, wearing a modest but very alluring smile. They shared a telling stare. He had remembered. She had told him months earlier, during one of their lengthy and comfortable conversations, how erotic she thought it was to catch a whiff of beer on a man's breath just seconds before he kissed her. The fact that he remembered that insignificant disclosure was one thing, but for him to actually follow through and indulge her fanciful whim was one of the sexiest things she had ever experienced.

His smile disappeared quickly, as once again he lowered his face to hers.

Her heart was pounding furiously in her chest as his delectable, tender lips finally met hers. At first, he teased her unmercifully with short, tiny tokens of wet affection, before he finally pressed his lips to hers in a heavenly, sweet embrace. She felt the electricity pass between them as the blissful circuits of their energies combined. He kissed her soft and long, handling her as though she might break beneath him.

She wrapped her arms around his bare back, running her hands across his smooth skin and digging her nails gently into his flesh.

His kiss became more urgent. His embrace was so thorough that she thought she might faint—his tongue probing, wanting, consuming her.

She whimpered with desire. Lost in the euphoria of his spell, she wondered how many beats her poor heart could skip and still sustain her life—although at the moment, she didn't care. She could think of no better place to die, than in his arms.

Her body clung to his, longing to be closer to him, to become one with him.

He raised his head and looked lovingly into her bedroom eyes. He watched her expression intently as he carefully entered her. She gasped from the torment of the pleasure.

"I'm sorry. Did I hurt you?" His concern was obvious as he pulled away.

"No ... no ... don't stop," she begged hoarsely.

Her pleading instigated a moan of arousal as he eased himself slowly back inside of her. Just as she had imagined he would be, he was gentle and caring, taking every precaution to insure that she felt nothing but pleasure from his penetration. Before he initiated any further movements, he leaned down and kissed her tenderly on the cheek.

"Just relax, darlin'," he instructed her seductively. "Tell me what you want ... how you ..."

Reaching up, she grabbed him around the neck and pulled him to her. She kissed him passionately. This time it was her tongue that initiated the seeking and the yearning. She clung to him desperately, afraid that she would never be able to convey to him how much she loved him. She kissed him with all the pent-up passion that had been smoldering beneath the surface since the first day they met.

"Wow!" he growled sexily when she finally released him. "I guess you wanted a kiss, huh?" His broad smile conveyed his obvious appreciation of her enthusiasm.

"Yeah, I did." She returned his smile with an enticing giggle. "Thank you."

"No thanks necessary, ma'am," he teased, his cheeks adorned with the sexiest dimples known to man.

Wrapping her legs around his body, his smile vanished instantly as she slowly pulled him closer and deeper into her.

"I want *you*, Jesse." She paused, staring seriously into his handsome face. "Just you."

"That I can give you, darlin'," he proclaimed, as he lowered his muscular body onto her, showering her neck and chest with titillating kisses.

Ever so gently, he immersed himself completely into her. After pausing momentarily, he began slow and deliberate movements, making love to her with such passionate gentleness that she wondered if he were only a dream—a tantalizing figment of her imagination.

Digging her nails into his back, she lifted her hips to meet each one of his pleasurable and fluid thrusts, each stroke creating a stimulating, moist friction inside of her. Languishing in the gratifying sensation of the bonding of their bodies, she could feel their forms meld together, seemingly filling every empty crevice of her body and heart.

She moaned with pleasure as his mouth found its way down her body claiming her breasts with his slippery, wet lips. She writhed deliriously beneath him as his tongue skillfully caressed her nipples in tandem with the motion of his lower body. Allowing her hands to slide purposefully down his back and onto his hips, she ran her palms over his taut, but supple buttocks. Grasping him with both hands, she forced him deeper into her with each of his inward motions.

He moaned loudly in response to her participation.

"God, you feel so good, baby," he confessed, his words coming out in breathless spurts.

She loved it when he called her baby. He'd only done it a few times. But when he did, it instigated a shudder of excitement to pass through her like a ghost in the wind.

"You feel good too, Jesse … Please don't stop."

"I won't, baby … I promise."

Her insistent words seemed to add fuel to his already flaming need, prompting his movements to increase in speed and intensity.

Quickly surpassing the limit of her defenses against his sensual advances, pulsations of unbridled pleasure swept over her. Mikayla's body throbbed around his, gripping and releasing him as the blissful release enveloped her. He covered her mouth in a hot, moist kiss, absorbing her screams of ecstasy.

Waiting for the climax to gradually fade, he lovingly stroked her trembling legs that were still wrapped tightly around his body. As he felt her relax beneath him, he watched her expression soften to that of sweet fulfillment.

He smiled down at her. Her romantic gaze reduced him to putty in her hands.

"Have I ever told you how much I love you?" he asked sweetly.

"No," she lied, wearing the cutest expression he had ever seen.

"Well, it's a lot," he grinned.

"Enough to change positions with me?" she asked, raising and lowering her eyebrows delightfully.

"Leaving me defenseless and at your tender mercy?" he beamed. "It would be my pleasure."

Sliding his hands beneath her shoulders, and with one quick movement, he was on his back and she was lying on top of him.

Giggling softly, she extended her arms and raised herself above him. Staring down into his mesmerizing eyes, her levity quickly dissipated. She lowered her lips to his and kissed him gently at first, gradually growing more thorough as her lust for him increased.

Relishing her affection, he returned her passionate embrace. He ran his hands over her enticing body, caressing her delicate arms and shoulders, trailing his fingers up and down the dainty indention of her spine. The sensation of her luscious body seduced him relentlessly. Unable to remain still any longer, he began to gyrate hungrily beneath her, desperately longing for the only movement that would satisfy his mounting desire.

Sensing his need, she tucked her knees beneath her and raised herself up and onto him, driving him deeper inside of her. Their sighs of pleasure united as she straddled him. The weight of her body bearing down onto him served only to intensify their union.

Struggling to contain his elation, he begged her for motion.

She leaned over him once again. As she began the slow and deliberate movement of her lower body, her breasts brushed lightly back and forth against his chest, arousing him to the brink of his tolerance.

Glancing down into his desperate eyes, his urgency for satisfaction was obvious. She had never wanted to please a man more in her life. Teasing him with one more kiss, she pressed her breasts solidly into his chest as she hastened her gyrations.

His body rose to meet her every downward action, his hands voraciously grasping her derriere to bring her back into him as she pulled away. He was desperate for her both physically and emotionally.

Their united moans of ecstasy filled the room, as finally the exhilaration of pleasure overtook them. He reached for her hands and grasped them tightly, intertwining their fingers together. Wave after wave of convulsive rapture passed between them, bonding and consummating their union.

"Kiss me, Mikayla," he begged in a raspy whisper.

Still clinging to his hands, she leaned down and lovingly kissed his lips. He returned her embrace with tenderness like she had never known.

When he finally released her, contented and exhausted, she rolled gently off of him and lay by his side, curled up next to him as close as she could possibly get.

Wrapping his strong arms around her, he pulled her even closer. He touched his lips to her damp forehead and then lifted her chin to face him.

Staring into her satisfied face, he breathed a long, complacent sigh.

"I love you," he stated softly. "God, how I love you."

"I love you too, baby," she uttered breathlessly. "More than I ever thought possible."

Pulling her to him, he kissed her once again. He kissed her so innocently, with such purity of love, that he stole her heart right out of her chest, claiming it for his own. She relinquished it willingly, knowing that it would never be broken while in his care.

She rested her head on his shoulder as they stroked and caressed each other without saying a word. Their connection had been so complete that neither could tell with certainty where one ended and the other began. They only knew that they loved each other with all of their heart and soul, and that was all they needed to know.

She fell blissfully asleep in his arms, content to slumber dreamlessly—her dreams already fulfilled.

❦   ❦   ❦

Mikayla awoke the following morning to the aromatic smell of coffee and sweet waffles filling her apartment. Stretching and yawning happily, she wondered, "Gosh, could this all be just a fantasy—a perfect and wonderful fantasy? What if it's not real?" Reacting quickly to the dreadful notion, she reached over and pinched herself on the arm, good and hard, just to make sure. She was eternally grateful for the immediate and welcome pain that the self-inflicted pinch produced. She wasn't dreaming. It was all real. Jesse was real, and he was happy and healthy, and he loved her. She knew that he did, because she knew that feeling very well—the unexplainable euphoria of being loved, completely and purely by another individual. There was nothing else on earth like it. It was more like a celestial awareness than a feeling really, totally unique and completely impossible to replicate any other way.

"Are you gonna stay in bed all day, sleepy head?" Jesse asked as he poked his head through her bedroom door. "Breakfast is ready and waitin' for ya. Do you want me to bring it up to you, or do you wanna come down to it?"

"I want *you* to come here to *me*," she said in a low sexy voice, motioning him over to the bed.

"Okay," he grinned devilishly. "That option works, too." It took him less than three strides to reach her. Instantly, he pulled her against him in a warm, enveloping embrace. He kissed her intensely, with almost as much desire as he had the night before.

She had no idea there were so many different types of kisses until him. He was a masterful kisser.

"I love you," he told her, as he breathed her name and embraced her so completely that she practically melted in his arms.

"I can't believe I'm saying this but … get dressed," he ordered jovially as he handed her the same nightgown that he had so effectively removed just a few hours earlier. "We gotta go downstairs. I got a present for ya."

Barely giving her time to slip the silky garment over her head, he lifted her effortlessly off the bed, cradled her in his arms, and carried her to the breakfast table.

"Do you want to eat first, or do you wanna open your gift first?" He was as excited as a child on Christmas morning.

"In keeping with the protocol of a typical female, I think I'd like the gift first, if you don't mind," she said teasingly.

"Great! That's what I hoped you'd say. Enjoy your coffee, and I'll go get it."

He returned seconds later with his gift, looking visibly pleased with himself. Anxiously, he placed a long, white cylindrical container into her hands.

"I hope you like it, darlin'," he whispered as he planted a tender, moist kiss on her forehead.

"Since it's from you, I'm sure I will," she stated with confidence.

She looked at him inquisitively as she pulled the stopper-type closure from the end of the cylinder and shook the container gently. Several large, rolled sheets of papers promptly spilled onto her lap.

Moving quickly, Jesse cleared the table in front of her, removing the plates and cups and giving her room to spread the papers out for easy viewing.

Carefully unrolling the stark white sheets, Mikayla discovered that they were blueprints—detailed floor plans for the renovation of a two-story house.

While examining the layout, she noticed the small identification title block in the lower left corner of the page. Her heart began to pound in her chest as she read the words that described the remodeling of the structure. As though her racing heart were pumping water instead of blood, the tears began to flow freely down her face.

"Oh my God, Jesse. How did you ...? How could you have possibly known this?" she asked, her garbled words exiting her mouth intermittently between the gasping sobs of joy. "Nobody knew about this but Granny Mae and me. It was our secret dream."

"Well, apparently Granny Mae must have told Mrs. Gregory, because she shared it with me." Excitedly, he began describing the plans spread out before her, which were already meticulously detailed in black and white. "Things are still in the very early stages of construction, so you can change anything you don't like. I want everything to be exactly the way you and your grandmother dreamed it would be," he said lovingly.

She had been quiet for the past several minutes as he pointed and explained. The only sound escaping her was an occasional sob or sigh.

"Are you all right, Mikayla?" His tone reflected his hesitantly. "You like your present, don't ya?"

"Of course I like it, baby. I just don't know what to say to such a gallant gesture. I just … I don't think I deserve you," she told him tearfully.

"Deserve *me*? Are you kidding? You deserve much better than an old, battle-worn soldier like me," he said wearing a faint smile. "But I love you, Mikayla. I've been waiting all of my life to love you. You're my dream come true. Now I want to do the same thing for you. All I want you to do is to dream 'Granny Mae's Bed and Breakfast' into existence for me. You can do that, can't you?"

She couldn't speak. She could barely force oxygen into her body, much less coax words back out of it, so she just tearfully nodded her head in agreement.

"Thank you, darlin'." Tenderly he kissed her damp cheek. "Now you know why a 'yes' answer was so important to me yesterday when I asked if you wanted to go back home to Alabama. If you had said 'no,' this would've been a really lousy gift," he told her with a hearty laugh.

It did her heart good to hear him laugh. It was like music to her ears. She could listen to him laugh for the rest of her life.

"I hope you don't mind." He grinned at her adoringly. "But I took the liberty of hirin' on some of the staff already."

"You did?" She was quite shocked that he had done so this early in the stage of construction.

"Yep … take a look at the last blueprint."

On the very last page of the plans was a large, color photograph. Standing there in the picture were the three other people she held most near and dear to her heart. They were posing side by side, wearing the most enormous grins that she had ever seen them wear. Beneath each picture was their name and title: Rick Owens, Manager; Bessie Gregory, Kitchen Manager; and a very pregnant Diana Owens, Concierge. Diana was smiling—a genuine smile—Mikayla could tell it was real—blood sisters know these things.

Shaking her head in disbelief at Jesse's generosity, Mikayla leapt to her feet. She grabbed him around the neck and held him tightly, treasuring him and loving him with every molecule of her heart. "Thank you, my love," she whispered into his ear. *Thank you, God*, she mouthed silently, over and over again.

Jesse returned her embrace, lovingly running his strong but gentle hands over every inch of her body within his tender reach. Instinctively, he bent his head down closer to her, his sensual breath lightly grazing her skin as he exhaled.

Nuzzling his face against her cheek, he began laying warm, moist kisses on her skin as he made his way up to her ear. Softly, he began singing into her ear, his deep, sexy, baritone voice reverberating up and down her spine. After only the first few lines of the enchanting lyrics to "All I Have to Do Is Dream," he lulled her into a state of fantasy.

God, he sang like an angel. She had no idea he could sing so beautifully. She found herself wondering how many more wonderful secrets she would ultimately discover about this man she loved so much.

Soothingly, he began swaying to the melody of the song. With the charisma of a pied piper, he prompted her body to follow his intoxicating lead.

They danced as he sang adoringly into her ear, the lyrics proclaiming his undying love and desire. She lost herself in the romance and tenderness of the moment, savoring every single melodious note that came out of his mouth.

Hoping to prolong the feeling of ecstasy, he repeated the chorus once again, but this time he improvised the ending by adding four of his own heartfelt words—and not just words of love this time, but a request—a life-altering question—one that required an answer. Although he had fully expected to be extremely nervous at that particular moment, he wasn't in the least. In fact, he had never felt more serene and complete. It didn't matter to him that he was gambling with his heart; he would risk it gladly for a chance to win her hand. He waited patiently for her response.

Pausing for an instant, it took her mind a moment to wrap itself around what she thought she just heard. *Did he just propose to me?* she wondered silently, although she was fairly certain that he had.

He repeated the words quietly into her ear. "Will you marry me?"

Leaning back slightly, she gazed into his longing eyes. "Were those last four words from the original lyrics to the song?" she asked sweetly.

"No, Mikayla … those words were from my heart."

He stared at her, watching contentedly as a soft, bewitching smile slowly graced her exquisite face. He was certain that he could look at her face for the rest of his life and every day find something different that he loved about it. But right now he just wished she would answer his question, so that his waiting heart could start beating again.

"Yes, baby, I'll marry you," she answered blissfully. "I would've married you a year ago if you had asked me."

She smiled tenderly at him, wondering how she could be so blessed. Reaching up, she gently touched his face and caressed his cheek with her thumb before lovingly kissing him. He was heaven-sent, she was sure of it—sent by God at Granny Mae's request. He had to be. There was no other explanation for him.

Jesse gathered her close to his firm body, devouring her in his passionate embrace. Beginning at her ear, he began covering her cheek with warm, wet kisses. Leaving a trail of smoldering heat on her skin, he forged a path down the side of her neck, pausing to softly nibble on her shoulder. The sensation made her weak in the knees.

"Jesse," she breathed his name longingly.

"Hmmm …?" he murmured, seemingly unwilling to forsake the taste of her skin in order to properly form words.

"I like what you're doing."

'You do?" he asked, raising his head slightly and releasing a very sexy chuckle. "Well, that's good, 'cause I like doin' it"

"Will you kiss me like that for as long as I want?"

Moving his moist lips to her ear, he whispered seductively, "Darlin', I plan to kiss you till you beg me to stop."

"You promise?"

"I promise."

She sighed contentedly at his response. "Am I mistaken, Ranger Daulton, or are you attempting to seduce me?" she cooed.

With a dangerous growl to his voice, he threatened, "There's a danger of it, baby. How am I doin'?" His breaths were beginning to quicken as he returned to tormenting her with his lips.

"I think if you don't make your move soon, I'm going to have to make it for you," she answered seductively. "Where in the world did you learn to do what you're doing to me?"

"This?" He chuckled sexily, "This is nothin' … have you ever heard of the ancient art of tantric lovemaking?" He nestled his face in the crook of her neck, making tiny little circles on her skin with the tip of his tongue.

"No, I haven't," she answered hastily, totally lacking for words at the moment. "What is …?"

"It's just a little somethin' I picked up over in the Middle East," he replied mysteriously. As he raised his head to gaze seductively into her eyes, an ornery expression slowly possessed his handsome face. "I think you're gonna like it." He gave her a sexy wink.

She returned his dazzling, dimpled smile. "I think you're right," she said dreamily, falling hopelessly in love with him all over again. Finally, at last, she had found her prince.

The End

GRANNY MAE'S RECIPES

GRANNY MAE'S BLUEBERRY DROP BISCUITS WITH BLUEBERRY BUTTER CREAM

INGREDIENTS

For biscuits:

2 cups of all-purpose flour
1 tablespoon of bakin' powder
1 teaspoon of salt
¼ cup of sugar
½ stick of butter, really cold and cut into little pieces
1 cup of buttermilk
1 egg
1 pint of fresh blueberries

For topping:

1 large package of cream cheese, softened
2 tablespoons of butter, softened
3 heapin' tablespoons of blueberry preserves

PREPARATION

Preheat oven to 400º.

In a large mixin' bowl, add all of the dry ingredients: flour, bakin' powder, salt, and sugar. Stir with a spoon until mixed up.

Cut the cold butter into the dry mixture with a fork or pastry cutter. The mixture should be crumbly lookin', and the butter should be about the size of a small pea. Don't use your hands 'cause they're too warm and they'll melt your butter, and you don't want that.

In another bowl, mix the buttermilk and egg together, and then add that to the flour mixture. Stir it with your hands just enough to mix the ingredients. Don't overmix the dough, or your biscuits will be tough. Stir the berries in real easy so you don't mash 'em.

Using an ice cream scooper, drop the biscuits on a greased bakin' sheet.

Bake for 15 to 20 minutes or until golden brown. Be careful not to burn 'em.

While the biscuits are bakin', mix up the butter cream ingredients.

Spread the hot biscuits with butter cream, and enjoy!

Serves 9 people if each person only eats 1 biscuit, which ain't likely.

GRANNY MAE'S BUTTERMILK SMASHED POTATOES

INGREDIENTS

6 large taters, peeled and quartered
½ cup of canned cream
½ stick of butter
Barely 1 cup of buttermilk
3 good pinches of salt
Couple dashes of pepper

PREPARATION

Cook the taters in a pot of cold water with several pinches of salt, until the taters fall apart when you stick 'em with a fork.

Warm the cream and butter in a little saucepan. Don't get it too hot, or it will scorch.

Drain the taters, and mash with a hand masher. Make them as chunky or as smooth as you want 'em.

Stir in the warm milk and butter. Then add the buttermilk until the potatoes are as creamy as you want 'em.

Add plenty of salt and pepper. Taters taste awful without enough salt.

Serves 5 to 6 people unless they are real hungry or all men; then it will only serve 4 or 5.

GRANNY MAE'S FRESH CORN PUDDIN'

INGREDIENTS

5 ears of corn on the cob
2 eggs
1 small onion, chopped up
1 palmful of sugar
3 good pinches of salt
2 cups of sweet milk
1 tablespoon of butter, melted
6 crackers, crumbled up

PREPARATION

Preheat oven to 350º.

Shuck your corn right before you start to cook it. Corn gets tough real fast after it's been shucked, so don't ever shuck it way ahead of time. The best way to cook corn is to start with a big pot of cold water. Don't ever add salt to your corn water. It'll make your corn tough. But do add about a half a palm of sugar and a squirt or two of lemon juice to the water. Put your corn in the pot of cold water, and heat it up to a boil. Let it boil for 2 or 3 minutes, and then just let your corn stand in the hot water for 10 more minutes.

After your corn has cooled enough to handle, cut it off the cob with a real sharp knife.

In a big bowl, add all of the other stuff to the corn: eggs, onion, sugar, salt, milk, butter, and crackers. Stir it up good.

Pour it into a 1-1/2 quart buttered bakin' dish, and bake for about an hour or so at 350º.

Serves only 4 to 5 people 'cause everybody loves corn puddin'.

GRANNY MAE'S GLAZED BRUSSELS SPROUTS

INGREDIENTS

2 tablespoons of butter
3 pieces of bacon, cut into little pieces
1-1/2 pounds of Brussels sprouts, cut in half
Couple pinches of salt and pepper
Barely 1 cup of raisins
2 cups of chicken broth

PREPARATION

Heat the butter in a big fry pan, and add a touch of oil to keep the butter from burnin'. Add the bacon and cook till done. Then take the bacon out of the pan and set it aside.

Add the sprouts to the pan, and cook for about 5 minutes or until they start to turn brown.

Add the raisins and broth, and cook the sprouts till they get tender, about 15 more minutes or so.

Add the bacon back to the pan.

Add a couple pinches of salt and pepper.

This recipe is guaranteed to turn any sprouts-hater into a lover with the first mouthful!

Serves 5 to 6 sprouts-lovers.

GRANNY MAE'S SOUTHERN COTTAGE MEAT LOAF

INGREDIENTS

For meat loaf:

1-1/2 pounds of hamburger meat
½ cup of ketchup
½ cup of tomater juice
2 eggs
1-1/2 cups of fresh bread crumbs
¼ cup of oats
1 small onion, chopped up
1 tablespoon of yeller mustard
2 or 3 good pinches of salt
Couple dashes of pepper

For topping:

½ cup of ketchup
2 palmfuls of brown sugar
1 teaspoon of yeller mustard

PREPARATION

Preheat oven to 400º.

In a large bowl, stir up the ketchup, tomater juice, eggs, bread crumbs, oats, onions, mustard, and salt and pepper.

Add the hamburger meat to the bowl, and mix it thoroughly with your hands.

Pour it into an 8" × 8" glass dish, and press it down till it's flat and there ain't no cracks.

In a little bowl, combine the toppin' ingredients: ketchup, brown sugar, and mustard. Then spread it over the meat loaf.

Bake at 400° for 50 to 60 minutes.

Drain off the fat, and let the meat loaf sit for a few minutes before cutting it or it will crumble, and you don't want that.

Serves 5 to 6 people unless they are real hungry; then it will only serve 4 or 5.

GRANNY MAE'S SOUTHERN FRIED CORNBREAD

INGREDIENTS

1-1/2 cups of self-risin' cornmeal
½ tablespoon of bakin' soda
1 egg
Enough buttermilk to moisten the mix real good

PREPARATION

Preheat oven to 450°.

Heat up ½ inch of bacon grease in a 9" iron skillet. Get it good and hot.

Mix up the meal, soda, egg, and buttermilk in a bowl.

Add about 1/3 of the hot grease to the meal mixture. Stir it up real fast and pour it into the skillet. Don't get scared if the grease bubbles up around the edges; it's supposed to do that.

Bake in the oven for about 12 minutes or until it's raised up a little and a nice golden brown on top.

When it's done, turn it out on a warm plate.

Cut it up and eat it with supper while it's still good and hot.

If you got leftover cornbread, be sure to keep it. Later on that evenin' or the next day, crumble it up in a bowl and pour some sweet milk or buttermilk over it. It's really good that way, too.

Makes 8 slices if you cut it like a pie or one more if you cut it into squares.

GRANNY MAE'S OLD-FASHIONED OATMEAL CAKE

INGREDIENTS

For cake:

1 cup of quick cookin' oats
1-1/2 cups of boiling water
(Mix oats and water in a separate bowl and let them cool while preparin'
the rest of the ingredients.)
1 cup of brown sugar
1 cup of white sugar
2 eggs
1 stick of butter, softened
1 teaspoon of vanilla
¾ cup of self-risin' flour
¾ cup of all-purpose flour
½ teaspoon of salt
1 teaspoon of soda
1 teaspoon of cinnamon

For icin':

1 stick of butter, melted
1 cup of coconut
1 cup of brown sugar
1 cup of chopped pecans
Few spoonfuls of milk to make the icin' spreadable

PREPARATION

Preheat oven to 350°.

Mix by hand the oats, sugars, eggs, butter, and vanilla together. Then sift in the flours, salt, soda, and cinnamon. Stir it up by hand.

Pour into a 13" × 9" greased and floured pan.

Bake at 350º for 30 to 35 minutes.

Mix up the icin' ingredients. Spread it on while the cake's still hot.

Return cake to the oven for an additional 5 minutes or until the icin' is simmerin'.

GRANNY MAE'S QUICK AND FRESH PEACH COBBLER

INGREDIENTS

8–10 fresh peaches, peeled and sliced
1-1/2 cups of biscuit bakin' mix
¾ cups of sweet milk
½ cup of sugar
2 tablespoons of butter, melted
Dash of cinnamon, nutmeg, and sugar

PREPARATION

Preheat oven to 400°.

Put the peaches in a large bowl and sprinkle with cinnamon, nutmeg, and sugar to coat.

Pour the peaches into an 8" × 8" greased bakin' dish.

Place the dish of peaches in the oven till they're hot and bubbly.

Stir together the bakin' mix, sweet milk, sugar, and butter.

Spoon the crust mix on top of the hot peaches and kinda spread it out.

Return the dish to the oven for an additional 25 minutes or until golden brown.

Top with homemade peach ice cream and serve. Yummy!

It won't serve very many, 'cause everybody takes a big helpin'.

GRANNY MAE'S FAMOUS LOW-CALORIE PECAN PIE

INGREDIENTS

For crust:

1 cup of all-purpose flour
2-1/2 tablespoons of sugar
½ teaspoon of bakin' powder
¼ teaspoon of salt
¼ cup of low-fat milk
1 tablespoon of margarine

For fillin':

1 large egg
4 large egg whites
1 cup of dark brown corn syrup
2/3 cups of dark brown sugar
¼ teaspoon of salt
1 cup of pecan halves
1-1/2 teaspoons of vanilla

PREPARATION

Preheat oven to 350º.

In a large bowl, add the flour, sugar, bakin' powder, and salt.

Add the milk and margarine and toss with a fork.

Form the crust mixture into a ball on plastic wrap, and cover with more plastic wrap. Roll the dough into an 11" circle, and put it in the freezer for 10 minutes to let it get good and cold.

Then remove one side of the plastic wrap and fit the dough into a 9-inch pie plate coated with a thin layer of butter. Fold the edges under, and pinch into pretty peaks with two of your fingers.

For the fillin': beat the eggs, corn syrup, brown sugar, and salt with an electric mixer, and then stir in the pecan and vanilla by hand. Pour the mixture into the crust.

Bake at 350° for 20 minutes. Then cover it with foil and bake it for 20 more minutes, or until you can insert a butter knife 1 inch from the edge and it comes out clean. Don't overbake it, or the fillin' will be gooey.

Serves 10 dietin' women—only 1 slice each.

MIKAYLA'S FAVORITE SOUTHERN SUICIDE DRINK

INGREDIENTS

1 jigger of Southern Comfort Whiskey
1 jigger of Jack Daniels Whiskey
1 jigger of orange juice
1 jigger of lemon-lime soft drink
½ jigger of peach schnapps
½ jigger of grenadine syrup

PREPARATION

Pour over the rocks. Stir and serve with a twist of orange.

LEX'S CALIFORNIA MARTINI

INGREDIENTS

3 jiggers of vodka
1 jigger of red wine
1 tablespoon of rum
4 dashes of orange bitters

PREPARATION

Put ingredients in a shaker with ice, and strain into a chilled martini glass. Garnish with a twist of orange.

A NOTE FROM THE AUTHOR

In my quest for realism and authenticity in the creation of Jesse, I submerged myself in research. I spent many months reading books and articles, watching documentaries, and carrying on personal conversations with some of the most fascinating and downright lovable American veterans you would ever want to meet—my daddy being one of them. At one point during my search for the truth, I got creative and located some real Army Rangers who were more than willing to share their invaluable, expert knowledge with *me*—a perfect stranger.

Anyway, my perseverance and hard work culminated into the single coolest experience of my life when on May 13, 2006, I had the awesome privilege of attending the Open House festivities and demonstrations at the Fifth U.S. Army Ranger Training Battalion in Dahlonega, Georgia. I was beside myself with excitement at least three months in advance, so when the day finally arrived, you can imagine my overwhelming awe and delight. You gotta understand, I had spent a year of my life fashioning and creating this awesome, heroic character of Ranger Jesse in my mind, only to find myself at the Open House literally surrounded by a whole battalion of 'em. I felt like a kid in a candy store—that is until these combat-trained, highly motivated, in-your-face Rangers got down to business and showed me what they were truly made of. It was then that I realized I was not there merely to *look* … but to *see*. The demonstrations were the most awesome displays of strength, skill, commitment, discipline, and teamwork that I've ever seen in my life. It was truly a humbling and eye-opening experience to see these soldiers in action.

It's something that I will never forget. I've already made plans to go back next year.

I feel the need to single out one specific Ranger so that I can better explain to you the caliber of individuals that I'm talking about here. Sgt. John P. Tompkins (pictured with me on the left) was my first Ranger contact and unfortunately was shackled with more than his fair share of the burden of my endless questions. It is blatantly apparent to me that John has been blessed with the patience of Job. I still find it hard to believe that he wasn't stumped by one single question—or that he didn't tell me to buzz off many months ago.

I was fortunate enough to meet John and his wife, in person, at the Open House at the Fifth Battalion. He was kind enough to spend the day with me, explaining the exhibits and displays, and—you guessed it—bearing the brunt of my never-ending curiosity for all things army.

I left the Fifth Ranger Training Battalion and Dahlonega, Georgia, that day with a head full of knowledge, a heart full of pride for America's finest, and my very own official—and highly coveted—black and gold Army Ranger Tab. I received this Tab not because I asked for it, not because I earned it, and certainly not because I deserved it … but because my friend John felt me worthy enough to give me his.

I've been told that a Ranger giving you his hard-earned Ranger Tab is the ultimate display of friendship and respect. I can't tell you how pleasantly shocked and honored I was with John's gift. The emotion of that moment, I'm certain, will bring a tear to my eye each and every time my heart feels the need to remind me of it. Even the way that he gave it to me was special. He didn't make a big "to-do" about giving it to me. Instead, he tucked it away amidst the pages of a book that he was loaning to me. He watched as I thumbed through the book and waited for me to discover the treasure he had hidden inside. When I did, he just smiled and humbly accepted my heartfelt hug of gratitude.

I will cherish my Ranger Tab and my Ranger buddies (John, Perry, Justin, and Brendan) for the rest of my life. Thanks, guys!

BIBLIOGRAPHY

"All I Have to Do is Dream," Song Title, referenced in Chapter 23.

Cyrus, Billy Ray, Artist. "Achy Breaky Heart," Song Title, referenced in Chapter 5.

Gingrich, Justin. The company name of Ranger Knives, the company's Web site: www.rangerknives.com, the company's insignia with the initials "RK", and the owner's name, Justin, as referenced in Chapter 14, are used with written permission by the owner, Justin Gingrich.

Reeves, Julie and Craig, Danny, writers of song lyrics, "Love Leaves No One Behind" (based on the novel by Claudia Pemberton). The song lyrics are included at the beginning of the book (following the dedication) and are used with written permission by the song writers Julie Reeves and Danny Craig.

(On the Back Cover)
(Staff Sergeant Ross L. Martin on the left, myself in the center,
and Specialist Ulmet D. Daneshpayeh on the right)
These Rangers participated in the demonstrations at the U.S. Army
Ranger Training Battalion Open House and were gracious enough to
have their picture taken with me.

Please visit the author's website at:
www.writingsbyclaudia.com

or email at:
claudia@writingsbyclaudia.com

ABOUT THE AUTHOR

Claudia Pemberton resides in West Virginia and works for the Cabell County Public School System. She is a very proud member of the Military Writer's Society of America; Romance Writers of America; and the American Authors Association. Unable to bid farewell to Mikayla and Jesse, Claudia is working on a sequel to *Love Leaves No One Behind*, her first novel.

978-0-595-41402-4
0-595-41402-8

Printed in the United States
122953LV00003B/52-69/A

9 780595 414024